Tahmima Anam was born in Dhaka, Bangladesh, in 1975. She attended Harvard University where she earned a PhD in Social Anthropology. She lives in London. *A Golden Age* is her first novel.

A GOLDEN AGE

Rehana Haque is throwing a party in the rose-filled garden of the house she has built, while beyond her doorstep the city is buzzing with excitement after the recent elections. None of the guests at Rehana's party can foresee what will happen in the days and months that follow. For this is East Pakistan in 1971, a country on the brink of war. And this family's life is about to change for ever. Set against the backdrop of the Bangladesh War of Independence, *A Golden Age* is a story of passion and revolution, of hope, faith and unexpected heroism.

TAHMIMA ANAM

◆

A GOLDEN AGE

Complete and Unabridged

CHARNWOOD
Leicester

First published in Great Britain in 2007 by
John Murray (Publishers)
London

First Charnwood Edition
published 2007
by arrangement with
John Murray (Publishers)
a division of Hodder Headline
London

British Library CIP Data

Anam, Tahmima
  A golden age.—Large print ed.—
  Charnwood library series
  1. Bangladesh—History—Revolution, *1971*—
  Fiction 2. Bangladesh—Social conditions—
  Fiction 3. Large type books
  I. Title
  823.9'2 [F]

  ISBN 978–1–84617–914–3

Published by
F. A. Thorpe (Publishing)
Anstey, Leicestershire

Set by Words & Graphics Ltd.
Anstey, Leicestershire
Printed and bound in Great Britain by
T. J. International Ltd., Padstow, Cornwall

This book is printed on acid-free paper

For my parents,
Shaheen and Mahfuz Anam,
who planted hope in my heart

EAST & WEST PAKISTAN IN 1971

CHINA

NEPAL

BHUTAN

PIA FLIGHT 010

amuna

Ganga (Ganges)

Brahmaputra

NECK

E. PAKISTAN (BANGLADESH)

CHICKEN

Agartala

Dhaka

Calcutta

Salt Lake

BURMA

Bay
of
Bengal

Freedom, you are
an arbour in the garden, the koel's song,
glistening leaves on banyan trees,
my notebook of poetry, to scribble as I please.

Shamsur Rahman, *Shadhinota Tumi*

March 1959

Prologue

Dear Husband,
  I lost our children today.

* * *

Outside the courthouse Rehana bought two kites, one red and one blue, from Khan Brothers Variety Store and Confectioners. The man behind the counter wrapped them up in brown paper and jute ribbon. Rehana tucked the packets under her arm and hailed a rickshaw. As she was climbing in, she saw the lawyer running towards her.

'Mrs Haque, I am very sorry.' He sounded sincere.

Rehana couldn't bring herself to say it was all right.

'You must find some money. That is the only way. Find some money, and then we will try again. These bastards don't move without a little grease.'

Money. Rehana stepped into the rickshaw and lifted the hood over her head. 'Dhanmondi,' she said, her voice in a thin quiver. 'Road Number 5.'

When she got home, the children were sitting together on the sofa with their knees lined up. Maya's feet hovered above the floor. Sohail was looking down at his palms and counting the very small lines. He saw Rehana and smiled but did not rise from his chair, or call out, as Maya did, 'Ammoo! Why were you so long?'

Rehana had decided it would not be wise to cry in front of the children, so she had done her crying in the rickshaw, in sobs that caused her to hold on to the narrow frame of the seat and open her mouth in a loud, wailing O. The rickshaw-puller had turned around and asked, as if he was genuinely concerned, whether she would like to stop for a glass of water. Rehana had never tasted roadside water. She refused him mutely, wondering if he had children, a thought that made her lean her head against the side of the rickshaw hood and knock repeatedly in time to the bumps on the road. Now, confronted with the sight of them, she fought the pinch in her jaw and the acrid taste that flooded her mouth. She fought the fierce stinging of her eyes, the closing of her throat. She fought all of these as she handed them the wrapped-up, triangular packets.

'Thank you, Ammoo jaan,' Maya said, ripping into hers. Sohail did not open his. He rested it on his lap and stroked the brown paper.

'You are going to live with Faiz Chacha,' Rehana said evenly. 'In Lahore.'

'Lahore!' Maya said.

'I'm so sorry,' Rehana said to her son.

'When will we come back?'

'Soon, I promise.' Pray to God, she wanted to say. 'They are coming for you on Thursday.'

'I don't want to.'

Rehana bit down on her tongue. 'You have to go,' she said. 'Go and be brave. You can fly your kite, beta, and I will see it, all the way from Lahore. It's a special kite. You have to be very good. Very good and very brave. Only the bravest children get windy days. And one day it will be so windy you will fly all the way back to me. You don't believe me? Wait and see.'

★ ★ ★

Dear Husband,
Our children are no longer our children.

★ ★ ★

How would she begin to tell him?

She got back into the rickshaw with the children. 'Azimpur Koborstan,' she said.

The graveyard was dotted with dusk mourners. They tossed flowers on the wet pelts of grass that grew over their loved ones. In the next row a man with a white cap cried into his hands. Beside him, an old woman clutched a spray of bokul.

Rehana held the round palms of her children.

'Say goodbye to your father,' she said, pointing to Iqbal's grave.

5

Sohail raised his fingers to his face. 'La-ill'ahah Ill'allah.'

'Maya, you too.'

★ ★ ★

My children are no longer my children.

★ ★ ★

The judge said Rehana had not properly coped with the death of her husband. She was too young to take care of the children on her own. She had not taught them the proper lessons about Jannat and the afterlife.

Maya chased a butterfly into the next row. Rehana seized her elbow. 'Say goodbye to your father.'

'Goodbye, Abboo,' Maya said, her eyes liquid, moving with the butterfly.

★ ★ ★

'Mrs Haque,' the judge had asked, 'what would your husband want?'

He would want them to be safe, she had said. Yes, he would want them to be safe.

Faiz had said, 'It's not safe here, milord. Martial law, strikes, people on the streets — not safe. That is why my wife and I want to take the children to Lahore.'

Lahore, the garden city with new roads and perfect buildings. It was a thousand miles away on the other side of India. Faiz was her husband's elder brother. He was a barrister, and very rich. His wife was tall, pouty-lipped and barren. She looked hungrily at the children.

Faiz had never liked Rehana. It had something to do with Iqbal's devotion to her. Leaving her slippers outside the bathroom door when she went to bathe. Pressing her feet with olive oil. Speaking only in gentle tones. Everyone noticed; Faiz would say, *Brother, you are spoiling your wife*, and Mrs Chowdhury, who lived opposite their house in Dhanmondi, would sigh and declare, *Your husband is a saint*.

Faiz told the judge about *Cleopatra*. Rehana had taken the children to see *Cleopatra*. Was *Cleopatra* a suitable film for young children? She saw the judge picturing Elizabeth Taylor's breasts. And then Faiz told the story about the coin. That eight years ago Iqbal had been presented with a proposal of marriage to one Rehana Ali of Calcutta, a young woman from an aristocratic family whose father had lost an immense fortune to bad counsel and even worse luck. Iqbal was already thirty-six; he had a successful insurance business — why not marry? Why not indeed. He had tossed a coin, glanced quickly at the result and gone to sleep. The next morning he sent a message to say he agreed.

Rehana had never believed this story, because Iqbal was not the type to gamble. He was an insurance man; he dealt in security. The avoidance of accident. The sidestepping of consequence. Perhaps he had been different before he married. Perhaps that was why Faiz

7

was upset. His brother was no longer his brother.

She should have burned some chillies and circled them over his head. Or slaughtered a goat, at the very least. But she hadn't done either, and so he had died, sinking to his knees in front of the house one January day, his walking stick rolling into the gutter, his hand over his waistcoat searching for the pocket watch, as though he wanted to record the hour of his leaving her. 'Maf kar do,' he whispered to her. *Forgive me.*

And there she was, a widow, nothing to recommend her, no family near by. Her parents were dead; her three sisters lived in Karachi. That was when Faiz and Parveen had offered to take the children. Rehana could see them during the holidays. 'Just for a few years,' Parveen said, 'Give you time to recover.' As though it were an illness, something curable, like what was happening to the country.

When Rehana refused, Faiz and Parveen had taken the matter to court.

'Milord,' Faiz said to the judge, 'Mrs Haque is distressed; she needs her rest. We are thinking only of the children.'

She had married a man she had not expected to love; loved a man she had not expected to lose; lived a life of moderation, a life of few surprises. She had asked her father to find her a husband with little ambition. Someone whose fortunes had nowhere to go.

★   ★   ★

8

It was getting dark; the gravestone shadows lapped at their feet.

'Ammoo, I'm hungry,' Maya said.

Rehana had thought to bring a packet of glucose biscuits. 'Here,' she said, peeling away the pink wrapper.

Sohail stood statue-still and stared into his father's grave. 'Let's go home,' he said.

'Just a few minutes.' She hadn't finished explaining it to Iqbal. 'Why don't you see if you can get those kites up?'

The children drifted to an empty field at the edge of the graveyard, unwinding the spools of thread attached to their kites.

Rehana began again.

★ ★ ★

Dear Husband,

I have given up the only thing you left me. When the judge asked me if I knew for certain whether I would be able to care for them, I could not bring myself to say yes. I was mute, and in my silence he saw my hesitation. That is why he gave them away. It was me; my fault. No other's. I don't blame your brother for wanting them. Who would not want them? They are the spitting image of you.

★ ★ ★

After the verdict, in that hot room with the dust-furred ceiling fans, the black shine of velvet benches, the tattered grey wig of the judge, she

9

had fallen to her knees. She had not been able to convince anyone that even though she was poor, and friendless in this town and the only thing left to her was a wild, untamed plot of land so recently reclaimed from the paddy she had to burn the insects that marched on to her small bungalow porch every morning when she woke to pray, she could still be a mother to her children. She had not explained to the children where exactly their father had gone, and she had let them stay home from school, and she had taken them to watch *Cleopatra*, but she could still be their mother; she would find a way to overcome her grief, her poverty, her youth; she would find a way to love them all alone. But no one had believed her, and in a few weeks they would travel across the continent, and she didn't know when she would ever see them again.

★ ★ ★

Faiz and Parveen took the children to Lahore a few days later on Pakistan International Airlines Flight 010. Rehana watched them leave from an airport window made foggy by hair oil and goodbye fingerprints. She waved a small wave, wondering when the world would stop ending. Maya and Sohail, their kites tucked under their arms, fastened their seatbelts and sailed gracefully into the sky, crossing the flooded delta below.

The next day Parveen called to say they had arrived safely, but Rehana could hear very little aside from the crackle of the long-distance line, and the cultivated, genteel laugh that conveyed both confidence and an awkward regret.

★ ★ ★

In the days that followed, people came to see her: Iqbal's business acquaintances; old men claiming to be friends of her father; distant relatives with wagging, so-sorry tongues; her gin-rummy friends from the Dhaka Gymkhana Club; even the lawyer. Grief tourists, Rehana thought, and pretended not to hear them scratching at the door.

All but Mrs Chowdhury, who came dragging a sad, tearful daughter. She held Rehana in the rolling fat of her arms and scolded her daughter for sulking.

'Silvi, it's not the end of the world. They'll be back.' And then she turned to Rehana. 'At least you had a few good years. My bastard husband left me when I couldn't give him a son. Took one look at this one, and I never saw him again.'

Rehana sat immobile, staring into the garden. Mrs Chowdhury finally said, 'We should let the poor girl rest.'

Silvi idled behind the kitchen door. 'Nine years old!' Mrs Chowdhury cried out. 'Too old to sulk, too young to be heart-broken. What, you think no boy will ever ask to marry you again?'

'Let her stay,' Rehana said; 'we can eat together.' She tried to imagine what she might feed the child. She hadn't been shopping. There was just a weak, watery dal and some bitter gourd.

11

'You said we would see *Roman Holiday*.'
'Next time, Silvi, OK?'
'If they ever come back. OK.'
She left. Rehana didn't see her to the door.

★　★　★

Rehana watched the days go by. She began letters to Sohail and Maya:

The mangoes will be perfect this year. It has been hot and raining at all the right times. I can already smell the tree.

She threw that one away. She also threw away the one that began:

My dearest children, how I miss you.

She wrote cheerful, newsy letters. The children should not be confused. They should know these important facts:

She was going to get them back soon.

The world was still a generally friendly place.

Silvi had not forgotten them.

The neighbourhood was exactly as it had always been.

Her memories of the children were scrambled and vague. The more she clutched at them, the more distant they became. She tried to stick to facts: Maya's favourite colour is blue, Sohail's is red. Sohail has a small scar on his chin, just below the ridge. She had teased him and said, 'This is a scar only your wife will see, because she will stand just beneath you and look up,' and he had said, very seriously, 'What if she is a very tall girl?'

Her son had a sense of humour. No, he was

completely unfunny. He barely ever smiled. Which was it?

She took comfort in telling them apart. She remembered which was the loud, demanding child, which the quiet, watchful one. The one who sang to birds to see if they would sing back. The one whose fingernails she had to check, because she liked the taste of mud. The one who caught chills, whether the day was cold or fiercely hot. The one who sucked red juice from the tiny flowers of the ixora bush. The one who spoke; the one who wouldn't; the one who loved Clark Gable; the one who loved Dilip Kumar, and stray dogs, and crows that landed on the gate with sharp, clicking talons, and milk-rice, and Baby ice-cream.

And she couldn't get off her mind all the times Iqbal had fretted over them, making them wear sweaters when it wasn't even cold, having the doctor visit every month to put his ear to their little chests, holding hands on busy roads and empty roads — *just in case, just in case, just in case*. And then there was that train journey that they almost didn't take.

It was Maya's fourth birthday, and Iqbal's new Vauxhall had just arrived from England. It was on a special consignment of fifty cars brought to Dhaka from the Vauxhall factory in Wandsworth, London, in 1957. Iqbal had seen an advertisement that told him about the smart new car with the restyled radiator and the winding handles. There was a photograph. He fell in love with the car: the smooth curves, the side-view mirrors that jutted out of the frame. He imagined driving

13

it into their garage, a big ribbon tied around the top, the horn blaring. But when it arrived, he was too nervous to drive the car and decided to leave it in the hands of a driver he hired for the purpose, an ex-employee of the British Consul-General who had driven His Excellency's Rolls-Royce and was an expert behind the wheel. His name was Kamal. It was Kamal who was driving the Vauxhall the day Maya waved to her father from the window of the Tejgaon — Phulbaria rail carriage.

As a special birthday treat for Maya, they had decided to take a train ride between a new station on the fringes of the city and Phulbaria Central; tracks had just been opened, and it was now a short trip from the brightly painted station built by a hopeful government to the crumbling colonial building that housed the old carriages of the Raj. It was to be their very first train ride.

On the appointed day Rehana made kabab rolls and Iqbal counted clouds, hoping to declare an incoming storm and cancel the whole affair. But there was only a cool October breeze and a scattering of lacy, translucent threads in the sky. Kamal started the car and opened the doors for them. Iqbal instructed everyone to sit in the back. Maya entered first, in her birthday dress, which Rehana had sewn of pale blue satin. There was a netted petticoat, which made the dress puff out at an unlikely angle. Blue ribbons were fastened to her hair, and she had managed to convince Rehana to dab her mouth with the lightest frost of pink lipstick; this she attempted to safeguard by keeping her lips held in a stiff

14

pout. Rehana settled into the car, balancing the food on her lap, and motioned for Iqbal and Sohail to hurry up. But they were having some sort of argument outside.

'Abboo, there's no space at the back.'

'You can't sit in front, it's too dangerous.'

'Oof, Abboo, I'm not a baby any more!' Sohail stomped a foot on the ground.

'Accidents can happen, doesn't matter if you are big boy or small. Accident doesn't discriminate.'

Rehana rolled down the window. 'Sohail, do as your abboo says.'

In the end Sohail piled sullenly into the car, with Iqbal following. It was tight, with all four of them in the back. Maya's dress swelled out in front of her like a small blue high-tide. Iqbal's white sharkskin suit was getting crumpled. Really, Rehana thought, he should have just let the poor boy sit in front with the driver. It was so hot. She rolled down the window defiantly and motioned for Sohail to do the same on his side. Maya's ribbons lapped gently in the breeze.

By the time they had reached Tejgaon, Iqbal had begun to worry about the journey again. If they were stuck on the train, how would anyone know? What if Kamal was late in arriving at the station? He mentally calculated the odds of this happening. As Kamal drove them up to the Tejgaon Station, he had an idea.

'Rehana, you go with the children. I have decided to stay.'

'What's that?'

'I will stay in the car with Kamal. We'll drive

15

beside the train. That way, if anything happens, you can just leave the train and ride in the car.' Ingenious!

So that is what they did. She remembered it clearly: the man in the car, his family on the train, the train carriage on the new rail line and the new foreign car on the adjacent road, the taste of kabab rolls and lemonade lingering lazily on their tongues, and her husband, beaming to himself, satisfied at last that no harm would come to his family, because he, Iqbal, had made absolutely sure.

March 1971

Shona with her back to the sun

Every year, Rehana held a party at Road 5 to mark the day she had returned to Dhaka with the children. She saved her meat rations and made biryani. She rented chairs and called the jilapiwallah to fry the hot, looping sweets in the garden. There was a red-and-yellow tent in case of rain, lemonade in case of heat, cucumber salad, spicy yoghurt. The guests were always the same: her neighbour Mrs Chowdhury and her daughter Silvi; her tenants, the Senguptas, and their son, Mithun; and Mrs Rahman and Mrs Akram, better known as the gin-rummy ladies.

So, on the first morning of March, as on the first morning of every March for a decade, Rehana rose before dawn and slipped into the garden. She shivered a little and rubbed her elbows as she made her way across the lawn. Winter still lingered on the leaves and in the wisps of fog that rolled over the delta and hung low over the bungalow.

She dipped her fingers into the rosebush, heavy with dew, and plucked a flower. She held it in her hand as she wandered through the rest of the garden, ducking between the wall-hugging jasmine and the hibiscus, crossing the tiny vegetable patch that was giving them the last of the season's cauliflower, zigzagging past the mango tree, the lemon tree, the shouting-green banana tree.

She looked up at the building that would slowly, over the course of the day, cast a long shadow over her little bungalow. *Shona*. She could still hear Mrs Chowdhury telling her to build the new house at the back of her property. 'Such a big plot,' she'd said, peering out of the window; 'you can't even see the boundary it's so far away. You don't need all that space.'

'Should I sell it?'

Mrs Chowdhury snapped her tongue. 'Na, don't sell it.'

'Then what?'

'Build another house.'

'What would I do with another house?'

'Rent, my dear. Rent it out.'

Now there were two gates, two driveways, two houses. The new driveway was a narrow passage that opened into the back of Rehana's plot. On the plot stood the house she had built to save her children. It towered above the bungalow, its two whitewashed storeys overlooking the smaller house. Like the bungalow, it had been built with its back to the sun. The house was nearly ten years old now, and a little faded. Ten monsoons had softened its edges and drawn meandering, old-age seams into the walls. But every day, as Rehana woke for the dawn Azaan, or when she went to put the washing in the garden, or when, after bathing, she fanned out her long hair on the back of a veranda chair, Rehana looked at the house with pride and a little ache. It was there to remind her of what she had lost, and what she had won. And how much the victory had cost. That is why she had named it *Shona*, gold. It wasn't just because of what it had taken to build the house, but for all the precious things she wanted never to lose again.

Rehana turned back to the bungalow and entered the drawing room. She ran her palm across the flat fur of the velvet sofa, the dimpled wood of the dining table. The scratched, loved, faded whitewash of the veranda wall.

She unfurled her prayer mat, pointed it westwards and sank to her knees.

This was the start of the ritual: wake before sunrise, feel her way around the house; pray; wake the children.

They were not children any more. She had to keep reminding herself of this fact. At nineteen and seventeen, they were almost grown up. She clung greedily to the *almost*, but she knew it would not last long, this hovering, flirting with adulthood. Already they were beings apart, fast on their way to shedding the fierce, hungry mother-need.

★   ★   ★

21

Rehana lifted the mosquito net and nudged Maya's shoulder. 'Wake up, jaan,' she said. 'It's our anniversary!'

She went to Sohail's room and knocked, but he was already awake. 'For you,' she said, holding out the rose.

While the children took turns in the bath, Rehana ironed their new clothes. This year she had chosen an egg-blue sari for herself and a blue georgette with yellow polka dots for Maya. For Sohail there was a brown kurta-pyjama. She had embroidered the purple flowers on the collar herself.

'Ammoo,' Maya said, 'I have to go to campus after the party — I can't wear this.'

'I'm sure your activist friends won't mind if you don't wear white for one day.'

'You wouldn't understand,' she retorted, tucking the sari under her elbow anyway.

After they had all bathed and put on their new clothes, the children took turns touching Rehana's feet. 'God bless you,' she said, hugging them tightly, their strong, tanned arms around her neck almost beyond her imagination.

They were both taller than her. Maya had passed Rehana by a few inches, and Sohail was a full head and shoulders above them both; Rehana was often reminded of the moment she'd met Iqbal, hunched over the wedding dais, how he had towered over her like a thunder cloud. But in fact Sohail had grown to resemble Rehana. He was pale and had her small nose and her slightly crooked teeth; his hair was fashioned into a wave at the top of his head, the crest

22

threatening to tip over his eyelids. Sometimes, like today, he wore kurta-pyjamas, but usually he was seen in more fashionable attire: tight, long-collared shirts and even tighter trousers that hung over his shoes and drew tracks in the dust.

It was Maya who looked more like her father. She had his chestnut skin and deep-set eyes that made her look serious even when she was trying to say something funny or make a joke — which rarely happened — but Rehana had often seen her friends pause and look at each other, wondering whether to laugh.

They took two rickshaws. Maya and Sohail climbed into the first and Rehana followed. She liked being behind them, watching their shoulders knocking through the rolled-up flap on the back of the rickshaw.

She hadn't seen her own sisters for years now. Marzia had come to Dhaka a few years after the children's return. She had brought photos of her own children, plump twin boys with big faces and windswept hair. She kept talking about the smell of salt in the Karachi streets, and the burned taste of kababs on Clifton Beach, and, even though she devoured Rehana's dimer halwa and swallowed the sweet Dhaka air with relish, she kept asking, again and again, why Rehana hadn't gone to live in Karachi when her husband had died. 'Everyone is there,' she'd said. 'Your whole family.'

When they parted at the airport Rehana had felt empty; she wanted to long for Marzia to stay, to cry and beg to be taken with her, but in the end she was just relieved to see her go. Marzia had behaved as though Rehana had betrayed them all; she had said things like, 'Your Urdu is not as good as it used to be; must be all that Bengali you're speaking.' She had pronounced it *Bungali*. And when she had referred to the servants at her house, she had said, 'Yes, we're very lucky, we have two *Bungalis*; Rokeya only has one and it's never enough, you know, the houses out there are so big.'

Still, there wasn't a day that went by that Rehana didn't think of them, out there in the sprawling, parched western wing of their country. She held them to her by a loose bit of feeling, not fully connected, not entirely severed. She wrote them letters. *Dear sisters*, she would begin. She never finished one; she never sent one. She kept the letters in a biscuit tin under her bed, beside the winter blankets and the dried rice balls.

The rickshaws crossed Road 5 and made their way through Mirpur Road, blue-black and newly paved. The shops nudging the road were beginning to open, their shutters rattling up, the shopkeepers clearing their noses in the outside gutters.

* * *

A sign above the graveyard said WOMEN NO ADMITTANCE. Beside it, the caretaker leaned his elbow on a new length of wooden fencing painted a dull yellow and already smattered with flecks of mud. He gave Rehana a salaam and said, 'Hot day.' She nodded and gave him five annas. They wove through the gravestones. As she passed them, Rehana recognized old friends and noted a few new arrivals.

There was a man who had been visiting his wife every day for forty-three years. She had died, it was rumoured, in childbirth. The man was very old now, but he made the unsteady walk to his wife's grave, laid down a small square of pati and sat facing her for hours at a time. So Rehana had always considered herself the second-most devoted mourner at the graveyard. She had never met the man, but once, after he'd left, she had approached his wife's grave. BEGUM HAKIM ULLAH HOSSAIN, the headstone read, WIFE AND MOTHER.

Over the years Rehana had made sure Iqbal's was one of the best-tended squares in the graveyard. She began by doing what everyone else did: laying roses on his gravestone. But every time she came back to find the sight of the rotten flowers, she felt she had somehow betrayed him. She didn't want to see dead things when she came to visit. So she planted a few seeds around the edge of the plot, and a few weeks later the tiny white bokul flowers appeared, casting themselves resolutely upwards, as though pointing the way. Rehana came back regularly with her trowel and her watering can, trimming and perfecting the little white border.

Now she stood at the foot of Iqbal's grave, facing the headstone that said, in black letters, MUHAMMAD IQBAL HAQUE. Sohail was on her left, Maya on her right. They cupped their hands and held them up.

This was the part when her throat always tightened.

My dear Husband, she began. Here are your two grown children. Mahshallah, it is the tenth year of their return.

Your son is now nineteen. Your daughter is seventeen. They are healthy and obedient.

Last time I was here I told you about the elections. Right now we are waiting for Mujib to be declared Prime Minister. There have been many delays. Your children are waiting for the government to change. Inshallah, once that happens they will be able to return to their studies.

She paused, took a deep breath. Steadied herself.

There was so much more she could say. I still miss you every day. Why did you leave me all alone. Why.

But she didn't. If he was listening he would know it all anyway.

She pressed her palms to her face. Goodbye, Husband.

When she looked up, Rehana saw Sohail brush a few tears from his cheek. Maya was stroking the headstone. Then she bent down and kissed it at the top, where the dome was highest.

★ ★ ★

They returned to the bungalow to get ready for the guests. Maya dusted the drawing-room furniture, and Sohail helped the decorators to put up the tent in the garden. Rehana had made

26

the biryani the night before, layering the ingredients and sealing the pot with flour paste. It had taken six or seven hours to cook; now she peeled back the seal, lifted the lid, and mixed up the layers of meat, potato and rice so that they were evenly distributed.

She counted out the plates. There would be about twenty people altogether. She was always nervous before this party; since she'd stopped going to the Gymkhana Club, it was one of the few times a year she saw her friends.

They had understood her absence from the club after Iqbal's death. They came to her instead; Mrs Rahman, Rehana remembered, often brought cake. Hard, inedible cake that would sit brick-like on the dining table, collecting flies and scraps of dust. Mrs Chowdhury brought Silvi. And Mrs Akram, the youngest of them, skirted awkwardly around her, brushing the stink of bad fortune from the air with a flapping hand-fan.

After the children came back, there was, the gin-rummy ladies said, no reason for Rehana to stay away. So she tried once, a few months after she returned from Lahore, to revive the old group.

★   ★   ★

Mrs Chowdhury had been in a particularly festive mood that day, a smile playing in her eyes. 'I have a surprise!' she said to Rehana. Rehana had ignored her. Must be a new sweetshop she'd discovered. Best laddoos in town, she could almost hear her say. She felt awkward and nervous; it was hot inside, and the fans pulsing from the ceiling didn't seem to be doing much good. She had been to the club many times before, but suddenly it was all very strange, and she was a little annoyed with Mrs Chowdhury for appearing so cheerful.

The square card table was decorated with flower-patterned tiles. The names of the flowers were written underneath with a curling, feminine hand. Bougainvillea, they declared. English rose. Daffodil.

Rehana had sat facing a row of yellow tulips. Across from her, Mrs Chowdhury was perched between the asters and the lilacs. Mrs Rahman shuffled over a row of dahlias. Mrs Akram made up the fourth, reapplying her lipstick in a thin sliver of mirror.

'OK,' Mrs Rahman said to Rehana. 'Cut.'

Rehana divided the stack in two. Mrs Rahman shuffled again, raising her arm high and bringing it down again with a slap.

'Face cards ten, low ace, as usual,' she said, tossing cards to the four corners of the table.

There was a knock. A waiter wearing a coat that used to be white came in with a tray of teacups and a plate of biscuits. 'Finally,' Mrs Chowdhury giggled. 'Just leave it here. No need to pour. Go. *Go*.' She lifted her bag from where it sat on the floor and pulled out a small silver flask. She unscrewed the top and tipped its tea-coloured contents into the four cups. She topped up the cups with real tea. Then like a chemist, she added milk. 'There we are!' she said with a flourish.

'What is it?' Mrs Akram asked, looking up from her mirror.

'Whisky, you idiot,' Mrs Rahman said. 'What's the matter with you — drink. God knows we deserve it.'

Rehana saw Mrs Rahman trying to catch her eye. No one moved; Mrs Chowdhury sighed and lifted a cup from the tray. 'All right, then, as you wish.' She looked up at the ceiling with its furry cornice. 'I just thought Rehana needed a little mischief. After all, she won't get married!'

This last statement caused Mrs Akram to giggle. She did it nervously, in muffled, half-snorting bursts, with a hand over her mouth.

Rehana could smell the sugary aroma of the whisky rising from the cups. 'All right,' she said. 'I'll have one.'

'Really?' Mrs Chowdhury almost squealed with joy.

'Yes, sure. I've tried it before.' Iqbal had once given her a taste. He'd held the glass to her mouth, withdrawing it as soon as the liquid touched her lips. It was like a feverish kiss. She picked up the teacup now and sipped tentatively. The others saw her doing it and followed, smiling into their cups. Mrs Chowdhury gulped hers down and clapped.

They began to play. Rehana won the first game with four aces and a suite of hearts. Mrs Rahman won the second, and at the end of the third Mrs Chowdhury said, 'RUMMY!' but there was a four missing in her row of spades.

She said it didn't matter, she'd brought the whisky, that had to count for something. Then Mrs Akram, who had to use two hands to hold up all of her cards, said, 'But it's still a mystery, no, why our Rehana here refuses to choose a bridegroom?'

Rehana thought Mrs Chowdhury would come to her defence, but she said, 'It's true, Rehana, we are always worried about you — what's the matter?'

Rehana found they were all pointing their faces at her with fixed, devouring stares. The whisky flooded into her stomach at that moment, as Rehana realized she no longer had the energy to laugh it off and be cheerful; she didn't want to blush and bite her lip and pretend to be coy. The truth was, she had no intention of remarrying. There was that one time she had considered it, before she'd built Shona. But ever since the children had returned, the urge to be loved in that way had disappeared from her altogether. It was too risky. It could too easily go wrong. And the thought that some man might be cruel to her children was enough to make the bile rise in her throat.

She didn't say any of this to the gin-rummy ladies. She just stopped attending the card parties. She complained of a headache, and then Maya caught the chicken pox, and so of course Sohail had to have it too, and soon they stopped asking altogether. By then Mrs Sengupta had taken her place at the table. Rehana tried to ignore her certainty that they were muttering about her refusal to marry and her general aloofness as they tossed the cards to the middle of the table and sipped their whisky-studded tea. She knew she must seem strange and remote to them. That they must wonder what was wrong. But even if she tried to explain it to them she knew they could never understand. It had never happened to anyone else.

★   ★   ★

Mrs Chowdhury arrived first. From the kitchen Rehana heard her twisting the latch on the gate. 'Maya, keep an eye on the biryani,' she said, and hurried to the front door.

'Sweeten your tongue, Rehana,' Mrs Chowdhury said, squeezing through the doorway, 'I have some news!' She held out a box of laddoos. A tall man in a military uniform followed her in. Behind him was Mrs Chowdhury's daughter, Silvi, overdressed for the occasion in a ropy gold necklace and a pair of ruby earrings.

Mrs Chowdhury waved towards the uniformed man. 'My son-in-law!' she giggled, causing a ripple through her neck, her chin and her bottom lip. She stuffed a piece of laddoo into Rehana's mouth.

'Really — oh.' The laddoo was like a lump of candy; it travelled coldly down Rehana's throat. 'You told me you were accepting proposals, but I didn't know things would happen so quickly.' She swallowed and tried to smile. 'Congratulations.'

'Well — they're not engaged yet. But I wanted

31

you to be the first to know.'

The uniformed man greeted her. 'As-Salaam Alaikum.' His mouth was rubber-band tight. Just above was the neatly sewn scar of a cleft lip.

'Walaikum As-Salaam,' Rehana replied. 'Please, come in, sit down.' She didn't quite know what to say next, so settled on more pleasantries. 'I'm very glad you could come.'

'Silvi, you sit here,' Mrs Chowdhury instructed, 'and jamaibabu, you sit beside her.'

Silvi and the uniformed man did as they were told.

'The boy came over last week,' Mrs Chowdhury whispered, 'with his mother and his aunt. Very handsome, don't you think? Doesn't talk very much, but then I was thinking, that is just perfect for my shy Silvi. They're two of a kind — and he's a lieutenant!' She tittered and the ripples returned, spreading to her cheeks.

Just as Rehana was trying to think of how she would break the news to Sohail, the Senguptas crossed the garden and knocked on the drawing-room window. Their son Mithun was in tow, dragging his feet in the grass.

'Hello — it's us.'

'Come in, come in,' Rehana said, grateful for the distraction.

Mrs Sengupta was wearing a peacock-blue sari and a sleeveless blouse that showed off her gleaming, ebony shoulders. Taller than her husband by at least three inches, she took advantage of her height by mounting a pair of platform heels and cutting her hair short so that it revealed the ridged length of her neck, which was adorned with a heavy gold mangalsutra, the ornament that identified her as married, and Hindu, and rich. Her husband, by contrast, was a squat man with tiny, wringing hands.

'Mithun, would you like some lemonade?' Rehana asked, turning her attention to the boy.

Mithun put a hot hand on Rehana's wrist. 'Tea, please. I have a headache.'

'I don't think you're allowed tea, beta.'

'No — that's right,' his mother said. 'What's got into you?'

'You said it was a *special occasion*.'

'True,' Rehana said. 'It is a special occasion. How about an orange cola?' She left to get the drinks while Mrs Chowdhury repeated her news to the Senguptas.

Sohail and Maya were slicing cucumbers in the kitchen.

Rehana's only thought was to get Sohail out of the house. She couldn't think beyond that; eventually he would have to return, but she just needed time to come up with a way to tell him the news first, to somehow soften the blow. 'Sohail,' she said, 'I need you to pick up some sweets from Alauddin.'

'Aren't we having jilapi?'

She cleared her throat and attempted to sound bossy. 'I don't think it'll be enough — you know how people like a little something sweet after biryani.'

'It's all the way on the other side of town — I'll be at least an hour.'

'Don't worry, people will stay all afternoon. You'll be back in time.' She gave him a few notes. 'Take a rickshaw,' she said. He turned towards the drawing room, more irritated than suspicious. 'No, go out through the back or you'll be held up for hours if Mrs Chowdhury gets hold of you.' She watched him guiltily as he shrugged and ducked out of the kitchen.

Maya could not be duped. 'What's going on, Ammoo?' She sat squatting behind the curved blade of the boti, her polka-dot sari wound around her ankles.

Rehana peered out of the kitchen window to make sure Sohail was out of earshot. 'Silvi's getting married.'

'*What?*'

'I know. It's all of a sudden. I knew Mrs Chowdhury was looking for a boy, but they've hardly met.'

'And Silvi agreed?' Maya jabbed aggressively at her cucumber.

Rehana nodded.

'God. My poor brother. What should we do?'

'I don't know. Just make sure he doesn't bump into them when he comes back.'

★   ★   ★

In the drawing room Rehana found that Mrs Rahman and Mrs Akram had already arrived. The two went everywhere together, and always without their husbands or their children, wearing fugitive looks and sighing about escaping from home. Rehana was happy to see the room filling up; it made her resist the urge to stare at Silvi and her fiancé. And now there

34

was the food to distract them all.

'Lunch is ready,' she announced, setting the heavy tray of biryani on the table. The guests made their way across the room as Rehana filled up the plates and passed them around.

'A wedding in the neighbourhood,' Mrs Akram said; 'you must be the first — what fun we'll have!'

Rehana piled on the biryani. 'Let me take your plate, Mr Sengupta. You must have some more.' Rehana had prepared a special vegetarian dish for the Senguptas.

'Enough! Your tenants will be eating you out of house and home,' he protested, putting his hand over his plate.

'It's been ten years,' Rehana said. 'Time you stopped calling yourselves tenants.' She made for the kitchen to replenish the biryani.

Rehana found Silvi lingering in the corridor. 'It's really good this year, khala-moni.' She always addressed Rehana as khalamoni, as though Mrs Chowdhury and Rehana were real sisters. Silvi still had a pale, ashen complexion, though the pallor suited her; without it, her light eyes might have been eclipsed, but, as it was, they reflected the sun and shone like bright, chalky pinpoints.

'Thank you — I made it in such a hurry.' Rehana's eyes lingered on Silvi, searching for an answer to the question she couldn't bring herself to ask.

'I wouldn't have guessed — it's delicious. You make the best biryani in Dhaka.'

Rehana nodded, accepting the compliment.

Silvi glanced down at herself and straightened her necklace.

There was a long silence. 'So. You're getting married,' Rehana said finally. She tried to sound cheerful.

'Yes, I . . . ' Silvi stammered, 'well, my mother was worried. I don't like her to worry. She has high blood pressure, you know.'

'Well, she looks very pleased,' Rehana said. She cupped Silvi's cheek, felt it yielding under her fingers. 'You've made her very happy.'

★ ★ ★

Sohail arrived with the sweets after the guests had collapsed under the shade of the tent. Rehana tried to intercept him at the gate, but she was carrying a handful of plates and Mrs Chowdhury got to him first.

'Sohail!' Mrs Chowdhury grabbed Sohail's arm. 'Where have you been? I have news. Silvi's getting married!'

Rehana saw Sohail brushing the hair back from his forehead with raking fingers. His other hand, holding the sweets box, rocked back and forth.

'Come, come, you must meet him. Sabeer, this is Mrs Haque's son, Sohail. A very old friend of Silvi — they were inseparable as children — Sohail, baba, this is Lieutenant Sabeer Mustafa.'

'Welcome to the family,' Sohail said.

'Thank you,' Sabeer replied, standing up and straightening his uniform.

36

'Sohail, jaan, will you help me with these plates?' Rehana attempted to hand him the stack.

'Well,' he said, ignoring her, 'I've just got tickets to tomorrow's cricket match. Pakistan vs England MCC.' He fanned out the tickets and waved them in the air. 'Who wants to come? Lieutenant, will you join us?'

'No, I'm afraid I'm on duty tomorrow,' Sabeer said.

'Silvi? Will you?' Sohail pointed the tickets at her.

'I don't think so,' Mrs Chowdhury said, jumping in. 'We have a lot of preparations to make.'

'I'll come,' Mrs Sengupta said cheerfully. 'Your mother will come too, won't you, Rehana?'

'I'll come as well. I'm afraid there's no room for you after all, Silvi,' Maya said pointedly. 'Another time perhaps.'

There was a long silence as Maya and Rehana finished clearing the rest of the plates. Rehana was hoping someone would begin a conversation, something to change the subject, but no one was saying anything. Mrs Rahman and Mrs Akram passed around the box of sweets. Finally Mr Sengupta brought up everyone's favorite topic: the election.

'How are things on the student front, Sohail?' he asked.

'It's uncertain, Uncle,' Sohail replied, his eyes darting around the garden. 'It's been two months since Mujib won the election. They should have convened the national assembly by now and

37

made him Prime Minister, but they keep delaying. Some of the students are urging Mujib to take more drastic action.' He suddenly looked weary; his shirtsleeves were crumpled, as though someone had grabbed his arms and pulled him into a tight embrace.

'Drastic action?'

'He should declare independence.'

'But he's won the election — surely now his demands will be met?' Mr Sengupta said.

'Yes,' Sohail said. 'But they've postponed the assembly too many times.'

Sohail looked as if he were about to start speechifying again. Rehana felt her face growing hot.

'Mujib is a canny politician,' Mrs Rahman interjected. 'He must know something we don't.'

'Perhaps there's still a chance for diplomacy,' Mr Sengupta said.

'Diplomacy? Forgive me, Chacha. You think Bhutto and Yahya want diplomacy?'

Sohail seemed on the point of turning away from the conversation when Sabeer raised his hand. 'You think we can make it as our own country?' he asked. Rehana wondered if Sohail would take the bait.

He did. 'If you knew anything about the country you would know that West Pakistan is bleeding us out. We earn most of the foreign exchange. We grow the rice, we make the jute, and yet we get nothing — no schools, no hospitals, no army. We can't even speak our own bloody language!'

Rehana waited for Sabeer to say something,

something aggressive and blunt; his military training would have taught him that, but he turned away instead, fingering the buttons on his uniform.

'Cyclone, young fellow,' Mr Sengupta interrupted, attempting to make peace. 'Nature. We live in a low-lying delta. And we have bad luck.'

'Starvation is not caused by God. It is caused by irresponsible governments.' Sohail rolled and unrolled the sleeve of his kurta. Rehana wondered if he was going to go on talking about the country's fortunes, the jute money, the cyclone. But he looked as though he'd run out of air. 'What we have here is an emergency,' he said in a tired voice. 'There is no possibility of reconciliation now. Mujib should have declared independence.'

Rehana had ordered two crates of orange cola, which she hurriedly passed around. She had to get the party back on course. The guests gratefully accepted the drinks and began to sip. They clinked the small glass bottles and smiled hesitantly into their straws. Their saris and kurtas flapped in the sugary March breeze, and the evening regained its still feeling, like the heavy pause before a mighty thunderclap.

★   ★   ★

The gin-rummy ladies offered to help Rehana put away the biryani. She wasn't sure she wanted the company, but they insisted, and she was too tired to protest.

'You didn't do a very good job of finishing the

food,' Rehana complained, examining the trays of rice. 'I'll have to send all of this to the mosque.'

'You might make up a packet for me,' Mrs Chowdhury said. 'You know how much I love it the next day.'

'I've already put some aside for you,' Rehana said, presenting her with a cardboard box. She saw Mrs Chowdhury eyeing it for size, calculating the number of meals she might make of it.

'There's still a lot left over.' Perhaps she hadn't done such a good job with the biryani this year after all.

'Just invite a few of Sohail's friends to dinner,' Mrs Rahman said. 'I'm sure they'll have no trouble finishing up the lot.'

'You know, I had no idea he was so involved in student politics,' Mrs Akram said, sorting through the glasses and the empty bottles of soda.

'He isn't,' Rehana replied, heaving a pile of plates into the washbasin. 'He's been trying to stay out of it.' She picked up the top plate and began to circulate a sponge around its rim.

'Sounded quite heated to me,' Mrs Rahman said.

'Well, you know, he's young and full of ideas.' Rehana felt a bit defensive. It was always difficult for the rest of them to understand: Mrs Akram's children were still in school, Mrs Rahman's three children had all married sensibly, and Silvi hardly strayed out of her mother's grasp. Her own children seemed a little out of control by comparison. 'It's just in the air — all this talk about delaying the assembly — the students are getting nervous, they're worried the elections won't be honoured.'

'He sounds quite involved to me,' Mrs Rahman insisted. 'And your Maya is in the Chattra League, no?'

Mrs Chowdhury decided to come to Rehana's rescue. 'What she's saying is — why doesn't the boy waste his time chasing girls instead!'

The kitchen suddenly grew quiet.

Rehana turned around and caught Mrs Chowdhury's eye. 'What?' she said. 'What?'

No one replied. Rehana realized they were making a space for her to say something. She opened her mouth and tried, but she couldn't think of the right sequence of words.

Mrs Rahman broke the silence. 'Are you the last to know?' she said.

'Know what?'

Rehana thought she might still be able to stop the conversation there, but something kept her swirling the plates with her back to the room. Let them have it out.

'Sohail is in love with your daughter,' she heard Mrs Rahman say.

'Ohhhh,' Mrs Chowdhury laughed, 'that. Don't be silly — that was just a childish thing.'

Rehana kept moving the sponge in circles. No one said anything; Rehana thought she could hear them all holding their breath, waiting for her to speak, but she was mesmerized by her plate and her sponge and the little orange flecks of rice that floated like petals in the dishwater.

'Well,' Mrs Chowdhury said finally, noisily heaving herself upright. 'I didn't know. The girl never told me.'

'You had no idea?' Mrs Rahman said.

'Of course I had no idea!'

Just then they heard heavy, running footsteps approaching the kitchen.

'Ammoo!'

It was Maya.

'Ammoo,' she said, panting and red-faced from the effort, 'Bhaiya's just sitting in the garden with his head in his hands.'

Lemonade, he needs lemonade. Rehana handed her daughter a clean glass. 'Here. Get some shorbot from the fridge.'

Maya must have sensed there was something going on in the kitchen because for once she just set off obediently, her chappals clacking behind her as she ran.

'Rehana,' Mrs Chowdhury said, 'you must believe me. I really didn't know.'

Rehana turned back to the washbasin and picked up another plate.

'She didn't say anything,' Mrs Chowdhury repeated, 'and he's so young — just a student — surely it's foolish to think — '

'So you did know,' Mrs Akram said.

'No, I didn't.' Rehana felt Mrs Chowdhury approach her. 'Rehana agrees with me, don't you, my dear — that it would be a bad idea? I'm sure she discouraged her son as well.'

Rehana swallowed the lump in her throat. 'Yes, of course you're right.' What could she do now? Just save her son from any further humiliation.

'See — she agrees,' Mrs Chowdhury announced.

Mrs Rahman shook her head. She began spooning the leftover biryani out of the giant metal pot it had been cooked in. The kitchen swelled with its perfume, and quickly the room shrank and the air was tight, filled with the remains of the afternoon heat, the buzzing of the bulb, Mrs Chowdhury's loud sighing.

'I don't know what the fuss is about. There's no way — no way — they couldn't be serious.'

Rehana finished rinsing her plate and began working on another. She thought that it must be the cleanest plate in the world. Mrs Akram picked it up and wiped it with the end of her sari.

'He's too busy with his politics — he'll never make a good husband. Anyway, he's younger than her.'

Rehana couldn't bear the conversation any longer. 'Please, Mrs Chowdhury — don't worry. It was just a misunderstanding.'

'That's right,' Mrs Chowdhury said, satisfied. 'Nobody forced Silvi.' Then she turned abruptly on her heel. 'I'm tired. Goodnight, everyone. Khoda Hafez.' She bustled away, knocking a row of empty pickle jars as she rounded the corner.

Mrs Rahman was elbow-deep in the biryani pot. 'Rehana,' she began, 'I'm so sorry — '

'Let's not speak of it.'

Mrs Rahman and Mrs Akram looked at each other as though this was exactly what they'd expected her to say.

43

'You don't speak of it. But I can say it's a shame.'

'Please.' Rehana chewed the inside of her lip. She gripped her plate; the soap slipped between her fingers. 'I'll take care of the rest — the children will help — it's getting late, I shouldn't keep you.' She brushed her cheek with the back of her wrist, where it itched.

'Let's go,' Mrs Akram said. 'Come on.' She peeled Mrs Rahman's arm out of the biryani dish.

'Goodnight, Rehana,' they said softly.

'Goodnight, friends,' she whispered back. She wasn't sure if they'd heard her.

★　★　★

Later, after the children had fallen asleep, Rehana climbed under her mosquito net and pulled the katha up to her chin.

She lingered over the Silvi episode, wondering if there was something she could have done. Sohail had avoided her all evening and gone to bed without his tea. She thought she saw a small accusation in the set of his mouth as he said goodnight.

He'll never make a good husband, she heard Mrs Chowdhury say. Too much politics.

The comment had stung because it was probably true. Lately the children had little time for anything but the struggle. It had started when Sohail entered the university. Ever since '48, the Pakistani authorities had ruled the eastern wing of the country like a colony. First

44

they tried to force everyone to speak Urdu instead of Bengali. They took the jute money from Bengal and spent it on factories in Karachi and Islamabad. One general after another made promises they had no intention of keeping. The Dhaka University students had been involved in the protests from the very beginning, so it was no surprise Sohail had got caught up, and Maya too. Even Rehana could see the logic: what sense did it make to have a country in two halves, poised on either side of India like a pair of horns?

But in 1970, when the cyclone hit, it was as though everything came into focus. Rehana remembered the day Sohail and Maya had returned from the rescue operation: the red in their eyes as they told her how they had waited for the food trucks to come and watched as the water rose and the bodies washed up on the shore; how they had realized, with mounting panic, that the food wouldn't come because it had never been sent.

The next day Maya had joined the student Communist Party. She donated all of her clothes to the cyclone victims and began wearing only white saris. Rehana hated to see the white saris on her daughter, but Maya didn't notice. She swallowed, like sugar, every idea passed to her by the party elders. *Uprising. Revolution.* She bandied the words about as though she had discovered a lost, ancient language.

As for Sohail, he would have made a powerful student leader. But he had refused to join any of the student movements, claiming he couldn't be

45

swayed by one faction or another. He was unmoved by the differences between the various Communist parties: the parties that sided with Peking, the ones that sided with Moscow, the Mao-lovers, the Mao-haters, the Marxist — Leninists, the Stalinists, the Bolshevists. It might have been a problem, but Sohail collected friends and offended no one. He was popular and well loved by everyone. Mullahs and bad-boys. Communists and bullies and good-for-nothings. Arts faculty, science faculty. Physicists, engineers, painters, anthropologists. Girls and boys. Girls, especially. His fellow students might have interpreted Sohail's absence from their meetings as a sign of disloyalty, but no one who knew him doubted his commitment to the cause. Sohail loved Bengal. He may have inherited his mother's love of Urdu poetry, but it was nothing to the love he had for all things Bengali: the swimming mud of the delta; the translucent, bony river fish; the shocking green palette of the paddy and the open, aching blue of the sky over flat land.

People said his popularity had something to do with his being handsome, but Rehana was convinced it had more to do with the sound of his voice and the manner in which he spoke, a gentle, whispering baritone. And he always held his hands behind his back in a posture of deference, fixing his gaze on whomever he was addressing, the effect disarming and magical and the reason women followed him from Curzon Hall to Madhu's Canteen every afternoon when he went to meet his friends under the giant banyan tree where every major student movement in Dhaka had ever been born.

But Sohail loved Silvi. He had loved her when they had watched *Cleopatra* in the summer after his father died, and he loved her when he came back from Lahore and they saw Audrey Hepburn in *Roman Holiday*; he loved her at school, where her roll number was 33 and her uniform slate and blue, and he loved her when her breasts began pushing against the V of her school uniform dupatta; he loved her still when he discovered poetry and when she wrote him letters sealed with India ink lip prints; he loved her at the university when they rode home together in rickshaws, their knees knocking together over potholes; and he loved her when she started to read the Koran, and he loved her when she agreed to marry according to her mother's wishes; and he even loved her after that, when she closed the shutters of her bedroom and refused to come to the window when he rapped, gently, with the rubber end of his pencil.

Yes, it was probably true. He was still a student, and too young. And he would recover from this first heartache, as men so easily do. Still, Rehana thought, the party could hardly be called a success. It was supposed to be a celebration of the children's return, that ten-year-old day when she brought them back.

As she lay in the dark, the story of their return began to play itself out like an old film reel, rusty and clicking but with the images still intact, still potent. This was the end of the ritual: a recounting of the past, an attempt at a reckoning.

★ ★ ★

First, Rehana had sold Iqbal's precious Vauxhall. Mrs Akram had convinced her husband to buy it. 'Sell us the car,' she said to Rehana, 'it's almost new — I've seen my husband eyeing it. I could convince him to give you a thousand.' At first Rehana refused, but after paying the lawyer she had exactly 250 rupees left. She said yes. 'Tell your husband to take it away when I'm at the bazaar tomorrow morning,' she told Mrs Akram; 'I don't want to see it go.' And when she returned that afternoon it was gone, leaving only a dark oily stain in the middle of the driveway and four bare patches where the wheels had been.

The Vauxhall brought her a thousand rupees. Still not enough money to bring the children back, raise them, keep them in ribbons and socks and uniforms. Not nearly enough. She pawned the rest of her jewels: the sun-shaped locket and matching earrings, the ruby ring, a few gold chains. She counted the total: 2,652. Still not enough. She sold the carved teak mirror frame above her dressing table, an antique from the house in Wellington Square, sent on a cart to Dhaka after her wedding, with a note from her father: *I'm sorry, this is all I could save.* The mirror always reminded her of her father's last days in the Calcutta mansion, knocking around the empty rooms, his footsteps spelling defeat, as one truckload after another disappeared down the alley, bound for the coffers of the people to whom he owed money, or gold, or acres.

Then Mrs Chowdhury had her idea.

Rehana hired an architect. It was May, two months after the court case. Make the house as big as possible, was Rehana's only request. Make it grand. The workers arrived in July and began to dig the foundations, their backs like black pearls in the dense midsummer heat. They poured cement into the hole. Metal girders to support the structure. Wooden scaffolding for the walls. But by August the money was gone.

She went to the bank for a loan. She tried Habib Bank first, then United and National banks. She had no guarantor. She could mortgage the land, they said. She wouldn't mortgage the land. Then a round-faced man with an oily forehead said yes and took her to his office at the back of a building, where he slipped his hand under her elbow like a question mark, to which she too almost said yes, until he came close and she smelled his curry breath and saw the cigarette tracks on his teeth. She leaped out of the room, still gripping the instrument she had brought along to sign the papers, a green metal fountain pen with a letter opener at the top.

Months passed. A stubble of moss covered the cement foundations. September, October. The monsoon washed through, turning the bricks to sand, the sandbags to bricks, forming a fetid, stagnant pond where the mosaic floor of the house should have been. Rehana stood at its

49

edge and watched the tadpoles swimming like lines of ink, the thin garden snakes curling around the girders, snapping the mosquito-laced air.

And then she found the money. Exactly how was a secret she had kept all these years, because she wanted to remember what she had done, how far she had gone, to get her children back, and also because the burden of it, she knew, should be only hers.

After that the house seemed to go up on its own: by the end of the year the walls had been raised; two months later the plaster was smooth; by March the fierce spring heat was drying the blue-grey whitewash, and Rehana was looking on as her carpenter Abdul scratched the letters on to a smoothed piece of mahogany she had saved from the building of the front door. *Shona*, she said, and he asked, 'Your mother's name?' 'No,' she replied, 'just the name of the house.' For all that she had lost, and all that she wanted never to lose again.

Mr and Mrs Sengupta had replied to Rehana's advertisement in the *Pakistan Observer*. BRAND-NEW 4-BED HOUSE IN DHANMONDI. DRAWING-DINING, KITCHEN, LARGE LAWN. 6-MTH ADVANCE REQUIRED.

Mr Sengupta owned a tea plantation in Sylhet. He would be away for weeks at a time and would be grateful if Rehana could look in on his young wife. They had been married a few months; he was looking for just such a place, where the neighbours might provide his wife with some companionship.

50

Supriya Sengupta did not appear to need looking after. She was writing a novel, she said to Rehana. She wanted to be just like Royeya Sakhawat Hossain — had Rehana read *Sultana's Dream?*

Rehana had not read *Sultana's Dream*. But she nodded and told them she needed six months' rent in advance. Mr Sengupta handed her the money in a toffee-coloured envelope. She passed him a set of keys. The next day she paid a visit to the judge, and then, clutching the court order in her hands, she packed her bags, boarded the next morning's PIA flight and set off to rescue her children.

She remembered the reunion exactly. They were playing hula hoops on the lawn. Their faces were darker and their legs were longer and her heart had stopped at the sight of them, and even now, a decade later, she was sometimes frozen in that moment of disbelief, at the possibility that she might discover them, repossess them, bring them home and become their mother again.

And that was how it had happened. Rehana finished telling herself the story and waited for the tears to dry up on her cheeks.

By some miracle they were in the lead.

When Azmat Rana scored his first half-century, dashing past the stumps with his knees raised high and the dust swirling around his feet, the stadium pitched and roared. People stood up

51

and howled, thumped their feet and beat crude drums they had brought along, all the while whistling and chanting 'Joy Bangla! Joy Bangla! Joy Bangla!' By the time he had scored his second, the announcer could not be heard over the shouting, the air electric with the shock and pleasure of victory.

The oval-shaped stadium was packed with families who'd arrived with picnics and cones full of spicy puffed rice, come to clap, feel the sun burning the tops of their heads, peer into the glittering afternoon and watch their heroes at play.

Rehana had made chicken sandwiches. She opened the paper-wrapped package and passed it to Sohail, who was sitting in the next row with his friend Aref and Aref's brother, Joy. 'Very nice,' Sohail said, taking a bite. He gave her the barest hint of a smile and passed the sandwiches to his friends.

Rehana, Maya and Mrs Sengupta were sitting together. 'Have they set a wedding date?' Mrs Sengupta asked.

'No,' Rehana muttered.

'She's so young,' Mrs Sengupta said, rolling her sunglasses to the top of her head. 'What's the rush?'

Rehana wanted to agree, but instead she squeezed Mrs Sengupta's elbow. 'Let's have some drinks,' she said.

Sohail waved to the drinks boy. 'Who wants lemonade and who wants orange?' He counted the raised hands and reached into his pocket.

'No, please, I insist,' Mrs Sengupta said,

holding out her hand.

'Oh,' Sohail said, 'all right.' And he sat down.

Now the crowd was cheering and blocking Rehana's view with its waving arms. She wanted to get a good look at Azmat while he was still at the crease, so she climbed up on to the bench and peered over the long rows of dark heads in front of her, her hand raised to her eyes. Giddiness was everywhere. Rehana felt a laugh start at her feet and climb up her legs. She began to giggle with her mouth open. She tilted her head back and squinted at the sun, brilliant, invisible in its mid-afternoon blaze. It might be, she thought, the happiest day of her life. Never mind all that hangama with Silvi; Sohail would soon forget it. Look at him now, linking hands with his friends and cheering at the cricket. Rehana fanned her face, heating up as the afternoon bloomed on.

Maya, turning to look beside her, was startled to find her mother climbing down from the bench. 'Ammoo, what are you doing?'

'I told you before, I love Azmat Rana. So handsome, he reminds me of your father. We are definitely winning today. Have some more lemonade, Maya,' she said, passing her daughter the bottle. Always too sober, she thought to herself. What's the big deal? Only a little cheering.

* * *

Nigel Gifford, arm wooden against his side, prepared to run at Azmat Rana.

Maya settled back into her seat and stared at the pitch with her arms crossed in front of her. In the next row Sohail was arguing with his friends. They were saying something about the military-industrial complex. Sohail was insisting it didn't matter whether they were a part of Pakistan or not; the injustices towards the poor would continue unless they changed the way the economy was organized. Rehana could almost recite the speech from memory. Aref said the important thing was that the assembly should convene as soon as possible and make Mujib Prime Minister. Without that, the whole election would be revealed as a sham, and who knew what would happen.

Just as Nigel Gifford raised his right hand and prepared to release the worn red ball from his fingertips and send it, straight as a bullet, through the air to Azmat, who waited with bent knees and bat tilted against the sharp, cloudless afternoon sun, the crowd shifted, tensed. They felt it together, in the open intimacy of the packed stadium.

People began to get up and wave their fists in the air. A roar climbed through the stadium. They didn't appear to be cheering for the players. The players stared up from the pitch, their shoulders raised in confusion. Rehana looked around her, and the crowd, a moment ago a mass of cheering fans, looked restless; their eyes were angry white specks; the cricket was forgotten, the puffed rice, the picnics, the drums. It was as though everyone knew before they knew; it almost didn't matter what, just that their huge, runaway joy suddenly had to go.

Someone threw a brick on to the field. Someone else threw a cracked wooden stick. Bits of torn newspaper floated down from an aisle above them. 'What's happening?' Rehana heard Sohail ask. He nudged the knot of men who had already begun to clog the aisle.

'We don't know,' one of them answered, 'something on the radio — '

Rehana began to pack up the sandwiches. 'Let's go, Ammoo,' Sohail said; 'forget the things.' People were climbing over the stalls. The throng heaved towards the doors, choking the exits. Sohail, Aref and Joy pushed against the crowd and cleared a path.

The cricket stopped, and the players, peeling off their gloves and their caps, scattered to the edge of the field. No one saw the sun breaking through the clouds and shining on Azmat Rana, who gazed in the direction of the Ramna Racecourse, where they had all gathered a few weeks before to celebrate Sheikh Mujib's victory. And they did not hear the announcer trying to calm them down and remind them to Please Remain Seated.

As they moved towards the exits, they were jostled and pushed against one another. Rehana, holding Maya's slippery elbow, lost sight of Mrs Sengupta. She tried to keep track of Sohail's head, the thick brushstroke of his hair. The smell of sweat and stale breath enveloped her. She resisted the urge to panic and run back inside. Armpits and elbows collided; backs met faces and dangling children's feet. Rehana held tightly

55

to Maya's arm and pushed her way through the tunnel and down the stairs. In the car park Sohail was waving and gathering them together. 'Stay behind me!' he was saying. 'I know where the car is.' His voice was flattened by the lost and searching people.

Sohail took the wheel of Mrs Sengupta's 1959 Skoda Octavia. Joy and Aref crowded into the front seat. Rehana, Maya and Mrs Sengupta squeezed into the back. Rehana saw Maya reaching for the handle and said, 'Keep the window up.'

They turned out of the stadium and on to Paltan Road. 'I want to see what's happening,' Maya said.

'You can see from here.' It was stuffy inside the car, but at least they were safe. Rehana was used to seeing crowds on the streets — they'd had so many processions in the months leading up to the election — yet today was somehow different; there was a hint of calamity in the air. She tried to catch Sohail's eye in the mirror, but he was concentrating on the road, his hands curled around the steering wheel.

They entered the university compound. The car sped past Curzon Hall, Iqbal Hall, Rokeya Hall. In front of the Teacher — Student Centre, they saw a wave of people in white clothes and black armbands carrying banners, making fists and chanting in circular, overlapping beats. Maya cupped her hands against the window and shouted, 'Joy Bangla! Joy Sheikh Mujib!'

The procession was heading towards them. Sohail looked over his shoulder and tried to back

56

up, but they were stuck in front of a line of cars. The chants rose, the words slowly becoming audible.

Maya tried to identify the people in the crowd. 'Who is it? Chattra League?'

'I can't tell,' Sohail said; 'should we get out?'

Rehana shook her head. 'We're safer in the car. Let's stay inside.' Mrs Sengupta nodded in agreement. Maya kept shifting between her seat and the rear window, pressing her face against the glass. Rehana knew it was no use telling her to stop; she was just grateful the girl didn't break open the door.

Within minutes they were swallowed. As they snaked past, people knocked against the hood of the car. They pounded the boot. Bared their teeth and pressed their faces against the glass. 'Joy Bangla!' they shouted. 'Death to Pakistan! Death to dictatorship!' Their breaths made clouds on the glass.

Someone recognized Sohail. He rapped with his knuckles. 'Dost!'

Maya slapped the window. 'Jhinu!'

The boy made binoculars with his hands and peered inside. 'What are you doing in the car?' he shouted.

Sohail opened his window and the boy stuck his fingers through the gap. 'I'm just taking my mother and my sister home,' Sohail said. 'What's going on?'

'You haven't heard? Assembly postponed indefinitely.'

'What?'

'Sala. Bastard Bhutto's convinced Yahya there

can't be a Bengali running Pakistan.'

'What?' Maya said. 'Election cancelled?'

Joy and Aref started firing questions at Jhinu, asking what he thought Mujib was going to do. They all kept saying we knew, *we knew* this was going to happen. It was only a few moments, a few sentences, but Rehana had the feeling they were deciding something important. She kept telling herself she was still in charge, that nothing would be done without her consent. She pitched forward on the seat.

'Sohail, beta, the crowd is thinning, perhaps we should go?'

Sohail was rapping the steering wheel with his fingers, whispering something to Joy. He turned around. 'OK, Ammoo, let's go.'

Good. She would find a way to make sure he didn't go back.

'We'll join you,' he said to the boy in the window; 'we're just coming.'

'Hurry up — we'll be at the TSC later.'

'Why don't you boys go ahead? I'll drive,' Mrs Sengupta said.

'Na, Supriya, let the boys take us home,' Rehana said.

'Nonsense,' Mrs Sengupta insisted. 'They'll just have to come all the way back. Pull over, Sohail.'

Rehana cursed the day Mr Sengupta had taught his wife to drive. She just wanted them all home. 'Really,' she said, 'do you think it's safe for us to go by ourselves?'

'Of course it's safe. We'll be in the car, what could happen?'

'Ammoo,' Sohail said a little eagerly, 'you'll be OK?'

'Yes,' Rehana replied. It came out weakly, but he didn't seem to need much convincing.

They waited until the last of the procession passed. Sohail parked the car in front of Rokeya Hall and left the engine running. 'Are you sure?'

'Yes, don't worry,' Mrs Sengupta said. 'I'll get them home. You join your friends. Jao.'

'OK. Ammoo — I'll just find out what's happening and come straight home.'

Rehana fought off a wave of panic. 'Be careful, beta.'

'Don't worry. Bye!'

'Khoda Hafez.'

Mrs Sengupta was already at the front of the car, waiting to take the wheel. She held out the door for Rehana with a flourish. 'Don't worry so much!' she said.

Suddenly a thin, lungi-clad boy bolted past. Mrs Sengupta's sari slid from her shoulder, exposing her blouse and her bare stomach, and, as she bent to rearrange herself, she slipped and tumbled forward, her head knocking against the wheel before she could stretch out her arms to break the fall.

Rehana rushed to her side and struggled to lift her up. 'Are you hurt?' She pulled Mrs Sengupta into the driver's seat and slammed the doors. 'Are you hurt?' she repeated.

'No, it's nothing,' Mrs Sengupta said, 'just a little dirty.'

'Here, take my handkerchief.'

'Just an accident. Nothing to worry.' She took

the handkerchief and began to wipe the mud from her palms.

'Supriya,' Rehana said, 'you've lost your teep.'

'Oh.' Mrs Sengupta touched her forehead and then looked into the folds of her sari. 'I hadn't realized.' She rolled down her window and hurriedly brushed a few stray tears from her eyes. 'Just a little startled,' she said, laughing nervously. Then she adjusted her seat, checked her reflection in the mirror and cupped her palm over the gear.

Rehana looked back to check on Maya. Her daughter was watching the retreating procession as it crossed the university intersection and headed towards Nilkhet.

★ ★ ★

Waiting for them in front of the bungalow gate was Sharmeen, a tall young woman with broad shoulders and a tough, ageless face. She was a student at the art college, famous on campus for her political posters, and Maya's best friend, or *comrade*, as she liked to be called.

'Where've you been?' Sharmeen said, as they tumbled out of the car. She was struggling with a giant roll of paper. Mrs Sengupta smoothed the back of her head. From across the road, Mrs Chowdhury's cocker spaniels, Romeo and Juliet, began to bark.

Maya hugged Sharmeen. 'We were driving back from the cricket match. We got stuck in Paltan.'

'I came to find you as soon as I heard. Help me with this?'

'I don't think you can get back,' Maya said, catching one end of the roll.

'Don't worry,' Rehana said, unlatching the gate, 'you can stay here.' It was an unnecessary invitation; Sharmeen was always staying over. There was a mattress under Rehana's bed that hardly ever gathered dust. Her toothbrush was in the cabinet behind the bathroom mirror.

They'd been best friends since Maya's first day at Vikarunnessa Noon School. The children had just arrived from Lahore, and Rehana decided it was time for them to learn Bengali. Not the fractured Bengali they picked up at the sweetshop and the playground but proper, school Bengali. So Maya was sent to Vikarunnessa, where the nuns were weathered and the girls wore hard braids and white knee socks. On that first day Maya stood up behind her desk and announced: 'My name is Sheherezade Haque Maya. I was named after a famous storyteller. My father is dead. I am Lahore-returned. We have a big house called Shona.' She was met with a vibrating silence as the girls shuffled and cocked their ears at her strained, accented Bengali. And then, chased by cries of 'Bihari! Bihari!', she fled into a far corner of the hockey field, her uniform skirt billowing around her legs, and that is where Sharmeen had found her, sitting inside her hula hoop, chewing on a piece of dried mango.

'Can I have some?'

'I already licked the whole thing.'

'Doesn't matter.' Sharmeen pinched with two fingers the wet leather of mango and popped it into her mouth. 'So. Your father's dead? Mine too.'

'How did yours go?'

'Typhoid. Yours?'

'Heart-attack.'

And their friendship was sealed.

Maya had always regarded Sharmeen with awe, as though she could never quite figure out why Sharmeen chose her when there were so many other stern young women in the movement. But Maya had underestimated Sharmeen's need to be adored. She didn't question, as Rehana often did, the fact that Sharmeen spent so many of her holidays at the bungalow in Dhanmondi instead of at home with her own family. It appeared the girl had nowhere else to go. Rehana accepted Sharmeen's presence in the house, and, even though she wasn't particularly fond of her, she liked to think of herself as the kind of person who took in strays.

In the drawing room Sharmeen and Maya locked arms and surveyed the poster.

'It's perfect,' Maya said.

'I think it needs more colour here,' Sharmeen said, pointing with her brush to a blank area of the canvas. Her hands were amphibious, the fingers green and stuck together with paint.

'Maybe — but it could signify, you know, the space of possibility — the future,' Maya said.

'You don't think that's too abstract?'

'Probably.' She shrugged her shoulders to

indicate that people who didn't understand the significance of the blank space didn't deserve to know the meaning of the poster.

Rehana retreated to her room; her head was throbbing, and she couldn't get the sight of Mrs Sengupta's fallen sari and her shocked mouth out of her head. And Sohail, drumming his fingers against that steering wheel. What was he doing now? Probably adding a voice of reason, she told herself. That was what he always did. He was so persuasive. If the students wanted to riot, he would tell them they shouldn't tear down their own classrooms just to prove a point. He would slowly shift the language of the conversation, so that they were no longer shouting about revenge and saying things like *who do they think they are.*

Rehana stroked her forehead in time to the rotating ceiling fan. I'll just close my eyes for one minute, she thought. And then I'll wake up and worry again.

* * *

By the time she emerged from her room a few hours later it was dark outside, the hum of a gentle storm rustling the leaves in the garden. She followed the voices to the drawing room and found it crammed with Sohail's friends.

'Salaam-Alaikum, Auntie,' they said in scattered chorus. No one was smoking, but the cigarette stink clung to the air. Maya and Sharmeen were bent over another sheet of paper. Aref was unpacking his guitar.

'Ammoo,' Sohail said, raising his voice over the throng, 'Mujib has called a meeting on the 7th. You should come.'

'Me? Why?'

'Because history will be made.'

'Yes, Auntie,' Aref said, twisting a knob on his guitar. 'You must be there — it's going to be even bigger than the last one.'

'You go,' Rehana said a little nervously. 'Tell me about it afterwards.' She suddenly felt awkward, like she had stumbled into the Men Only room at the Gymkhana.

'Ma, seriously,' Maya interjected, 'you can't miss it — Mujib might declare independence.'

'I don't know — we'll see, OK? Do you all need anything? Are you hungry?'

'Don't worry about us, Ammoo,' Sohail said, waving to her. 'We feed on the revolution.'

As she turned back to the kitchen, Rehana wondered if she should attend the meeting. They were always telling her to come with them to their rallies and their get-togethers, but, not being young or part of the student movement, and not having attended the conferences of the Nationalist Party or the elections of the student unions, and not, like Sohail and Maya, having read the *Communist Manifesto* and sat for hours under the banyan tree debating the finer points of the resistance, she did not have the proper trappings of a nationalist. She did not have the youth or the appearance or the words. The correct words, though by now familiar to her, did not glide easily from her tongue: 'comrade', 'proletariat', 'revolution'. They were hard, precise words and did not capture Rehana's ambiguous feelings about the country she had adopted. She spoke, with fluency, the Urdu of the enemy. She was unable to pretend, as she saw so many others doing, that she could replace her mixed tongue with a pure Bengali one, so that the Muslim salutation, *As-Salaam Alaikum* was replaced by the neutral *Adaab*, or even *Nomoshkar*, the Hindu greeting. Rehana's tongue was too confused for these changes. She could not give up her love of Urdu, its lyrical lilts, its double meanings, its furrowed beat.

No, Rehana did not have the exactness to become a true revolutionary. But she had realized long ago that, while the children would remain fixed at the centre of her life, she would gradually fade out of theirs. In the meantime she wanted to hold on for as long as she could, especially now that their dreams had suddenly grown so spacious. She turned into the kitchen and wondered how she would feed all those hungry dreamers.

★ ★ ★

'Ammoo, we have a present for you,' Sohail said, after they'd all eaten. Rehana had decided on khichuri, which was quick and meant there was no need to cook the dal separately. And she'd made omelettes with chilli and fried onions. The whole lot had been devoured in seconds.

'What?' Rehana said.

Sohail pulled out a large bag from underneath his chair. He unfolded the packet and held up a rectangular length of cloth. It was a rich, muddy green, the colour of the lowest leaves in the mangrove. Sewn into the middle was a circle, a little uneven, in red. Inside the circle was a yellow cut-out map of East Pakistan.

'This is our flag, Ammoo.' And he opened his arms to show her its full length. Aref took hold of one side, and they stretched it across the room. A few people clapped. 'Joy Bangla!' someone shouted. A flag without a country, Rehana thought, but didn't say. Maya whooped, draped the flag around her shoulders and ran to find a bamboo pole so they could secure it to the rooftop.

⋆ ⋆ ⋆

The days following the cricket match were full of strikes and processions, curfews disobeyed and slogans shouted from blaring megaphones. Sohail and Maya spent most of their days at the university, returning home late every night, talking excitedly about the change in the air. But Dhanmondi was quiet, and things mostly went on as normal. Occasionally Mrs Chowdhury would arrive at Rehana's doorstep with a mountain of small brown packets containing the latest shopping for Silvi's wedding. One sari after another was purchased, then the blouses and petticoats to match, and the lace trim to go around the sleeves of the blouses, and the matching clips for her hair. One day Mrs Chowdhury appeared with only her handbag, and on that day Rehana knew she'd been to the jeweller. She pulled out two red boxes covered in velvet and opened them with a snap, and Rehana had to ooh and aah at the locket and the pair of earrings that winked from inside.

Despite her initial reluctance, Rehana found herself at the racecourse on the 7th of March. She arrived early but the field was already full. It was as though the whole country had turned up: people flooded the grounds and all Rehana could see for miles was a vast sea of shining black heads, glowing in the sunshine like a restless horizon of darkness.

Sheikh Mujib was a tiny white figure in the distance. In the years since he'd become the leader of the movement, his short black coat, his reedy voice and the finger he always pointed at the sky had become familiar sights, but there was still a thrill at seeing him in the flesh. As he made his way on to the stage, the crowd bucked, and Rehana watched as he waved his arms to quiet and reassure his people. *His*. They belonged to him now; they were his charge, his children. They called him father. They loved him the way orphans dream of their lost parents: without promise, only hope. He cleared his throat and began to speak. Rehana could barely hear him amid the shouts of the crowd, the whistles and the cheers; the afternoon sun beating down on the cloud of flags that dotted the racecourse ground seemed to make his words bend and quiver in the heat. 'Make every home a fortress,' she could just hear him say.

The scene appeared before Rehana like a glamorous black-and-white picture; there was the white of Mujib's kurta-pyjama, the black of his short coat, the black — she knew, though she could not see — of his thick-framed glasses, the white of the tent pitched to cover the stage. By the end she found herself shouting *Joy Bangla, Joy Bangla, Joy Bangla* with the crowd, the rhythm of her words chiming with the hard thump of her chest, and she recognized, at once, the incendiary thrill of shouting. Maya looked over at her mother and flashed her a wide, encouraging smile. Rehana suddenly felt young, plunged into a world of limitless possibility.

At thirty-eight, Rehana's body had finally caught up with its history. People who did not know used to assume she was a student, or that she was unmarried, because she didn't wear a wedding ring or a single piece of gold jewellery, but no longer. She had gained a little weight, and she enjoyed the occasional heaviness of her limbs, the stubborn, outward curve of her belly, the slight effort of movement, an awareness of breath and bone. Her new, comfortable shape came with new imperfections: the bowed line between nose and chin, the slight shadow above her lip, the thickening of her waist and ankles. All fortunate developments for Rehana, as they signified the battle-weary body of a woman who had passed years in the effort to raise her children.

Maya leaned over and held her mother's hand — not, as she sometimes did, for a reassuring squeeze but in solidarity, and suddenly Rehana felt sure it would all resolve itself: Sheikh Mujib would be Prime Minister, and the country would

68

go on being her home, and the children would go on being her children. In no time at all the world would right itself, and they would go on living ordinary, unexceptional lives.

25 March 1971

Operation Searchlight

They blamed it on a sudden, collective deafness. How else could they explain the military planes that had landed at the airport, the soldiers told they were saving the world? How else could they explain not knowing, not hearing? And later they would say they should have heard the birds leaping out of trees and flying eastwards, and the crickets fleeing, and the bats folding up, and the grass-green tiktikis hiding in crevices, under house slippers.

But they didn't, and this is how it happened:

On the 25th Mrs Chowdhury invited them all to dinner in honour of Lieutenant Sabeer. All day there had been strange rumours floating around the city. Mujib was in talks about the election, and no one was saying whether the talking was coming to anything; across Mirpur Road, at the Bengal Rifles Compound, the place they have always called Peelkhana, there was speculation about a military attack; some students had come out with bricks and broken chairs from the dormitories, trying to construct a makeshift barricade.

It was a bad night for a party, but Mrs Chowdhury insisted. The couple hadn't been formally engaged, she said, not with all the troubles; nothing elaborate, just a small ceremony, maybe a ring for Silvi. She roasted an entire lamb, which sat on the table with a tomato stuffed between its jaws. Rehana did not feel she could say no; Sohail agreed to come as well — probably to test himself, Rehana thought. He avoided looking at Silvi and Sabeer and kept his eyes fixed on the lamb. Maya's mood was especially black; she had been forced to leave Sharmeen at Rokeya Hall, where confetti was being thrown out of windows and a group of Bauls were singing at the bottom of the stairwell. She complained of the quiet in the neighbourhood, as though no one in Dhanmondi knew or cared they were on the verge of a revolution. She wanted to be on the streets, distributing leaflets and singing 'We Shall Overcome'.

The neighbours assembled around the table. Silvi was dressed in a heavy turquoise salwaar-kameez. Lieutenant Sabeer wore his uniform, as usual. Mr and Mrs Sengupta put Mithun to bed in Silvi's bedroom and turned their attention to the aromas floating in from the kitchen.

The party was quietly expectant. But no one heard anything, not even the sound of guava trees dropping their fruit, as they always do in March.

'Well, then, let's raise our glasses to Silvi and

Sabeer, my beloved daughter, and my soon-to-be son-in-law. May God bless you both.'

They raised their glasses of milk shorbot. Rehana sat beside Sohail and tried to catch his wrist to give it a squeeze. But his hands were on the table, and he said, 'Here's to our country. May it emerge from this trial and stand strong.'

'Hear, hear,' said Mr Sengupta, leaning back and stroking his belly.

'And to the proletariat! And to the revolution!' Maya said, standing up and draining her glass in a hurry.

'OK, OK,' Mrs Chowdhury said, 'now let's eat.'

While Mrs Chowdhury plunged her knife into the lamb's glossy, rippled back, a slow procession of jeeps and tanks crawled through the city; it snaked out of the cantonment, crossed the railroad tracks into Bonani, where it split up, one line straying through Elephant Road, through Quaid-e-Azam Avenue, and into the university compound. The other line made its way towards Peelkhana, green jeeps with green men waving the green Pakistan flag, a flapping sickle with its lavish, bent smile.

Oblivious, they devoured the roast lamb, smacking their lips and sucking on the bones. Later they would remark upon the crudeness of their hunger. After dinner Mrs Chowdhury instructed Silvi and Sabeer to sit beside each other on the double sofa. She gave Silvi a garland of jasmine and told her to place it around Sabeer's neck. Sabeer dipped his head, and Silvi slipped the garland over it. Everyone clapped, except Maya, who was looking up at the ceiling and singing quietly to herself. Amar Shonar Bangla . . . *My golden Bengal, how I adore you.*

At ten o'clock the tanks began to fire.

It was the sound of a thousand New Year firecrackers, of metal pipes being dragged across a stone road, of chillies popping in a smoking pan.

'Ya'allah!' Mrs Chowdhury cried. 'What's happening?'

'Everybody stay where you are,' Sabeer said.

'I want to go home,' Mrs Sengupta said. 'Let's take Mithun and go.' She gathered the child in her arms and made for the door.

'Ammoo,' Maya said, 'it's coming from Road 2.'

There was loud, thunderous bang. 'Hai Allah! Hai Allah!' Mrs Chowdhury said. 'This is it, we are all finished.'

Then they couldn't hear each other over the sound of the bullets. Mithun woke up and began to cry softly. His mother cradled him against her breast, whispering with her lips to his forehead. Outside, Romeo and Juliet were barking hoarsely at the shelling.

'Everybody stay calm,' Sabeer said, 'stay calm and stay where you are. Sohail and I are going to the roof to see what's happening.'

'I want to go home,' Mrs Sengupta said.

Rehana saw Sabeer's chair clatter to the ground as he rushed to the stairwell; his boots pounded, and Sohail's chappals clapped, as they made their way to the roof. 'Don't go up there!'

76

Mrs Chowdhury said, but they were already gone.

Flashes of light came through the window and illuminated the room. Mrs Chowdhury's lamb roast was a half-eaten corpse with naked ribs and a picked-over leg. The tomato was gone but the mouth was still open. Mrs Chowdhury looked as though she might lunge under the dining table, but instead she sank deeper into her chair, her hand clasped to her breast. 'Allah! Allah! Allah!' she said.

'What's happening, what's happening,' they kept repeating.

The shelling at Peelkhana was close enough to make Rehana's chest rattle. She heard shouts. A siren sounded in a looping, circular wail. Fiery sparks illuminated the horizon; a deep sound like faraway thunder reverberated through the air; then came smoke, and a small hush, as though it was over. But it wasn't. Seconds later it started all over again. Rehana wanted to hold her children. She wanted to put her hands over their ears. But Maya was glued to the window, and Sohail was on the roof with Sabeer. She could hear the two sets of footsteps echoing dully from above.

Maya picked up the telephone. 'Phone's dead,' she declared. Then she turned to the transistor, but there was only a low, humming static.

From Mrs Chowdhury's roof, Sohail and Lieutenant Sabeer watched the fires of the lit-up city. Suddenly they heard everything: the killing of small children, the slow movement of clouds, the death of women, the sigh of fleeing birds, the rush of blood on the pavements.

Sohail spoke first. 'We'll have to wait till the curfew's lifted.'

Sabeer looked down at his uniform. The green was dark, almost invisible, but the sickle, the grin, shone whitely against his chest, the crimson sky, the blinking horizon. 'I'm an officer of the Pakistan Army,' he said at last.

'What will you do?'

'I'm not sure.' The scar above his lip rippled as he twisted his mouth.

'Desertion is punishable by death,' Sohail said.

'I don't care about that. I just never thought it would come to this.'

Sohail did not rebuke Sabeer for not knowing better.

They returned to the party. Mrs Chowdhury was still supine on the dining chair; Mrs Sengupta was at Mithun's bedside with her hand on his chest. Maya took the radio to the kitchen to see if she could get a signal. Rehana was with her; she was putting ice into a glass for Silvi, who was nervous and thirsty.

There was nothing to do. They waited. Maya crouched stubbornly in front of the radio; Sabeer paced the drawing room, pulling aside curtains, opening and closing windows. Silvi perched on the sofa, rocking back and forth on her hands. Mr Sengupta lit a thin brown cigarillo.

Finally Mrs Chowdhury rose from her chair as though she had just had a revelation.

'There's going to be trouble, lots of trouble,' she said to Sabeer. The pitch of her voice told

78

Rehana she was about to make an announcement. 'You know it. I want you to make sure nothing will happen to my daughter.'

'Your daughter will be safe.'

'How can you be sure?'

'Of course I'm sure.' He turned to Silvi, who nodded silently into the floor.

'But what if something happens to you? What if they come for her?'

'Who?'

'Who knows? People! The army!' And she collapsed again into the chair.

'Ma,' Sabeer said, 'nothing will happen to Silvi.'

'There's only one way to be sure. You must marry her tonight.'

'*Marry?*'

'You don't understand, you're just a child, but I've been through things like this. The thing to do is to make sure all the unmarried girls are safe. You think this gate will keep the hoodlums out?' Mrs Chowdhury's voice climbed to a shaky trill.

Rehana saw her whispering something to the Lieutenant. She pointed to Silvi, hung her head, raised it, raised her finger, brought a handkerchief to her eyes. The Lieutenant nodded distractedly, patting Mrs Chowdhury's shoulder.

By midnight the shelling had slowed to a few staccato beats in the distance. Mrs Chowdhury ushered Sohail and Rehana to the kitchen. 'Sohail, I need you,' she said. 'Silvi needs to get married right away. You have to witness. There have to be two men. Mr Sengupta will be the

79

other witness. It isn't exactly right, but we'll have to make do.'

'Mrs Chowdhury,' Rehana said, 'is this really the time?' Her head spun with the absurdity of it.

'Of course this is the time. What better time is there? There may be no other time. No time left! What if the Lieutenant doesn't return for months? What if he *dies*?' And then: 'Why don't you select a few verses, Rehana? You read so well.'

As soon as Mrs Chowdhury left to change Silvi into a fresh sari, Maya muttered, 'This is ridiculous — you'd think Silvi would have more sense.'

Rehana reached for the shelf where she knew Silvi kept the Holy Book. 'Help me get it down, Sohail.'

'I don't love her any more,' Sohail said, as if she had asked him a question. And then he said, 'I stopped loving her the moment I heard about the soldier.'

Rehana kept silent but Maya looked up sharply, a challenge in the set of her mouth.

'I don't believe in violence,' Sohail announced, as though the two women he was addressing were new acquaintances. 'I can't support any kind of violence. And anyway it's her choice. Women must be allowed to choose for themselves.'

'Don't be a fool,' Maya said; 'you know she just buckled under the pressure. Really, the girl is very weak.'

'Shut up,' Sohail said.

Maya rolled her eyes and returned to the

radio. 'You go. I'm not having anything to do with this charade.'

Rehana opened the Holy Book.

Again Silvi and Sabeer were seated on the double sofa. Again Silvi looked down into her lap. Rehana could see her lip trembling, and she wanted to run over to the girl and ask her if she was sure, very sure she wanted to marry the Lieutenant, but just as she was about to cross the room, Silvi, in one of those rare interruptions to her sobriety, flashed a wide, toothy smile. The smile was for her mother, Rehana knew, but it worked to silence the doubts that were circulating around the room.

'Sohail,' Silvi said, louder than she needed to, 'why don't you take a photograph?'

'Do you have a camera?' Sohail asked.

'I still have yours,' Silvi replied, opening a drawer next to the sofa; 'you let me borrow, it, remember, because I wanted to take a photo of Romeo and Juliet?' She handed him his most prized possession, a Yashica Electro 35G Rehana had bought him for his eighteenth birthday.

'Of course,' Sohail said, taking the Yashica out of its case and hiding his face behind the lens. What did he see, Rehana wondered. Did he see regret on her lips, in the way her hands were arranged, in the brightness of her cheeks, in the ragged quickness of her breath? And what about Silvi? Would she miss the long silences between them, the love notes delivered through slats in the shutters?

Sohail pointed the camera at the couple on the sofa.

81

'Smile!' And there was a snap.

Just as Rehana was about to open the Holy Book the lights went out. She had to recite the marriage verses from memory: *He created for you mates from among yourselves, that you may dwell in tranquillity with them, and He has put love and mercy between your hearts.*

Silvi and Sabeer exchanged rings. Then Mrs Chowdhury said, 'Let's have a poem, Sohail!'

'No, khala-moni, really, I couldn't.'

'Come on, not even for an old friend?'

'Maybe music would be a better idea,' Rehana said, trying to rescue her son. 'Why don't you ask Maya to sing a ghazal?'

But Maya kept her back to them and pretended not to hear.

Under the veil, Silvi's shoulders shook violently.

'Sweetheart, don't be afraid,' Mrs Sengupta soothed. Silvi didn't look any more or less unhappy than any other bride.

'We are all family now. We must have a poem,' Mrs Chowdhury insisted.

Sohail faced the couple, closed his eyes and recited:

When you command me to sing it seems
    my heart will break with pride.
I look to your face and feel the wet salt of
    my tears.
My adoration spreads wings like a glad
    bird on its flight across the sea.
It is only in this, my voice, that I am wit-
    ness to you.

Drunk with the joy, sublime, of singing, I
*   forget myself and call you friend who are*
*   my lord.*
You have made me endless; such is your
*   pleasure.*

And that was it. They lingered in Mrs Chowdhury's drawing room, listening to the rat-tat-tat of the machine-guns. The night passed like a dream, no movement, no words passing between them.

★   ★   ★

With dawn the bullets quietened. The sun was making a slow rise in the east, preceded by blurred sky-stripes of pink and orange. Dust was settling on trees and rooftops. They decided to go home. Mrs Chowdhury was asleep on her chair, her hand under her chin. They slid open the front door and found Juliet pacing around a prone Romeo. Her head was bent; her ears brushed his face as she circled him. She grunted quietly, her nostrils moist and flared. Romeo didn't stir. Sohail put his hand on the dog's belly. 'He's dead,' he said; 'he must have had a heart-attack.'

At home, Rehana told the children they should try to get some sleep, but nobody shifted from the drawing room. In the afternoon a truck stopped in the front of the bungalow, its engine grinding. On the silent street, every sound was exaggerated. A megaphone squealed to life.

'Bengalis, take down your flags. Take down

your flags. Take down your flags. Flag-bearing is illegal. You will be arrested. Take down your flags.' The voice was thin and nasal. And then, as though an afterthought, it added, 'Take down your flags, you bastard traitors.'

'Maya — the flag!'

Maya ran to the roof in her bare feet.

A few minutes later she was lying on the floor with the flag wrapped around her shoulders. She raised her finger to the ceiling and counted mosquitoes. They could hear Juliet barking chaotically from Mrs Chowdhury's driveway.

They sat. They waited for something to happen. Sohail paced the veranda, the garden, the roof. Maya fell asleep in the flag. Rehana checked the fridge and tried to work out how long the food would last. She counted the chickens. She measured the level of the rice. Three days, she said to herself. I can make it last three days. She went back and measured again. She stacked up the onions, the pumpkin, the marrows. Five days.

The truck came back. 'Curfew will be lifted from 2 p.m. tomorrow afternoon for four hours. Curfew set for 6 p.m. Return to your homes at 6 p.m. Officers will shoot on sight. Repeat, shoot on sight. Curfew will be lifted from 2 p.m. to 6 p.m.'

Juliet howled at the truck as it backed out of Road 5.

As soon as the curfew was lifted, Sohail and Maya left for the university. Rehana watched from the window as Lieutenant Sabeer emerged from the gate with Silvi and said a short farewell.

Rehana stayed in the bungalow. She was wondering how many hours had passed since she'd slept, and whether she should be tired, when someone bolted through the door. It was Mrs Sengupta.

'We just couldn't turn them away.'

'Who?'

'You haven't seen? Go to the veranda.'

Rehana peered over the boundary wall into Shona's garden. Something was moving, rustling the grass. 'What is it?'

'People — refugees, Rehana.'

'How many?'

'Twenty, thirty, I'm not sure. They just started coming. Can they stay?'

'Of course. Of course they can stay.'

'I don't know any of them. But we're the only Hindus on the street.'

'Are there children?'

'A few. It's mostly families, a few stray people. They're not saying much.'

'I'm going to bring over some food.'

Rehana took her chickens out of the fridge. Two she made into a spicy curry with tomatoes, the third into a korma for the children. There wasn't any yoghurt; she used milk. She made cabbage and potato bhaji, fried the okra with onions, made a stew with the spinach and pumpkin. She worried for a moment about using up all the food, but she quickly brushed the thought away. Who knew what had happened to these people, what had led them here?

When she was finished, she took the trays of food to Shona, picking her way through the ragged blankets. There were children, just as she'd imagined, and women, and old men with wrinkled faces who looked at her and tried to smile in gratitude. But they didn't speak, not even to each other. They sat in silence, sifting through their loose bundles, calculating the sum of what they had salvaged.

Looking at them, Rehana had the sudden urge to know more. She felt she was only beginning to make sense of the night, the bombings, Mrs Chowdhury's hysteria. She wanted to know how these people had passed the night, how they had come to be there. A feeling of restlessness overcame her and she had to see it, whatever it was that was out there, what grief had caused these people to run from their homes and seek shelter on her doorstep.

★ ★ ★

'University,' she said simply.

'Better not, apa,' the rickshaw-wallah said.

'University,' she repeated, climbing in and pushing back the hood.

He shook his head and set off, turning on to Mirpur Road. There was very little traffic on the street. The few cars on the road had polite, murmuring engines. No one rang the horn. And when the rickshaw cut across Nilkhet, they let it pass with a wave.

Everything seems almost the same, Rehana thought. The New Market gate was shut, and the little shops around its entrance were boarded up, and the vendors selling jackfruit and amra were nowhere to be seen. Still, it could have been Friday afternoon, when everything closed down for the Jumma prayers; or it could have been another strike. They'd had so many strikes lately.

The rickshaw-wallah pedalled past the round-about before entering the university compound, and here the air began to change: there was a low-lying fog clinging to the pavement — no, it was smoke, whispering through the streets, leaving an ashy, sour taste in the mouth. It got thicker as the rickshaw-wallah brought Rehana closer to the dormitories; he stopped, unravelled the gamcha from his head and tied it around his face. He motioned for Rehana to do the same with her sari. She held the sari to her nose and with one hand clung tightly to the rickshaw frame, because the road was uneven here; when she looked down she saw scraps of litter scattered over the street. She thought she saw a prayer cap and a pair of unbroken spectacles. People must have dropped their things as they ran. She wanted to pick up the spectacles and wave them around, see if anybody was looking for them, but the rickshaw had already driven past. Now there was a thin length of red ribbon on the road; she leaned over; she couldn't be sure. It was glistening wet.

They continued and the rubble grew denser; Rehana became aware of the growing crowd on the street; the rickshaw-wallah strained to get them through the uneven road and the people that were laced around them. Now there were bricks and bits of plaster and layers of dust that had settled on the road and turned it grey-white.

They were in front of Curzon Hall. The wet ribbon had followed them all the way, and now it poured into a gutter, which was also red, and on the side of the gutter was a pair of hands, the fingers clasped together in prayer or begging, and next to the hands was a face. The mouth was tiny, only a pale pink smudge, like the introduction of a bruise.

It was a little girl. Her hair swallowed the top half of her face. Beneath the clumped-together strands Rehana could see an eye squeezed shut.

She wrenched herself away from it; she looked for only a minute, but it felt like so much longer, felt so close she thought she could smell the girl's breath escaping from her nostrils and from those too-small lips.

'Move on,' she said to the rickshaw-wallah. She didn't see anything after that. Later she would say she had *seen* it all: the corpses piled onto the pavement like cakes in a window; the rickshaw-pullers dead with their heels on rickshaw-pedals; the tank-sized holes in the dormitories, Rokeya Hall and Jagganath Hall and Mohsin Hall. But as they clattered through the compound her eyes had been closed, squeezed shut against the sight of her ruined city.

★ ★ ★

When Sohail and Maya returned, they were mute, their faces lined with ash. The story of the night unfolded slowly. First, Mujib had been arrested and flown to West Pakistan. The army had started its attack at the university, bombing the dormitories and the canteen and the Teacher-Student Centre. On their way to the old town, the tanks had bulldozed the slums that clung to each side of the Phulbaria rail track; they needed that rail line to get across the city, so they had swiped their guns through the cardboard and tin shacks, the flimsy homes held together with glue and cinema posters. And then they had gone into the Hindu neighbourhoods on jeeps because their tanks were too wide for the narrow lanes, and mounted on their jeeps they had fired through shutters and doorways and shirts and hearts.

In the evening Rehana and the children heard the announcement on the radio:

I, Major Zia, provisional Commander-in-Chief of the Bangladesh Liberation Army, hereby proclaim, on behalf of our great national leader Sheikh Mujibur Rahman, the independence of Bangladesh. I also declare we have already formed a sovereign, legal government under Sheikh Mujibur Rahman. I appeal to all nations to mobilize public opinion in their respective countries against the brutal genocide in Bangladesh.

So this was it: a war had come to find them. Whatever was going to happen had already happened; now they would have to live in its shadow. Rehana wrapped her arms around herself and squeezed tight, willing the old strength to rise up within her again.

April

Radio Free Bangladesh

The city slowly adjusted to occupied life. It adjusted to the stiff-backed soldiers who manned the streets, their uniforms starched, their pale faces grimacing. It adjusted to the tanks sitting fatly in the middle of roads, and to checkpoints where soldiers leaned into car windows and barked orders at drivers who held up their hands and shook their heads, protesting their innocence. And it adjusted to the silence, because there were no more speeches, or marches, or processions, just an eerie, still quietness, interrupted twice a day by the wail of the curfew siren; but otherwise all was ghostly, only the rustle of trees and the sizzle of the April sun to draw the line between day and night.

Wild rumours circulated in the quiet. The army had dug a mass grave to hide the bodies. There was a warehouse, somewhere on the outskirts of town, where they tortured the prisoners. The animals in Mirpur Zoo, even the Bengal tiger, had all died of fright. But no one seemed to know anything for sure. The newspapers announced, 'Yahya saves Pakistan!' and Dhaka, so long at the centre of the struggle, was now a besieged and vacant city that kept its knowledge close and hidden.

Those people who had never really been citizens of the city erased their faint tracks and returned to their villages. The butchers, the tailors, the milkmen, the rickshaw-pullers, the boys who painted cinema actresses on the back flaps of rickshaws and the even younger boys who made tea in rusting kettles on pavements — all left silently, snaking out of the city with bundles on their shoulders, children cradled against their backs.

As she witnessed the emptying of the city, Rehana counted her blessings.

The children were safe.

Mrs Chowdhury and Silvi.

The gin-rummy ladies. Mrs Akram had spent that night with the shutters closed and her hands over her ears. Later her husband would say she'd been hysterical, screaming about Kayamat, the end of the world. They'd had to tie her to the bedposts and press their hands over her mouth. She remembered none of it. When she came to see Rehana, two days after the curfew was lifted, she tried to hide the weals on her wrists by wearing wide, mirror-studded bangles. But she was alive.

Romeo was dead. Mrs Chowdhury had him buried under the tallest coconut tree in her garden.

Mrs Rahman had almost not been so lucky.

94

She had accepted an invitation to dine with an old schoolfriend. The school-friend's husband owned a tailoring shop in the old town, and they lived above it, on Nawabpur Road. At the last minute Mrs Rahman had pleaded a headache, dreading the choked roads she would have to pass through to get there, remembering the dreary furniture, the bony curry she'd been fed the last time. She felt guilty but consoled herself by resolving to send her friend a gift the very next day. A sari perhaps, or a pair of earrings.

Nawabpur Road was in the army's way as they passed through the old town on their way to Shakaripotti, the Hindu neighbourhood. Perhaps they had taken a wrong turn; perhaps they'd held their maps upside down; or maybe it was taking too long to get there and they were impatient, the blood leaping in their skins. They swiped with their machine-guns, back and forth, and one of their bullets found the house on Nawabpur Road. Mrs Rahman's schoolfriend escaped with a grazed cheek, but her husband, crouching under the dining table, did not.

Rehana's children were safe. That was the most important thing. She could not help feeling grateful to Mrs Chowdhury for holding Silvi's engagement party that night, keeping her children close to home, when they could so easily have been in one of the university halls.

Sohail and Maya accounted for their friends. Joy and Aref had been among the students who had heard rumours of an attack on the city. They had broken into their dormitory cafeteria and

95

stolen all the chairs, which they'd stacked at the mouth of Nilkhet Road. They set fire to glass bottles and hurled them into the streets. But when the tanks climbed over the barricades and splintered the chairs, they fled, weaving through the buildings and hiding in Curzon Hall. The bullets missed them.

But Sharmeen. Sharmeen could not be found.

At first Maya was vaguely irritated she'd missed everything. All her friends had stories of that night, and, while she kept saying, 'Good thing I wasn't on campus,' there was a slight regret at having been sidelined. She wanted some mark, some sign, that the thing had happened to her. A bruise on the cheek. A tear in her blouse. She waited for Sharmeen to show up at the gate, to give her a little of the moment.

But on the third day there was still no sign of her.

'It's all right,' Rehana soothed, not knowing what to say; 'there must be some explanation.' Everything she knew about Sharmeen prevented her from fearing for the girl. She was too big, too stormy, to simply vanish. Maya must have thought the same thing, because she refused to worry.

On the fourth day the Senguptas decided to leave. Rehana found them at Shona with their belongings strewn across the drawing-room floor, dotting Mrs Sengupta's pink rose-petal carpet.

'We have to go,' Mrs Sengupta began. It was obvious she had been the one to urge her husband to leave; she was nervous, drawing her achol over her shoulder and smoothing her pleats.

Rehana didn't say anything, only nodded.

'It's not safe for Hindus in the city,' Mr Sengupta explained. 'As you know.' The refugees had stayed a couple of days, making their home on the lawn, keeping vigil at night with hurricane lamps and lengths of wood they had saved from their door-frames. Then they too had left, for villages in the interior, or across the border to India. They had thanked Rehana for her kindness, gathered up their things and latched the gate behind them.

'Are you going to India?' Rehana asked.

Mr Sengupta made a show of being surprised. 'Why? No, why would we go to India? We are going to our village in Pabna. We haven't been to stay in a long while. Mithun should see his ancestral home, meet his cousins.' Mr Sengupta parted the net curtains on the window behind him and looked out at his son chasing a crow in the garden.

'Of course,' Rehana said, 'you know what is best. But there are disturbing reports. Burning villages. Targeting Hindus.'

'That's just a rumour. The city is dangerous, but they won't go that far inland,' he said. 'It takes two days just to reach the town — mud roads, nothing paved. Why would they bother?' And he made a sound somewhere between a short laugh and a snort.

'The people in your village,' Rehana said, pressing him a little, 'can you trust them?'

'My village people? Of course! My family has

been in that village for generations. Mrs Haque, would you have all Hindus flee to India?'

Rehana could see she had offended him. There was now a clear note of challenge, a probe, to see which side of things she was on. He crossed and uncrossed his legs. Mrs Sengupta was nervously fiddling with the hem of her sari. Looking at her, Rehana was reminded of herself at a younger, more confident age, when she'd had the luxury of retreating when she wanted to, allowing someone else to make decisions, declare the lines of argument.

Mrs Sengupta leaned over to Rehana and took her hand. 'We feel terribly about leaving you alone. Will you be all right?'

'Of course,' Rehana said, though it had just occurred to her that she would not have any money until the Senguptas returned. In the way Mrs Sengupta was looking at her, Rehana could tell this was the reason for the apology. Her friend took out an envelope and held it between her palms. 'Oh, no, Supriya, you mustn't do that.'

'It's the only way we could even consider leaving.' She turned to her husband. He appeared to have recovered and nodded vigorously. 'It's not much. But we couldn't leave you empty-handed.'

'I won't hear of it,' Rehana insisted, wondering how long she would have to pretend she didn't really need the money. She murmured a few more words of protest but took it in the end, warning the couple that if they stayed away too long she might find new tenants. The idea of

98

anyone moving to Dhaka at a time like this made everyone laugh.

'I'm sorry we've left such a mess,' Mrs Sengupta said, waving her arm around the room.

'Don't worry, Maya and I will take care of the rest.'

'Really?'

'Of course. Just take what you need. You'll be back soon, I know it.'

'Mithun!' Mr Sengupta called out into the garden. 'Say goodbye to your auntie!'

Despite her best efforts to appear casual, Rehana felt a sting in her eyes as she embraced Mrs Sengupta. 'God be with you,' she said, squeezing her friend's shoulder. 'I'll be waiting for you.'

By the middle of April they began to realize that the attack on Dhaka was only the beginning. The army was making its way across the country, subduing one district after another, leaving behind a trail of burning villages. And there were stories of boys running away from home to join the resistance, slipping away in the middle of the night with their shoes in their pockets, crossing the border to find Major Zia, who had made the announcement on the radio.

One day Joy and Aref came to the bungalow in a truck. It was filled with crates of different sizes, which they began unloading and stacking up against the gate.

'What's this?' Rehana asked.

'Auntie, we need your help,' Joy said. 'We need to store some things in your house.'

Sohail came out of his room. 'Where did you get them?'

'What's going on?' Rehana asked. They were all behaving as though it was perfectly ordinary. As if people arrived with trucks full of mysterious things every day.

'Ammoo,' Sohail said, 'we've heard reports of refugee camps across the border. They need medicine.'

'Where did you get these?'

Sohail waited for Joy to reply. Aref was counting the remaining boxes in the truck. 'PG Hospital.' He put his hands on his waist. There was a pause while the boys waited for Rehana to ask how they had convinced the doctors at PG hospital to give them a truckful of medicine.

She decided not to ask. If she asked, they would have to tell her they had stolen it. 'Good idea,' she said finally, 'bring it all inside. Do you boys want to stay for lunch?'

Aref beamed at Rehana from above. 'We knew you'd understand,' he said, blowing her a kiss.

The next day they came again. They carried eight crates of powdered milk, three boxes of cotton wool, four drums of rice, sixteen cases of dal. Buckets. Shovels. Rehana put the food in the passage between her bedroom and the kitchen. Now they had to walk sideways to get to the kitchen. The dining chairs were stacked on top of the table, the medicines stored underneath. They

100

started taking meals with plates on their laps.

Maya was soothed by the crowded house. She put her cheeks against the boxes of cotton wool, ran her finger along the tops of the medicine cases.

It had been almost two weeks, and Sharmeen was still missing. No one knew where the girl was, but she was making her presence felt at the bungalow, as they each silently imagined what might have happened to her. Still Maya refused to talk about it. She drifted through the house like a cloud of dust. Rehana tried to bring it up, but every time she approached Maya it felt like a trespass.

'Where is her mother?' Rehana asked finally.

'She's in Mymensingh.'

'Maybe Sharmeen went to see her?'

'I already contacted her family. She's not there.'

'Does she have brothers?'

'Not really.'

Sharmeen's mother, Rehana remembered, had remarried. There were other children. And a stepfather. That is why Sharmeen lived in the dormitory, and why she was always at the bungalow for Eid. And why her clothes were mixed up with Maya's in the cupboard. And her toothbrush in the bathroom cabinet. She had a stake in their house. Rehana knew all of this, but, as the picture of Sharmeen's life came into focus, she felt guilty for sometimes resenting her presence at the bungalow. She could have been warmer towards her. She might not have saved the girl, but she could have loved her.

101

She still didn't know what to do with Maya. 'Are you hungry?'

'No.'

Rehana did not know what else to say. If Maya would not discuss Sharmeen, Rehana could not console her. She could not find a way into her daughter's grief, drawn so tightly around her.

Rehana often wondered if she could help loving one child better. She had a blunt, tired love for her daughter. It was full of effort. Sohail was her first-born, and so tender, and Maya was so hard, all sympathy worked out of her by the throaty chants of the street march, the pitch of the slogan. Too many strong words had come out of her mouth. The ideas were like an affliction; they had taken her over so completely she had even changed physically: suddenly the angles of her face had moved, sharpened, so that she was no longer young, or even pretty. And she wore only widow's white, which always felt to Rehana like an insult.

She had only two remnants of a gentler self: the thick braid that snaked down her back like a swollen, black river, and her singing voice. Both had escaped being sacrificed. She often threatened her mother with photographs of women with short hair, the bob that stared out of magazine covers, the boy-cut some of her friends had dared to ask for at the parlour. But somehow, despite the threats, she had never lopped off the hair that so definitively identified her as Rehana's daughter, in its shine and its straightness, in its dark blue hue, its thickness and weight. Rehana had even caught Maya

102

caring for her hair, combing or massaging it with coconut oil, though if she herself ever offered to help she was met with a withering stare and a short 'nothing doing'.

And when she sang, Maya could not stop the tenderness from covering her features like a fine winter mist. There was nothing harsh in her voice — in fact, it was even a little girlish, defying the learning that had so hardened her spoken words. She opened her mouth, and from her lips, her throat, the immature heart, came sweet, rapturous song. She had learned her mother's ghazals, but her politics had turned her to the banned songs of Tagore, and these suited her better. For they did not demand the plaintive, mournful tenor of forsaken love but rather, a more innocent form of sentiment, which Tagore, uncomplicated lover of God, of earth, of beauty, had delivered in such abundance.

Her hands on the harmonium were delicate, square-tipped, her bitten-down nails paying homage to the seriousness of the task; her brows were knitted together in service of the song, and in the end it was only to the music that she was bound. In singing she was, if only briefly, a supplicant, as though in the presence of a divinity that even she, devout non-believer, had to somehow acknowledge.

Rehana thought of it as her biggest failure. That her daughter had not found a way into her heart.

* * *

On the day Joy and Aref appeared without the truck, they had another boy with them, a Hindu boy named Partho whose family had fled the city.

'Don't let them in,' Sohail said to Rehana, but they had already climbed over the gate. Aref was shifting from one foot to another and adjusting his round-rimmed glasses with the tip of his finger. There was a black bag between Partho and Joy.

She couldn't imagine why Sohail would shun his friends.

Joy cupped his hands around his mouth and shouted, 'Sohail! Dost! Aye na! Come out!'

When Sohail didn't reply, Rehana stepped through the veranda and asked them what they wanted. They looked rough, as though they hadn't bathed or changed clothes. Joy's hair curled like a comma above his head, and Aref's hung limp between his ears. Partho was staring past Rehana and into the windows of the bungalow to see if Sohail would emerge.

'As-Salaam Alaikum, Auntie,' Aref said. 'Sohail achhe?'

These were his friends. Surely he wouldn't mind if she invited them in. 'Do you want to come in?'

Joy and Aref looked at the black bag. 'No,' Joy replied, 'we'll stay here.'

Aref was fidgeting with a matchbox. He held a packet of cigarettes out to Partho, who shook his head. He lit one. 'Is he there?' he said.

Rehana considered lying but decided not to. 'I think he's upset.' She was annoyed at not

104

knowing the cause of this sudden change of heart. One minute he was glued to his friends, the next he didn't want to see them.

'We just want to talk. Can he come to the window?'

'I don't know, I'll see.' She went back through the house and found Sohail pacing the drawing room with the loose drawstring of his pyjamas flapping between his knees. 'Tell them to go away,' he said, tugging at the string.

'They've come all the way — '

'I don't care.'

Rehana paused for a moment, exasperated. 'OK, I give up. I'm going to Shona. You decide what to do with your friends.'

★ ★ ★

Rehana and Maya were at Shona, packing up the last of Mrs Sengupta's things, when Sohail entered. He hung in the doorway of the dining room, watching Rehana wrap Mrs Sengupta's plates in sheets of newspaper. The newspaper was mostly blank, giant banner advertisements for Tibet Soap and Brylcreem framing empty spaces.

Maya was helping Rehana put the wrapped plates into a crate, but as soon as she saw Sohail she abandoned the crate and put up her hands.

'What's happening?' she asked.

'Nothing. Aref and Joy came to see if we were all right. We're waiting to see how things will evolve.'

'Waiting for what?'

'The foreign journalists at the InterContinental Hotel saw everything. Can you believe those bastards? They didn't even try to cover their tracks. It'll be all over the international news.'

'Your friends. What did they want?'

'We need support from the UN.'

'Don't change the subject,' Maya needled. 'You're planning something.'

'Nothing — what would we be planning?'

'They had something — a package — Ammoo told me. Were they asking you to hide something?' She pressed him. Rehana knew he hated lying.

He looked straight at Maya, as though daring her to ask again.

'You're going, aren't you?'

Going? Where would he be going? Wait, Rehana wanted to say. I thought you were arguing about something small. Something insignificant. Not about going. If only they'd told me it was something to do with going, I would have stood at the door myself and refused to let them in.

Sohail pushed the hair from his eyes. Rehana fought the wave of panic crawling through her arms.

'Just tell me, bhaiya, please, I just want to know,' Maya said. She pointed her face to the box of plates, as though to say, *You owe me.*

* * *

'Ammoo,' Sohail said the next day, 'there's something I have to tell you.' The full moon was

106

hammocked over Dhaka; it shone through the windows of the bungalow, revealing the dark, speckled shadow on Sohail's chin, on his fist tightening and loosening.

'Don't tell me.'

He looked very sorry. 'I have to go.'

'Go? Where? Where will you go?'

'We heard there's a resistance across the border. All the Bengali regiments have mutinied. Didn't you hear Zia?'

'This is a thing between soldiers. What does it have to do with you?'

'They need volunteers. Aref and Joy and Partho are going too.'

'I thought you were a pacifist.' She clung to the word. Pacifist. Someone who does not rush off to join a war. Someone who stays behind and doesn't break his mother's heart.

'I really struggled, Ammoo, but I realized I don't have a choice.'

'Of course you have a choice. You always have a choice.' Rehana held her head in her hands and tried not to sound desperate. 'What if something happens to you?' She choked a little at the words. He had missed a button on his shirt. It was his favourite, a red-and-blue check, and as she leaned over to tuck the stray button through its loop he put his hand on her head, as though he were giving her his blessing. 'I thought you hated war,' Rehana said weakly.

'This isn't war. It's genocide.'

'Is it Silvi?'

'No, of course not.' He paused, seemed to hold his breath, then said, 'I can't sit back and do nothing, Ma. Everyone is fighting. Even people who weren't sure, people who wanted to stay with Pakistan.'

'How will you go?'

'Aref's cousin Raju has a car. He'll drive us to the border.'

He didn't say when. Maybe if she delayed him it wouldn't happen at all. She wanted so much for it to depend on her. 'I can't decide now. Can I decide later? Can I decide tomorrow? We'll go to the graveyard.'

'It won't be for a few days,' he said. 'Let's go to sleep now.'

Rehana nodded. And then she had a sudden thought: what if he left in the middle of the night, like the other boys, without telling her? It might be better. No. No, it wouldn't be better. 'Don't go without telling me.'

'I won't.'

'Promise.'

'I promise.'

'Promise on my life.'

'I promise on your life, Ammoo.'

★ ★ ★

The next day Rehana and Sohail took a rickshaw to the graveyard. Rehana was silent all the way, though in her head there was a shout. Don't go, the shout said. Please, don't go.

They passed a group of schoolboys on the street. Rehana wondered if their thoughts, like Sohail's, were full of war. If they turned the idea over in their mouths like sugar-candy. If they were waiting for the right moment to tell their mothers and disappear.

The graveyard was pristine, a crisp open sky above it.

Here is your son, she said to Iqbal. Surely you would not have wanted this. Your son wants to fight for his country. He says he has no choice. I want to, but cannot be angry with him. So I leave it to you.

The quiet rumbled in her ears; the brief rustle of the drying graveyard grasses, the tinkle of a passing rickshaw, the burning tip of the caretaker's biri as he lit it through the open glass of his kerosene lamp. The sounds roared; they screeched; they pierced. Please don't go.

'Don't go,' she finally said aloud. 'There must be another way you can help.'

Sohail looked at her as though to say, Let's not do this in front of Abboo. But Rehana was strengthened by Iqbal's presence. Of the two of them, he would have been the one to protest. He would have forbidden it — yes, forbidden. I forbid you to go, he would have said. I forbid it! She should try to utter that word; it had such an unyielding quality.

But of course she could forbid nothing. She was seized with a sudden, gripping exhaustion. 'I just keep hoping you'll change your mind.'

He was still wearing the red-and-blue check; the collar pointed to his shoes. She saw him arguing with himself, calculating the most noble thing to do. The thing that would require the most sacrifice. Weighing his guilt against his desire to go. He must be picturing her alone in the house, with only Maya as her silent companion. And then himself in an army uniform. Which would be worse? He would choose that.

Rehana realized that she too would have made the same calculation. She would have moved through the world in that same way, trying find the thing that denied her most. She suddenly saw how much like her he was in this. The knowledge was an open window.

Sohail was still battling. His hand was hovering over the pocket of his shirt. Iqbal's gravestone gleamed like the side of a ship.

'It's all right, baba,' was all she could think to say. 'Say goodbye to your father.'

Sohail cupped his hands and raised them to his face.

I cannot stop him. Perhaps if you were here, you would have done it. But I cannot. It is too great a thing.

★ ★ ★

In the afternoon Rehana watched as he packed his bags. Her fingers itched to help him so she tried to focus on something else. The books on his shelf. The posters hanging on the wall. Mao Tse-Tung. Che Guevara. Karl Marx. He wouldn't tell her when he was leaving, or how he was planning to get out of the city.

'It's better if you don't know,' he said.

She unearthed an irritated, argumentative version of herself. 'Why? Why is it better if I don't know?'

110

'Because that way if anyone asks, you can say you don't know.'

She was tired. She wanted to be stubborn. It reassured her to dictate the terms of his leaving. 'No. I have to be here when you go. Tell Aref and Joy to pick you up. There's no need for secrecy,' she said; 'just tell them to come here. I want to know the moment you step out of that door, the moment you cross that gate. I want to say Aytul Kursi and Surah Yahseen.'

'All right,' he sighed. He was folding his shirts.

All this time Maya was standing under the doorframe, her feet on the raised threshold.

'I have something for you,' she said. It was a package wrapped in delicate red paper. It looked soft.

'What is it?' Rehana asked.

'Open it later,' Maya said.

Rehana wanted a brother. Someone to give going-away presents to. Someone to love without worry.

* * *

Rehana went to see Mrs Chowdhury. She thought she might tell her the news: about Sohail, and the boys leaving their stolen supplies in her corridors, and Sharmeen disappearing. She imagined Mrs Chowdhury holding her hands and telling her it would all be put right, like she used to.

Mrs Chowdhury was sitting on her veranda, facing the coconut trees in her garden. When Rehana leaned over to kiss her cheek, she found

111

henna paste smeared into Mrs Chowdhury's hair.

'Any news of the Senguptas?' Her breath was eggy.

'Nothing. I thought they might write. Where is Silvi?' She hadn't seen Silvi since that night.

'In her room. Praying, probably. All she does these days.' Mrs Chowdhury waved away the plate of sliced papaya the cook had brought her. 'What's this? Bring me the samosas!'

'No fried things, khalamma. Silvi apa's orders.'

'I don't care. I'll eat samosas if I want to. Go!' And she snapped her fingers, which were heavy with generations of gold rings.

Rehana smiled indulgently at Mrs Chowdhury and realized that, in some quarters of the city, life was going on as before. Women were arguing for samosas. People were taking briefcases to work and frowning over their typewriters.

Mrs Chowdhury misunderstood Rehana's silence. 'Don't worry, darling. The Senguptas will soon return.'

'Times are bad, Mrs Chowdhury.'

'Nonsense. Things will soon return to normal. It will all be done in no time.'

The words, when they came, did not comfort Rehana. She wondered if Mrs Chowdhury had been out of the house since the massacre, if she'd seen the death-coated city. Her dog had died, that appeared to be the extent of it. Rehana felt waves of hot and cold pummel her; she gripped the seat and swayed.

'Oh, my dear, you're about to faint!' Mrs Chowdhury clapped again. 'Ei, get over here, you good-for-nothings, bring some ice water. Hurry!'

Rehana closed her eyes and waited; the ice water was put to her lips; she drank, pressed her back against the sofa. I'll just lie here for a few minutes, she told herself. Just a few minutes.

★ ★ ★

'Tomorrow,' Sohail whispered. 'We're leaving tomorrow.'

Even though she had left him alone to pack his bag, she could not help unzipping it to see what he'd taken. She counted a few shirts. A lungi. She felt the plastic of his toothbrush. It was like combing her hands through his hair. Satisfied, she left for the kitchen.

She had prepared a feast. It had kept her calm throughout the day. So much to do.

There was shrimp malai curry.

Polao.

Chitol fish, which she'd had to debone and shape into balls. Chicken roast. Shami kabab. Dal, extra thick.

This is my duty, she said to herself. Sending my son to war with a full stomach.

They ate.

Maya, whose clothes suddenly hung over her frame in limp, deflated folds, nudged her rice with a spoon. Rehana realized how much she had neglected her daughter. The food turned grainy and sour in her mouth. Sohail was the only one eating, smacking his fingers together and smiling into his plate.

They said nothing of what was about to happen.

After the sweets and the halwa, Sohail rubbed his hands together and prepared to go.

'They're going to meet me in Sadarghat.'

'Should I get you a rickshaw?'

'Na.'

Just let me go, she heard him say. He turned to Maya, who had set her mouth into a thin line. He gripped her shoulders. She looked brittle between his hands. When he pulled her towards himself, she crumpled.

'Get the bastards,' she whispered. Then she turned and left them.

The light flickered.

'I hate to let you go,' Rehana said. She saw him looking at the creases on her forehead, the ones she had named 1959 and 1960. And she saw the scar under his chin, the one he had named *Silvi*.

'Go,' she said finally. 'God goes with you.'

And then he was gone, his room tidied, the sheets tucked neatly into the mattress, his books lined up straight on the shelf, a small gap where *Ghazals of Mirza Ghalib* and *Collected Poems of Dylan Thomas* had sat beside each other, their frayed, loved, monsoon-waved pages pressed into line. She smiled at the choice. He had already memorized the poems and worn out the spines, but he would surely recite the verses to his soldier friends, who, despite being fierce and gun-wielding, would listen in rapt attention.

After Sohail left, Rehana resolved to confront her daughter. But Maya was evanescent; somehow even when she was sitting right in front of her it was as if she wasn't there. She behaved as though no one had told her that once the war began there would be nothing for her to do but wait. No one had told her that she would only be allowed to imagine it from a distance. No one had told her how lonely, how hot, how tiresome, the days would be. And no one had told her that her friend would be the first to go.

She began spending all her time at the university, leaving as soon as the morning curfew was lifted, ignoring the breakfast Rehana offered, bolting through the door with only a few rushed words, and every evening returning just before the siren, looking exhausted and tense. When Rehana asked her what she did all day she said she had *work to do.*

In truth, it was a relief when she left the house every morning. Even the trees seemed to relax. Rehana tried not to let her imagination run loose around the empty house. She spent the days in stunned efficiency, counting and recounting the supplies, listening to the radio and discovering the violence that had been wrought upon the country. The deaths. The arrests. The children with no parents. The mothers with empty laps. The ones who simply vanished, leaving behind a comb or a pair of shoes.

Mrs Akram and Mrs Rahman came to visit. 'Mrs Chowdhury said you've been upset,' Mrs Rahman began.

Sohail had instructed her not to say anything

115

about his departure. 'It's been very difficult. Everyone's gone — the Senguptas — and you remember that girl, Sharmeen, Maya's friend? We can't find her anywhere.'

'We should all go,' Mrs Akram said. 'It's not safe for our children.'

'Why should we go?' Mrs Rahman said. 'We don't have to run away like criminals. This is our city. Let them march around and pretend they've taken over — I'm not leaving. I passed by those soldiers on my way here — they're just little boys, younger than my own children. They expect me to be afraid!'

There was something comical about Mrs Rahman's bravado, but Rehana didn't feel like smiling.

'Will you go, Rehana?' Mrs Akram asked. 'Don't you have sisters in Pakistan?'

'Pakistan?' Mrs Rahman said. 'Why on earth should she go to Pakistan? You know what they would do to us over there?'

'No,' Rehana said slowly, as though she had given the matter some thought, 'I don't think so. The children would never hear of it.'

'I tell you, we should all stay here and take a stand.'

'What sort of a stand, exactly?' Mrs Akram asked.

'We should do something. I'm not giving up so easily.'

'Don't be foolish. You're just a housewife. What on earth could you possibly do?'

'You wait and see. I'm not just good for gin-rummy, I'll have you know.'

116

A few days later Rehana decided she'd had enough of Maya's secrecy, so she decided to confront her. She wanted to know what the girl was doing all day at the university. Rehana borrowed Mrs Chowdhury's car and ordered the driver to take her to the university campus. She didn't know where to look — in the bombed-out hostels, or the canteen, or the Teacher — Student Centre — but she was sure she would find her, and she couldn't stop thinking Maya must be doing something wrong. She was upset. She could be in trouble. Rehana would find out and put an end to it, whatever it was. Yes, she was worrying. Maybe for no reason. But better to make sure.

Rehana had only really been inside the university once, when Sohail had invited her to try the famous phuchkas at the canteen. He had bet her the university phuchkas were better than the ones at Horolika Snacks in Dhanmondi. Rehana said that wasn't possible. She and Iqbal had tried all the phuchkas in Dhaka and no one could beat Horolika Snacks. Sohail said that was over a decade ago and things had changed. Rehana didn't like to be reminded that things had changed and her husband was dead, but she was carried along by her son's enthusiasm and agreed to see for herself. They bought a dozen phuchkas at Horolika Snacks and balanced the boxes on their knees as they took a rickshaw to the university campus.

At the canteen Sohail ordered a dozen more.

He put the tiny cups of fried dough in a row in front of Rehana. Then he poured a little tamarind water into each one, licking his lips and clapping his hands together and saying, 'Horo-lika versus Dhaka University! Which will it be?' Some of the students stopped talking and looked over. The owner of the canteen stood up over his counter and cheered for himself. Then Sohail told Rehana that, in the interest of fairness, she should close her eyes and taste first one, then the other.

In the end she chose the canteen phuchkas. Things really had changed. And now the canteen, along with most of the other low buildings on the university campus, had been burned down on the night of the massacre.

Rehana didn't have to search for her daughter. She saw her as soon as the car entered the university gates. There was a line of girls, and Maya was in the front row, raising her knees higher than all the others and shouting louder than all the others. So this was what she'd been doing. She didn't look timid, or embarrassed that the gun she was holding was just a wooden stick. 'Hut-two-three-four! Hut! Hut! Hut!' she shouted.

Rehana told the driver to stop the car. She watched as the girls marched past. Some of them paused and peered through the window at Rehana. One smiled shyly; another waved. Maya, who kept her eyes straight ahead, didn't notice her mother. The girls stopped a few feet away from the car and moved their hands over the wooden sticks, pretending to load, aim, fire,

118

reload. They wore starched white saris with thin blue borders. They looked like washerwomen. They looked serious. None was as serious as Maya.

Rehana sat in the car and watched her daughter, waiting for the training, or whatever it was, to end. Once it was over she opened the car door and waved in Maya's direction. Maya was talking to a boy and didn't notice, but the boy, who was blowing smoke rings into the air, saw Rehana wave and whispered something to Maya. He pointed. Maya stalked over, her face coming together in a frown.

'Are you spying on me?' she said. The exercise had made her aggressive. Her braid was coming undone, and the stray hairs clung wetly to her forehead.

'No, I just — you've been away so much. It's dangerous, I just wanted to see where you were.'

'Well, now you know.' She brushed the hair from her face. 'I'm trying to contribute.'

'By doing this? Running around with wooden guns?'

As was her habit, Maya mounted an attack. 'Why did you bring us back here?'

'What do you mean?'

'From Lahore? Why did you bother to bring us back? You have no feeling for this place.'

What did she mean? 'This is my home. Your father's home.'

'Then why won't you let me do something?'

'I just want to protect you. Everything I've done I've done for you and your brother. Now please, get in the car, the curfew's about to ring.'

119

'I'm not coming.'

'What?'

'I'm not coming. You go home, I'll stay here.'

'You come with me right now. You get in the car.' Rehana felt the futility of it, but she insisted, grabbing Maya's elbow and pulling her towards the car. She was surprised at her own strength. Maya tried to wrench her arm away, and Rehana gripped harder. 'Don't make a scene,' she said coldly.

They said nothing to one another in the car. When they got home, Maya turned on her mother and began with a shout: 'You are not so good at this either. You couldn't keep my brother back, and you can't keep me!'

Keep me. The words were poisoned arrows.

'You don't know what you're saying.'

'You've been crazy — ever since — ever since Abboo died, you have this thing about keeping us at home. You're mad! You want to lock us up!'

Rehana tried to change the subject. 'I'm so sorry about Sharmeen, I know you're upset.'

'Don't speak about her. You could never understand.'

'Of course I understand.'

'I mean you could never understand what it's like for me and Sohail.'

'Leave your brother out of it.'

'Sohail,' she said, 'where is he now? Probably dead, killed by one of your Pak soldiers!'

It happened so quickly. She hadn't meant to hit so hard, and it was only when she saw the red flowering on Maya's cheek that she realized what she'd done.

Maya put her hand to her face, looking surprised, and then almost relieved. Then she said, 'You should have left us in Pakistan.'

Rehana wanted to say sorry for the slap. She wanted to shake her until Maya took it back. But she stayed quiet, only glaring at her daughter and hoping Maya would not see the weak tremble in her jaw.

★ ★ ★

Maya stopped speaking. There were no more pleasantries, no more 'good mornings' and 'I'm not hungrys'. With Sohail and the Senguptas gone, and Mrs Chowdhury and Silvi locked up in their house, Rehana felt a kinship with the deserted city. Maya took her plate and ate silently in Sohail's room. The light would stay on deep into the night, and Rehana began to know her daughter only through the line of pale yellow that crept in below the door, and through the small sounds she made: the click of the ceiling-fan switch, the swish of the bedcover as she peeled it back, the faint whistle of a turning page. It went on this way for two weeks, as April, with its dense, stifling heat, spooled out before them.

Then one day Maya suddenly announced: 'The soldiers need blankets. We're collecting old saris.'

'You're sewing kathas?'

'Yes. We need material. Things you'd throw away.'

Before she even realized it, Rehana had an

121

idea that led her to an old steel almirah she hadn't opened in years. She found the heavy key tucked behind the lowest shelf in the kitchen where she kept the emergency supplies of rice and dal. A life of variable fortunes had taught her never to finish anything. She always kept behind a tiny bit — a finger of ginger, a stick of cinnamon, a handful of rice — in case the next time she went to buy these things they somehow eluded her, through poverty or the unreliability of the country's fortunes.

The key, despite years of disuse, slid smoothly into the lock. As she turned it and twisted the handle to release the bolt, Rehana recognized the old sound of scraping metal, and she steadied herself for the smell of mothballs and silk. The doors rasped in protest as she swung them open and surveyed the contents of the almirah. Here were the saris Iqbal had given her in the eight years of their marriage. After his death, she had washed, ironed and hung them up in the order in which they had been presented to her.

She remembered each occasion, the sari arriving in the red-and-white cardboard box of the sari shop, still smelling of the attar of the market and the ash of young cigarette-smoking boys who were enlisted to bring down the starched saris from high shelves and drape them delicately around their youthful hips. They would sway in imitation of women, dangling the achol from outstretched arms to show off the elaborate embroidery, the swimming colours.

It had not been difficult to arrange the saris; as the years had gone by, Iqbal's prosperity, and his gratitude for his wife, had meant more and more daring purchases. Simple cottons became diaphanous chiffons, prints were given up in favour of embroidery, the threads of each sari always heavier than the last, the patterns more refined, the silk more serious, until, just a few weeks before his death, Iqbal had presented Rehana with the jewel of the collection, a blue Benarsi silk.

Rehana regarded the saris and tried to recall the feeling they had given her, of being at once enveloped and set free, the tight revolutions of material around her hips and legs limiting movement, the empty space between blouse and petticoat permitting unexpected sensations — the thrill of a breeze that has strayed low, through an open window, the knowledge of heat in strange places, the back, the exposed belly. It was the bringing together of night and day, the sari: as it concealed the skin, it also released it, so that one body, one woman, would know something of the complications of her sex.

The saris stared at Rehana like pictures in a photo album, evocative, a little accusing. She hadn't worn a single one in years. She was not sorry to lose them, just sorry she would never again have occasion to wear them. She piled the saris loosely into her arms, rushed into the drawing room and presented them to her daughter.

'Here. Blankets for your freedom fighters. I'll help you sew.'

Maya stared at her mother. 'I asked you for cottons,' she said quietly. 'What's the point of all this expensive material? The blankets will itch.'

'Put them inside. It will be winter before you know it, and the silk will keep everyone warm.'

The sight of the saris stirred something in Maya.

'Please don't give them away,' she said softly.

'Why not? You never wear anything but white.' Rehana was aware of a punishing note in her voice. Why, despite her best intentions, did the words to her daughter always sound so sharp?

Maya's face closed up. 'It's foolish to give these away. They're of no use; you should put them back.'

★ ★ ★

Rehana called Mrs Rahman and Mrs Akram to the bungalow. 'Follow me,' she said, leading them up the stairs to the roof. She had laid out a jute pati and a few cushions. The saris were stacked up in a basket. Beside the basket was Rehana's sewing box. The box contained a row of needles and a bundle of black spools. There were small pattern cutouts and a collection of thimbles. A tomato-shaped pin-cushion.

'What's all this?' Mrs Rahman said, sliding off her chappals and flopping on to the pati. 'You want to open a tailoring shop?'

'Don't you know? We're at war, and my daughter says I have to do something. To prove I belong here. So I'm doing something.' Rehana felt a tear crawling out of her eye; she tilted her head, sent it back. 'I'm doing something. Making blankets for the refugees.' She felt her lip curling

124

back on to her teeth.

'What's going on — where's Sohail?' Mrs Akram asked.

She was desperate to tell them. 'He isn't here — I sent him to Karachi.'

'Really? I thought — '

'Don't you know what they're doing to all the university boys? They're making them disappear. What would you have me do, just sit back and let them take him?'

'Rehana,' Mrs Rahman said, pointing to the silks, 'you don't have to use these. We can find some old cottons.'

Rehana dug in her heels. 'Why not? Everyone has to make sacrifices, why not me? It's my country too.'

'Of course it's your country — ' Mrs Akram began.

'My daughter doesn't think so.'

'She said that? She couldn't have meant it; you know how children are.'

'I slapped her.'

'Oh, Rehana.' Mrs Akram put a hand on Rehana's arm.

'I couldn't help it, I just did it. She's out of control.'

'Rehana, you must have patience,' Mrs Rahman said.

'Patience? I have nothing but patience for the children. Running around all over town, revolution this, democracy that — nothing but patience!'

'For Sohail, yes, but — '

'What are you saying?'

125

The two women exchanged cautious looks. 'We know she hasn't exactly been easy,' Mrs Rahman said. 'But you've always been — a little more unforgiving of Maya.'

'Unforgiving? Me? I'm only one person — I have to do everything — is it possible, humanly possible?' But she knew they were right. The knowledge burned inside her, but she couldn't bring herself to say it. You're right. I've been unfair. 'You want to help me,' she said instead. 'Sew.'

★ ★ ★

On the last day of April, it rained. Rehana watched the cotton clouds shout to a hungry, cracked earth. She imagined it raining on the human exodus on the Jessore Road and the Mymensingh Road and on the widows and the swollen bellies, trying to wash away the tears, falling in skyfuls over the slowly departing. And falling on her Sohail and his friends as they picked through the spring prairie grasses, through the low paddy, the bleached stacks of wheat, as they searched for the war with only their wet-toothed smiles, their poems, their death-defying youth.

May

Tikka Khan,
the Butcher of Bengal!

Mrs Rahman and Mrs Akram took to the sewing with the same enthusiasm they'd displayed for cards. They gathered at the bungalow every week, ready with their sewing kits. Mrs Rahman managed to get a steady supply of old saris from her various acquaintances and relations. She enlisted everyone she knew — her distant cousins, in-laws, her tailor — to make a contribution to the war effort. Of course, she was quick to point out, no one had been foolish enough to give away their best clothes.

Mrs Akram, whom they had always considered a little spoiled, surprised them by turning out the fastest stitches. And it was her idea to put sackcloths between the saris to make them more sturdy.

'Let's call ourselves the sewing sisters,' Mrs Akram said. 'Or, I know, Project Rooftop!'

'Arre, now you want to give it a name — aren't you the one who said we weren't good for anything but cards?'

'I never said that,' Mrs Akram protested, a needle between her lips. 'That is not the kind of faltu thing I would say.'

It was true, Rehana thought. It was not the sort of thing she would say any more. Already two months ago felt like the distant past. It was May. They had been at war since March. What was strange had become unstrange. They were used to seeing the green uniforms wherever they went; they were used to returning obediently to their homes at the peal of the curfew siren; and they were used to the dusty, empty streets, the closed shops, the hospitals with locked gates, the half-full baskets of the fruit vendors. The landscape of war was becoming familiar, and they had all found their ways to live with it.

Maya was still angry at Rehana. The silence banged around between them. They batted it back and forth. Sometimes, while she waited for Maya to return from the university, Rehana would resolve to say something, to make up; she could feel the tender words bubbling in her mouth. *I'm sorry I hit you.* But she couldn't utter them; as soon as the girl came home, as soon as Rehana saw her scowling face, the way she slammed the bolt through the door, the irritation flooded back. Why couldn't she smile, give a hint she might relent? But she didn't, and Rehana too was frozen, the words stuck somewhere between her heart and her mouth.

The more time went by, the harder it became. Rehana organized the house; she packaged the supplies the boys had left at the bungalow; she sewed her kathas. It was a lonely, stretched-out time. The only thing she and Maya did together now was listen to the radio. In the morning they would listen to BBC Bangla, and in the afternoon Voice of America. But the programme they waited for with most anticipation was the Free Bangla Radio transmission, every day at 4.30, broadcast from a secret, undisclosed location in the liberated zone.

The number of refugees flowing into West Bengal has reached one million. The International Red Cross has stated that the refugee camps along the border between India and Bangladesh are overcrowded and suffer from a lack of clean water, sanitation and proper medical facilities. Indian Prime Minister Indira Gandhi has pledged her support for the people of Bangladesh, stating that the freedom-loving Bengalis would soon triumph over the fascistic regime of the Pakistani dictators.

So by the time Sohail returned to Dhaka, the city had settled back into a sort of routine. He came in the middle of the night and stood at the foot of Rehana's bed. Later she would say she had known all along that he was there, that she'd deliberately kept her eyes closed, savouring the relief of having him back, and alive, but really she'd slept through the whole thing — his entrance through the gate, his stealthy sidestepping of the furniture and the medicine boxes, the deep breath he took before uttering her very favourite word.

'Ma.'

She pressed her cheek against his cheek. He smelled of petrol and cigarettes. At the touch of his shirt against her hand she felt a deep, piercing loneliness.

'Have you eaten?' she said, then laughed at herself. Still, she got up and darted into the kitchen while he went to wake Maya. She'd had only a moment to scrutinize him. He wore a grey shirt and a pair of blue trousers; they were both dirty and looked too big. His eyes were ringed dark brown, and he was growing a beard. There was something unmistakably foreign about him now, as though some other hands had begun to shape him, hands not as loving or as tender as hers. She couldn't help thinking back to the years he had been with Parveen. *My children have not always been my children*. The old wound pulsed inside her.

As she deliberated over what to cook, she heard him wake his sister. 'Bhaiya!' Maya cried out. It was the most cheerful thing she'd said in months. 'Tell me everything,' Rehana heard her say. 'Have you been to the battlefront?'

The food — egg curry, a few strips of fried eggplant, leftover dal — was soon on the table. Sohail rolled up his sleeves eagerly and between mouthfuls began to tell them about the freedom-fighter army.

'Joy drove us to the river and then we took the ferry. It was full of refugees. We heard the most terrible stories about that night. Lot of Hindus especially.'

'The Senguptas haven't come back,' Maya said.

132

Sohail nodded, paused for a moment as he took another bite and smiled gratefully at his mother. Then he glanced at the door, and she knew what he was thinking.

'She's fine. But we hardly see her.'

Sohail nodded and continued the story. 'We didn't know where to go, we just heard the Bengali regiments had crossed the border and were setting up camp. Raju's uncle is in the military. We thought we'd look for him. Three days later we found the camp. All the Bengali regiments in the east had mutinied. They were regrouping when we found them. It was just a temporary settlement at first, then we moved to Agartala, about fifteen miles further from the border. Now it's become like a small town — there's even a hospital, and barracks for the officers. And there are others, in Chittagong, Sylhet, Rajshahi. Seven sectors in all.'

'We've been listening on the radio,' Maya said.

'Where do you sleep?' Rehana asked. She could tell he wanted to talk about more important things, but she couldn't help herself.

'Tents, Ammoo. Not very comfortable. When I go back, you will have to give me some blankets, and a plate. I've been eating from banana leaves!'

So he was going back. Rehana tried not to show her disappointment. Here was her son, living such a strange life. He used to love Elvis Presley, she suddenly remembered. She leaned over the table and piled more rice on to his plate.

'Everyone has joined. Everyone.' And his eyes shone. 'All the young men, fighting side by side. No one cares who anyone is. They've all joined, the peasant and the soldier, together, just as we've been dreaming.' And then his face changed. 'But things are bad, you know.'

'And what will you do?' Maya asked.

He took a deep breath. 'I'm being trained. As a guerrilla.'

'Guerrilla?' She had a vague image of an outlaw. 'Is it dangerous?'

'Of course it's dangerous, Ammoo!' Maya exclaimed. 'War! What do you think?'

'I know what war is, Maya.'

'Aren't you even a little excited? A whole nation, coming together.'

'Excited? I'm not excited, I'm sick. I'm sick with worry. This is my *child*.' Rehana left the table and moved towards the kitchen, muttering something about sweets. She could hear her daughter sighing and Sohail whispering something, trying to make peace.

It began to occur to Rehana that any doubts Sohail once had about becoming a soldier had completely disappeared. As with everything else, he had taken it on with a kind of brutal devotion. He was a guerrilla. A man for his country. He would die, if he had to. Rehana wondered if she should begin to prepare herself, imagine a life without her son, carve out a hole where he used to be, familiarize herself with the shock of his absence. And as soon as she had this thought, she realized she had no choice. She could not give him up, not to fate or to nation, and if he chose to leave her anyway, there would be no way to prepare.

It was almost dawn by the time they finished eating.

'Get some rest, Sohail.'

He looked around, as though deciding whether to speak.

'Ammoo, Maya, I need to ask you something.'

He waved his hand and drew them closer. He dragged a chair towards himself and faced them, moving to close the curtains before sitting down. He switched off the lights and allowed the small flame of the kerosene lamp to trace shadows across his face.

He brought his palms together. 'Some of the guerrilla operations will take place here, in Dhaka,' he began. 'And we need a place in the city. To store arms. A safe place to hide out before and after the operations.' As he looked at his mother, there was no hesitation. 'Our mission is to disrupt the normal functioning of the city. Make sure the world knows what is going on. People will not just stand by and witness the rape of Bangladesh.' He took a deep breath, then continued, 'I've come here to find shelter and to recruit more men for the guerrilla regiment.'

Rehana imagined the journey Sohail had taken to come here, eluding the barricades around the city, the powerful searchlights that scanned the docks of the river, the green trucks with guntoting soldiers. She imagined someone in charge, a military man, taking one look at her son and knowing he would be the right one to send back to Dhaka. She wanted to be more

135

angry and less proud, but she found herself wanting to say yes, not just so that she would have Sohail's confidence, but because she could not blame anyone but herself for making him so fine, so ready to take charge. This was who she had hoped he would become, even if she had never imagined that her son, or the world, would come to this. And she knew what he was asking her.

'You want to use Shona.'

'Yes.'

Shona with her back to the sun. Shona that had given her the children. Proud, vacant Shona of the many dreams.

'The house is yours, Sohail. Your birthright.'

It didn't take long for Sohail to set up Shona as the Dhaka headquarters of the guerrilla operations. A few days after he arrived, Rehana watched as he and the other boys dug a ditch in the rough grass beside the rosebushes to store their weapons. They worked at night, using small torches to pierce the darkness. Once, Rehana's curiosity overcame her, and she peered inside one of the ditches, but all she saw was a set of rough wooden boxes and something shiny underneath, winking back at the sun, which beat its dry May heat. At Shona, Sohail and his friends prepared the back rooms for the new recruits. When the boys — she thought of them as boys, they were so young — needed something, they came to the bungalow and asked politely. A hammer. A glass of water. Soap. They never stayed long.

The activity at Shona kept Maya closer to home. She spent long hours helping the boys write press releases. They found her an old typewriter, and she could be seen hunched over it hungrily, scowling at the letters, hitting the keys hard with her two forefingers. Sounds like a machine-gun, Sohail said. At night, when Rehana insisted Maya eat with her at home, she carried the bulky typewriter back with her, the pages fluttering like the white wings of a summer bird.

Rehana watched the huddled figures that came in and out of Shona, imagining the conversations they were having, the plans, the secrets. She attempted to keep up with the activity next door by putting the bungalow in order. She rationed the money the Senguptas had left and kept a strict schedule for washing, cleaning, shopping, cooking. And there were the medical supplies to store. She found herself busy and preoccupied all the time. There were few opportunities to dwell on Sharmeen's disappearance, or Maya's anger, or Mrs Chowdhury and Silvi's silence next door.

The only problem was the sewing. Mrs Akram and Mrs Rahman were due to come to the bungalow with a new supply of saris, but they couldn't be told about Shona. Rehana felt guilty for keeping secrets from her friends, but Sohail said it was a matter of their safety; *you must pretend we're not here*, he said. Not here? It was all she could think about. But Rehana had to come up with a plan to keep her friends away.

There was only one thing to do, she decided: make pickles. The mangoes on the tree were just about ready: grassy-green and tongue-smackingly sour. She asked the boys to pick them from the tree. When they were younger, this was the children's job. Maya was by far the better climber: her foot would curl over the branches and hold her fast, while she stretched her arms and plucked the fruit, throwing it down to Rehana, who kept shouting, 'Be careful! Be careful!'

She would slice the green mangoes and cook them slowly with chillies and mustard seeds. Then she would stuff them into jars and leave them on the roof to ripen. There was a rule about not touching pickles during the monthlies. She couldn't remember who had told her that rule — her mother? — no, her mother had probably never sliced a mango in her brief, dreamy life. Must have been one of her sisters. Marzia, she was the best cook. And the enforcer of rules. But Rehana had decided long ago this was a stupid rule. It was hard enough to time the pickle-making anyway, between the readiness of the fruit and the weather, which had to be hot and dry.

As she recited the pickle recipe to herself, Rehana wondered what her sisters would make of her at this very moment. Guerrillas at Shona. Sewing kathas on the rooftop. Her daughter at rifle practice. The thought of their shocked faces made her want to laugh. She imagined the letter she would write. Dear sisters, she would say. Our countries are at war; yours and mine. We are on different sides now. I am making pickles for the war effort. You see how much I belong here and not to you.

The boys stripped the tree and brought her three groaning baskets of fruit. Rehana hunted down every glass jar she could find, and when she ran out of those she decided to use the clay vats that had held the yoghurt, back when there was fresh yoghurt at the market every day.

The pickle jars took up half of the roof. The nose-aching stench swelled to cover the rest. When Mrs Rahman and Mrs Akram came the next day, they would smell the drying pickles from the gate and refuse to sew.

★   ★   ★

The next day, while Rehana was checking to make sure the pickles had settled properly, she heard a small commotion at the gate. It must be Mrs Akram, she thought, wiping her hands on her achol. She was always early. She leaned over the railing and was about to wave when she saw not her friend climbing out of a rickshaw but someone else, a woman, getting out of a car. Perhaps she was at the wrong address. Rehana inched closer; she was about to call out to the woman, ask her if she was lost, when she saw her reaching over her head and unlatching the gate.

'Rehana?' the woman said.

She would know that voice anywhere. She

took the stairs two at a time, her heart clapping in her chest.

The woman was knocking at the door when Rehana approached from the garden. 'Parveen.'

'Rehana! Thank God!' Parveen clasped Rehana's hands and looked into her face with eager eyes. 'We were so worried.'

'Please,' Rehana said, 'come inside.' Stay calm, she told herself. This time she is not coming for your children. Rehana watched Parveen glide through the door and settle, with a sigh, on the sofa. Then she leaned her head against the cushion and turned her eyes to the room.

It was ten years, Rehana remembered. The decade was gone, like a breath, when she looked into that face; she was that trembling, stupid widow who gave up her children. Her mouth flooded with bitterness. 'What brings you to Dhaka?' she said, intending to sound cold but not angry.

'Why, the war, what do you think?' Parveen said. 'Your brother, Faiz, has been given a very important responsibility. Very important. We didn't want to come, of course, but you know Faiz, so dutiful. Always wants to serve his country.'

Rehana was confused. What responsibility, which country?

'We only came last week. Things have not arrived, house is still a mess, but I thought, I must go to see my sister. What will she think if she hears, na?'

Rehana didn't know what to say. 'Well, it's been a long time.'

140

'Too long!'

A pause stretched between them. Rehana did not want to bring up the children; let her ask, if she wants to know. When they had first come back, Rehana had refused to talk about those years apart. She hadn't wanted to know. She had only asked if they'd been fed properly, if they'd been beaten, if anything terrible had happened to them. She had checked them for bruises. Part of her, she knew, had wanted some physical symptom, some obvious mistreatment, that would tell her the children too bore marks of their long separation. She wanted to hear nothing about the little affections, the life that had passed between them in her absence. She especially didn't want to know if Parveen had been any good at being their mother.

'So,' Parveen said, slapping her hands on her knees. 'The children. They're well, by God's grace?'

'Yes, mahshallah, they are well.'

Rehana was about to tell Parveen that they weren't home, how sorry they would be to have missed her, but Parveen cut her short. 'And you still live here? That's your rented house, in the back?'

'Yes.'

'You have tenants?'

'Yes, the Senguptas.'

'Hindus?' Parveen grimaced. 'You gave your house to Hindus?'

'They've been my tenants for years,' Rehana said; 'they're like family.'

'Well, you do as you wish, Rehana, but I would

not trust my house to those people . . . ' She screwed up her face, as though she'd just taken a sip of bad milk.

Rehana ignored this last statement; she was busy trying to unmask the purpose of the visit, of Parveen's cavalier manner, all traces of the dirty history between them forgotten. But she really shouldn't have been surprised. This was often the way with families; they would try to destroy one another, and then they would pretend nothing had happened; carry on with their old habits, their casual humiliations, as Parveen was doing now, pointing her eyes to the shabby state of Rehana's furniture.

' . . . just as well we're getting rid of them.'

Rehana was drawn back to the conversation. 'Rid of who?'

'Haven't you been listening, Rehana? I'm talking about the dirty elements of our great nation. The Hindus, the Communists, the separatists! That is why your brother and I are here — it's a great duty, a privilege.'

This was the mission? Rehana's eyes flew to the window, to Shona. Parveen was a few short feet away from the guerrilla hideout. When she assured herself there wasn't any obvious movement in the next house, she relaxed, suddenly pleased at this deceit, to watch Parveen perched so comfortably, while next door the boys planted guns in the garden. She was about to offer her a snack, when there was a knock at the gate and the sound of it swinging open.

'Yoo-hoo! Sorry we're late.' It was Mrs Akram and Mrs Rahman. She heard them crossing the driveway. 'What on earth is that smell — Rehana, you opened a pickle factory on the roof or what?'

Rehana rushed to the door and ushered them in. 'Come in, come in. Meet my bhabi Parveen,' she said, trying to sound casual. 'Bhabi, these are my friends, Mrs Akram and Mrs Rahman.'

Mrs Rahman gave Parveen a frank, appraising look. 'Salaam-Alaikum,' she said in a headmistress voice.

'Salaam-Alaikum,' Mrs Akram echoed.

'We've all heard such a lot about you,' Mrs Rahman said. 'What brings you back to Dhaka? I thought you lived in Lahore.'

'We're here to fix things up!' Parveen said with a laugh.

'They've come to work for the army,' Rehana said, praying Mrs Rahman would keep her thoughts to herself.

'Ah, all right, I see,' Mrs Akram said. They stood awkwardly around the door, not knowing whether to sit down.

'What about those pickles?' Mrs Rahman said. 'The stench!'

'Oh, is that what it is?' Parveen said.

'Sorry, friends, we'll have to find somewhere else,' Rehana said.

'What possessed you?' Mrs Rahman asked. 'You must have been up all night.'

'Well, I thought I should just make as many as I could — who knows what will happen to my tree?'

This brought a nod of assent from Mrs Akram. 'So true,' she said, 'future is so uncertain.'

'But who will eat so many pickles?' Mrs Rahman asked. 'I'm getting a bellyache just thinking about it.'

'Maybe you can sell them,' Mrs Akram said.

'Arre, good idea, we can buy more thread.'

'We'll see,' Rehana said, eager to get rid of them both. Luckily Parveen was ignoring them; she had stood up and was making her way to the dining table, where Rehana had kept the leftover parathas from breakfast; Maya hadn't touched hers. 'So shall we postpone for a day or two, until we find somewhere more suitable?'

The gin-rummy ladies left, patting Rehana on the back, whispering, *Tell us all about it tomorrow*. A few minutes later Parveen took her leave too, inviting Rehana to bring the children to her new house. Everything happened so quickly that Rehana could almost convince herself it was a dream. And had Parveen's perfume trails not clung to the walls, or had her words not insinuated themselves into her ears, or had the sight of her shiny beaked hair, her gauzy sari, vanished, even faded, it might have been possible. But of course it was not, and Rehana was left to face the afternoon, replaying the scene, and wondering why, after all, Parveen had decided to come.

Another week passed in much the same manner as the last; Sohail and his friends went in and out of Shona; Rehana watched the pickles ripening on the rooftop; the May sun crashed through the windows every morning and threatened to suffocate them. Then Sohail appeared at the bungalow and said, 'We're ready, Ammoo.'

'Ready for what?'

'For the operation. I've recruited a team, and we've received our orders.'

Rehana hadn't given much thought to what they would actually do once they'd dug up the garden and readied the house. It already looked like work. But they had only been preparing. For this.

'What will you do?'

'We're planting an explosive at the InterCon Hotel. We're making a statement.' He put his hand to his cheek and rubbed his jaw.

'Statement? What sort of a statement? Will people get killed?'

'No. We're hoping there won't be any casualties.'

Now he was referring to dead people as casualties.

'Is it dangerous?'

'You want me to lie, don't you?'

Yes, please. 'Of course not.'

'It's not dangerous. I'm just the lookout.' He held her wrists. 'Thank you, Ammoo. I keep meaning to say that.'

'I'm just happy to have you near me.' She wanted to ask him to promise nothing would happen. That he would be safe. That he wouldn't get himself killed, or maimed, or something selfish like that. 'When will it happen?'

'Tomorrow, early morning — before sunrise.'

'I'll be praying,' was all she could think to say.

His hand was on his jaw again, and he seemed to consider something. 'Why don't you come before we set off? You can meet everyone.'

'Your friends wouldn't mind?'

'They'll be happy to get your blessings. Some of them haven't seen their own mothers in a long time.'

Rehana understood. She felt a flush of pride at being asked.

Sohail put his hand to his cheek again.

'Do you have a toothache?'

He grinned, then winced a little. 'Just a small one. Nothing to worry.'

A toothache is the sort of thing I used to worry about. Now I worry about your legs, your heart, your life.

⋆ ⋆ ⋆

Before dawn the next day Rehana crossed the garden and walked through the narrow iron gate she had built to divide the properties. She had made puris, half with potatoes, half with dal, and halwa. It felt foolish nowadays to take pride in cooking, but she couldn't resist taking pleasure in the domed rise of the puris, the perfect, vague sweetness of the halwa. It was her first time at Shona since the guerrillas had taken over. From the outside, nothing seemed different; she knew some of the plants had been dug up, but they'd settled back, even though they looked a little ragged and unkempt. I must remember to water everything tomorrow, she thought.

The first thing she noticed when she stepped inside was the thick darkness. The curtains were drawn, so that even the weak moonlight and the even weaker streetlights did not penetrate; it was like closing her eyes to sleep. As she adjusted to the darkness Rehana could make out shapes crouched on the floor. Then there were moving pinpoints of light: cigarettes, she gathered, from the smell.

'Hello?' she said into the darkness.

'Partho, turn on the light,' someone said. She heard a scratching sound, then saw the flame of a match. The hurricane lamp was lit.

The lamp was passed along. Each face glowed orange, one at a time, as though they were a cast of actors introducing themselves. They smiled or nodded at her; one raised his hand to his forehead and salaamed. She couldn't help thinking they all looked so happy. Not scared. Not as though they might be facing death, or worse. But as though they were about to play cricket and found themselves gifted with a cool afternoon. Casual. Carefree.

She tried, but could not tell them apart. They were a blur, shadows behind a veil of cigarette smoke, old and very young all at once. When the lamp was passed to him, Joy stood and approached Rehana. He held the light up, and she saw he was grinning. 'Such bodmashes we are, Auntie, making a mess of your house.'

'Don't be silly, beta. My house is yours. I don't see your brother.

'Aref is in Agartala,' Joy said. 'He's been assigned to another mission.'

Maya was already there; she began circulating with the plate of puris. Rehana thought of the last time they were gathered this way, with Maya leading the songs and Sharmeen pumping the harmonium. She wanted to cradle Maya in her arms. Tell her that she remembered.

Joy came up beside his brother. 'Someone will come to collect the boxes,' he said. 'And we'll be bringing in more donations.'

'We've heard about your sewing group,' Aref said; 'the muktis will really love those — if only you could see the camp, Auntie — nothing soft about those beds!'

The other boys laughed from the shadows.

'Oof,' one of them said, his mouth full of puri, 'and the food — the rootis are hard as sticks, and full of holes.'

Sohail tugged at Rehana's arm. 'Ammoo,' he said, 'this is our commanding officer.' He led her to a corner of the room. He whispered, 'He used to be a major in the Pak Army.'

'Hello,' the man said. He was standing directly in front of the lamp and she couldn't make out much, except the span of his shoulders and the firm grip he returned when she, not knowing how to greet him, offered her hand.

'Oh, hello,' she said, returning the squeeze.

'It's kind of you to give up your house, Mrs Haque,' the Major said.

'Yes, yes, of course.'

'The whole nation is grateful.'

He was probably thinking she had done it out of some sense of duty, and looking at him now, the tightness of his grip still ringing in her fingers, she wished it had been so; not that the act was any less noble, having been done out of love for her son; even so, it was somehow bigger, in this room, and in this tall man's presence, to have done something for the country and not just in the service of her children. Perhaps she really was doing it for the country.

From the distance, the sound of the muezzin interrupted her reverie and reminded her of the time. 'Please forgive me,' she announced to the huddled group, 'it's the morning Azaan. I have to pray. And we haven't had the halwa.'

'You finish saying your prayers and then we'll eat,' Sohail suggested.

'OK.' There was an awkward pause. 'Would any of you like to join me?' She glanced around; some of the boys were staring down at the ground. She was sure they needed some reassurance, some certainty, before going on their mission.

'Ma,' Sohail said finally, 'Partho is Hindu.'

'Doesn't matter,' Rehana heard someone say from the back of the room. Still no one moved.

Rehana was about to move to Mrs Sengupta's bedroom when the Major said, 'Why not? Mrs Haque, you stand in front.'

'Really? You don't mind?' Rehana was pleased, though she knew she really shouldn't; women weren't supposed to lead the prayer. But she went to the curtained window that faced west, and the boys lined up behind her. Even Maya joined in, standing between Sohail and Joy. Rehana pulled her sari over her head and tucked the end behind her ear.

God is Great.
I bear witness that there is none other
  worthy of worship.
Come to prayer, come to felicity.
Glory to you, O Allah. Blessed is your
  name, exalted is your majesty.
In you I seek refuge.
Holy are you, and magnificent.
Come to prayer, come to felicity.

Rehana couldn't sleep. Shortly after dawn she'd said goodbye to Sohail and his friends and counted, over and over like the long, repeated summer days, all the things that could possibly go wrong. The boys were too young; they were excitable; they were carried away by the thrill of danger, but what did they really know? She'd said all the prayers, Zohr and Asr and Magreb.

In the evening, when the Radio Free Bangladesh broadcaster announced that there had been an explosion at the InterContinental Hotel, Maya let out a whoop of joy and ran through the house, waving her green and red flag.

'Ammoo! Listen!' and she pressed the radio to Rehana's ear.

Foreign journalists have requested the permission of the government of Pakistan to access the front lines of the civil war after an explosion at the InterContinental Hotel revealed the extent of resistance to occupying forces. The government of Pakistan denies all reports of genocide, and President

150

Yahya Khan accuses Sheikh Mujib and his associates in Calcutta of spreading false propaganda against the Pakistan government.

So the operation was a success. But that still didn't mean they'd got away with it. Rehana closed her eyes and said Aytul Kursi for what felt like the thousandth time that day. She couldn't sleep. She thought she heard Maya in the other room. Ma! she was saying, I forgive you! I forgive you! Rehana leaped out of bed and ran to Maya's room and found her with fingers poised over her typewriter. Her heart was pounding painfully in her chest.

'What are you doing?' Maya asked, her head tilted. 'Did you see a ghost?'

★   ★   ★

When Rehana heard the noises coming from the driveway she knew something had gone wrong. She had been so sure that it had; it was almost a relief to discover she was right. It was an hour before dinner; she'd just put the rice on the stove. She bolted out of the kitchen and saw Sohail and Joy pushing a green car towards the house, the engine switched off. There were others in the car, though she couldn't make out their faces. Stricken, she ran across the garden and through the gate, meeting them just as they were taking the Major out of the car. Sohail and Joy were both covered in blood, and with them was a stranger, a slight man in a white coat,

151

looking terrified. The Major was between them, motionless and grey.

'Oh, God, he's died.'

Sohail dragged the man out by his shoulders. His head lolled to the side. 'Take his legs!' he whispered. Sweat was pouring down Sohail's face and pooling around his chin. Joy grabbed the Major's legs, and they pulled him to the front door.

'Goddammit!' Joy kept saying. 'Goddammit!'

They laid him across the rose-petal carpet. Someone had tied a cloth around his leg. He was awake, groaning, tossing his head; when he turned his face, Rehana saw there was a triangular splinter of wood lodged in his cheek. Sohail stood over him while Joy pointed a gun at the doctor.

'Fix it.'

'I can't. I need things — medicine, anaesthetic.'

'You'll have to make do with what you've got in the bag.'

The doctor was no older than the rest of them, probably hardly out of medical school, a thin, delicate boy with greasy hair.

'You have to take him to the hospital!' he said.

'Are you mad? Do you know how many people are looking for us?'

The doctor waved his arms. 'I can't. I can't do it.'

Rehana found herself kneeling beside the Major, looking the young doctor in the eye. 'Listen, this is an emergency. Just do your best.' She kept her gaze on him, until he nodded slowly.

'We have to get the shards out of his leg,' he said, looking only at her. 'There are several smaller traumas, but the main thing is the leg. And the face. I wouldn't know what to do with the face.'

'Just patch it up,' Joy said. 'We'll take him to the field hospital in the morning.'

'He can't go very far.'

'Fix it! We have to move out tonight!' Joy pressed the gun to the doctor's temple.

'Joy, baba, this man is trying to help,' Rehana said.

'Please, take the gun away. I'm on the right side.'

'Just fix it.'

'The gun! Take it away first!' The doctor blinked away tears.

Joy lowered the gun, but he kept his finger curled around the trigger.

The doctor took a syringe out of his bag and filled it with the contents of a small, upturned bottle. Then he went to work on the Major's leg. Rehana remained beside him, strangely unaffected by the sight of the Major's torn limb, the ragged flesh exposed, the whiteness of bone shining through the dimness of the room. She didn't hesitate when the doctor told her to peel back the Major's trousers and begin to clean the smaller wounds. He gave her a pair of tweezers and told her to pick out the shards. She bent over the leg, working quietly, ignoring the shudders coming from the Major.

When Rehana finished with the tweezers, the doctor started to stitch. 'Thank you, Mrs

Haque.' She could tell he wasn't just thanking her for helping to clean the wound.

The wood was still lodged in the Major's cheek.

Sohail whispered something to Joy, and he put down his gun, crouching instead and holding a kerosene lamp over the doctor's arm. 'Auntie,' Joy said, 'you go and take a break.'

Rehana went to Mrs Sengupta's kitchen for a glass of water. She was taking a giant gulp, sighing into the glass, when Sohail approached and hugged her tightly. She felt him crying into her shoulder.

'Ammoo,' he whispered, 'it was my fault.'

'What happened?'

'It was me. I was supposed to fix the timer on the explosive. But I got there and I just froze. I couldn't move. The Major pushed me aside and did it himself, but it was too late; he got caught up in the blast. It should have been me; I messed it up.'

Rehana didn't know what to say. She held his head, stroking it slowly.

'I don't know, I don't know if I can do this — I'm no good — the firing, training — I shouldn't have gone.'

'It's not your fault. Whatever it was, it can't have been your fault.'

'He saved my life,' Sohail said. 'I would've been dead without him.'

★ ★ ★

The doctor finished his work.

'I've sutured the wounds, but I can't promise

154

there won't be an infection. He needs medicine. And even then he might lose his leg.'

'Can we take him away?' Joy asked.

'Maybe a few roads, but no further.'

'There's a field hospital in Agartala, near our camp.'

'Across the border? Absolutely not.'

'Ammoo,' Sohail said, 'you have to let him stay here.'

Rehana was tired; there was blood everywhere; Mrs Sengupta's carpet was ruined. She wanted to feel sorry for the man, but she couldn't. He was so ugly, lying on the carpet, his mouth open horribly. But he had saved her son's life.

But it was Maya who said, 'No. He can't stay here.' She had been quiet ever since the boys arrived, hovering at the periphery of the scene. Now she was standing over the Major, pumping her fists.

'Maya, please,' Sohail said, 'there's no choice.'

'Then you stay. You stay here and take care of him. Don't make us do it.'

'We can't stay here. We're wanted men.'

'This is all your fault.'

'It is, it is my fault!' Sohail's eyes opened wide, red and ferocious. 'Ma, you have to take him. Please say you'll take him.'

Rehana was torn. 'You're sure there's nowhere else he can go?'

'Ma,' Maya gasped, 'you want another man dying in your house?'

Another man? Was she talking about her father?

'This man cannot be moved,' the doctor said.

He looked at Maya, who was leaning against her mother and breathing heavily, as though she'd been running. Then he said, 'I will stay. I will stay here and make sure he doesn't die.'

Rehana breathed a sigh of relief. 'What's your name?' she asked the doctor.

'Rajesh.'

'Maya. Maya, please look at me. Look at me. Dr Rajesh is going to stay here and take care of the Major. No one is going to die. OK? No one is dying. You wanted to do something, remember? You wanted to do something? Here it is. We'll take care of him. He saved your brother. Enough, enough. No crying.' And she stroked her daughter's hair.

Rehana opened her eyes and for a moment forgot where she was, only sensing the wrongness of the place, and then remembered, and woke with a start, moving the hair from her forehead, feeling for the frayed braid, untying, retying, out of habit. She was positioned awkwardly on the sofa. Looking across the room, she saw the rubble from the night before — the stained bandages, the muddy footprints across the floor, the little bits of plaster and wood from the explosion — and accounted for the tiredness in her limbs.

The Major was installed in Mithun's bedroom. When Rehana approached him, she saw the lace curtain was drawn, and in the early-morning light the pattern traced shadows across his face. There, on his forehead, a star-shaped flower; and there, across the thigh, a speckled row of hearts. He slept without a sound, immobile but for the lace shadow that stirred slightly with his every shallow breath.

In slumber, the Major was enormous. His arms and feet spilled out from the bed, his hands like spreading spider webs. The doctor had left just after dawn, declaring the Major stable and promising to return the next day with medicine and more bandages. The first night will be the worst, he had said. You must stay here.

And here she still was.

The night had made him no prettier. On his face, in a jagged, angry curve, was a scar. It travelled, meandering, from the outer edge of his left eyebrow to the corner of his upper lip. A bluish stain marked the other side of his face. The rest of him, except the bandaged leg, seemed strangely untouched, healthy in fact, the skin on the neck and arms taut and glowing in the pale morning sunlight.

Rehana looked at him and felt a surge of pride in his solid presence, as though he were a fallen angel, ugly and beaten, but maybe still a little blessed.

Suddenly she was hungry; she couldn't remember when she'd last eaten. She had a craving for lychees, not the dry ones they imported from China but the local variety with the smooth, leathery skin. The lychees made her think of other indulgences; perhaps she should buy some meat, some better rice. She would go to New Market. She felt the urge to venture to out, to leave the house and the sight of the night's chaos.

★ ★ ★

It was a bright day with no clouds at all, the sort of day when the sky is holding its breath and everything is still and perfectly clear. The market was the same as it had been ever since the start of the war: every week another shop or two closed, the vegetables dusty and shrivelled, the fish small and dull-eyed. But Rehana was buoyed by the thought of haggling with the vendors or finding some small treasure, a fresh chicken or a late-season papaya.

Her cheer left her as soon as she entered the market. Dotted among the stalls and the ferry-wallahs were men in army uniforms. They strolled through the market with rifles carelessly slung across their shoulders. She passed a sweetshop and saw a group of them sitting around a plastic table, laughing with their mouths so wide open she could see, even from a distance, the peaks of their teeth. One of them spat loudly into the gutter.

As she walked with her head down, trying not to catch anyone's eye, Rehana was annoyed at her fear, especially in this place, which had seen her through a decade of struggle. Here was where the material for the children's school uniforms had been bought, where she had calculated the week's rations and planned her cooking. It was where Iqbal had bought her

158

wedding sari — only twenty-two rupees, he'd confessed — where she had come to shop for Eid gifts, wedding presents, birthday clothes for the children. New Market was the very heart of the city for Rehana, its smells and winding alleys as familiar to her as her very own Dhanmondi. And now it was suddenly an alien place, the air heavy with menace. 'Watch out for the butchers,' Sohail had said; 'they're Urdu-speaking.'

'Why? I'm Urdu-speaking. So what?'

'Those people are army collaborators.'

Sohail was referring to the Urdu-speaking Biharis, who were rumoured to be siding with the army. The division of the city into sympathizers and collaborators sat uncomfortably with Rehana, but he told her there had to be some way of knowing who to suspect and who to trust. They could no longer trust their instincts. Or even their friends.

Rehana followed a narrow passageway into the butchers' quarter. The stalls were scattered haphazardly, cuts of meat hanging from each one like wet jewels. Rehana always took pleasure in buying meat; she would take her time examining the white pearl of bone, the rubied blood, the deep garnet sinews.

She found herself in front of her regular butcher.

'What's good today?' she asked. She looked down at the ground, so he wouldn't know it was her.

'Nice chop meat, memsaab. Also mutton is good today.'

Rehana thought of the Major, his sewn-up

cheek. 'I need bones. For soup.'

'You like soup? OK.'

It was so hot. Rehana saw the flies that hovered, then sank against the hanging meat, their buzzing amplified by the low ceiling of the market. She saw the butcher extending his arms and offering a piece he thought might impress her. It was the entire side of a small cow, a row of bones raised like curved teeth, the flesh sliced neatly so that its purple striations reflected the light. The smell of blood, metallic, laced with rot, assaulted Rehana. She shuddered and turned her face. The butcher recognized her instantly.

Rehana recalled why she had always bought her meat from this man. He was impeccably dressed; there was no blood anywhere on his shirt or on his hands. He wore a spotless white kurta, and a cap, as though he was on his way to the mosque.

'How are you, madam?' he asked in Urdu, and saw her start.

'Yes, well,' she answered quietly, and then, without meaning to, she said, 'We're having a war.'

'I know.' And when she stayed silent it was as though she was accusing him of something and he had to say, 'I have nowhere else, madam.' But the words were hollow, and Rehana realized how strange the language suddenly sounded: aggressive, insinuating. She saw that it was now the language of her enemy; hers and Sohail's and the Major's. She tried to feel something else, some tenderness for her poets, some sympathy for this man, only a meat-cutter after all.

'You have this,' he said, proffering the meat. And Rehana could see that he was afraid of her, and she was pleased, and then ashamed to be pleased. She quickly pulled out a five-rupee note and turned, waving away the flies that had suddenly collected around her head.

* * *

The Major was awake when she returned. Rehana could tell he was uncomfortable; he didn't turn his head when she entered, just blinked a few times and tried to move his mouth. His eyes were two black pearls. She turned on the ceiling fan and wiped the sweat that had gathered on his forehead. He needed water. She went outside to look for Maya, and found her frowning over a book and writing in its margins with a tiny, illegible scrawl.

'What are you doing?'

'Reading *Che Guevara Speaks*,' she said, exposing the spine.

'I asked you to look after the Major.'

'He's asleep.'

'No, he's awake.'

'Well, now you can take care of him.' And she returned to her book.

'You don't like him?'

'Why not?' she mumbled, not looking up. 'He's fighting for us.'

Rehana looked more closely at her daughter and tried — how many times had she done this? — to see something that might have escaped her. There was none of the panic of the night before,

161

nothing of the need.

It started to rain.

Sighing, Rehana took a glass of water to the Major, covering her head with a plastic sheet as she crossed the garden into the other house. As he drank, she noticed his lips were not as desperate as the rest of him. He thanked her with a relieved breath, and she looked at him as though he could not see her, with a frank stare.

★ ★ ★

Joy arrived in the evening. He rubbed his hand across his chest and asked for a word. 'I need to speak to you, Auntie,' he said. 'Thing is, the Pakistan Army think the Major is dead. They saw the building collapsing around him; there's no chance he survived.' He looked around the room, avoiding her eyes. 'We believe we can use this to our advantage.'

'What will you do?'

'He'll stay here until he recovers, if that's all right with you.'

She remembered the sight of the Major's leg. It could be weeks, even months. 'I thought it would be only a few days.'

'We could move him,' Joy said, 'but now that he's in hiding, it would be better if he stayed here.'

What had she got herself into? 'How long?' she asked.

'Maybe a month. And he can give out his orders — through me. I'll go back and forth.'

'What about Sohail?'

162

Joy rubbed his chest again. His fingernails were rimmed with black. 'That's the thing, see, it's dangerous now for him to come here so often. So we'll have to find him another place.'

'He can't stay here with you?'

'It puts everyone in danger. You, the Major, Maya. Anyway he'll mostly be in Agartala.'

Rehana threw up her hands. 'Do as you will, beta.'

★   ★   ★

As it turned out, it wasn't long before Rehana saw Sohail again. Just after lunch a few days later she received a telegram and spent the rest of the day with her head on the arm of the sofa, waiting for him. She knew he would come; he wouldn't make her do this alone. All afternoon she heard the clatter of Maya's typewriter; her strokes were getting faster, more confident.

By evening he was at the door. He stared emptily at Rehana and squeezed her hand. He was wearing a white kurta, like the butcher, except he had a green hat with a red metal star glued to the front.

When Maya came into the drawing room, she saw her brother staring into the garden.

'Hey, what are you doing here?'

He approached her and pulled her into his arms. Then he said, 'Sharmeen is in Dhaka.'

'What? How do you know?'

'I know.' A beat, and then: 'She's at the cantonment, Maya. The hospital.'

'Let's go, then.'

Nobody moved.

'Why are you sitting there? Let's go!' she started. 'She must be sick. How did she end up there? But you can tell me everything later.' And she flashed her teeth — a bluish tinge, like the sight of clouds. If she noticed her brother's bent head, she ignored it, smoothing the middle part in her hair and changing her sandals for outside shoes.

'Go go cholo cholo,' she said, in the mixed Bengali — English she used when she was nervous, or in a hurry.

'She's dead,' Sohail said finally. His beard, now dense like a solid black mantle, reflected the thickness of his eyebrows, the paleness of his skin.

Maya ran out into the garden and started speaking to them through the window.

'Why would she be in the hospital if she were dead?' She had to shout to make herself heard.

'She's been there, Maya. She's been there all along.'

'What? And you knew?'

'Yes. But there was no point in telling you. There wasn't anything we could do.'

'Why? Why didn't you tell me? I would have got her out of there myself.' Then, as though it had just occurred to her, she realized the truth was uglier than she had imagined. Rehana, seeing her daughter through the open window, knew that for ever afterwards Maya would remember where her brother had told her the news, there in the shade of the mango tree, the air expectant, just after rain, the sky dark as

164

though it were night, could only be night, but wasn't, and the pale glow of the jasmine and the bougainvillea, abundant, perfumed; the Major asleep, or dead, in a far corner of Shona.

And then he told her everything.

'She died in the hospital.' He would have gone outside to comfort her, but she gripped the window bars and held him with a terrible look.

'She was pregnant.'

'Pregnant?'

Maya turned her face away and kicked the foot of the tree. 'She hated men. She hated them! She hated sex, did you know that? She never had sex. Everyone else did, but not her.' Rehana wanted to flinch, or to tell Maya to shut up, but she stopped herself and just stared, letting a tear trickle slowly from her eye.

'I want to know their names.'

'Who?'

'The ones who raped her. I want to know.'

'They're soldiers, Maya. Tikka Khan's soldiers.'

'Tikka Khan,' Maya shouted, as though she were making an announcement, 'the Butcher of Bengal!' And then she kicked at the tree again, reached up and hugged a ropy branch, looking as though she might swing from it, but then just stood there with her arms raised and her face pressed against the bark.

★   ★   ★

That night Rehana dreamed of Iqbal. She dreamed he was knocking at the door. In life, he

165

had never knocked.

He would come home every evening at exactly six o'clock. Rehana, her eyes on the wall clock, would be ready with his evening refresher: a tumbler of whisky, at first with water, then soda and eventually, as the years passed, with two cubes of ice.

Even though she had been waiting for him all day and she knew he would not be late, she would sit quietly with her back to the door and her hands folded on her lap instead of staring out of the window or unfastening the latch or even waiting on the veranda so he could see her as soon as he stepped through the gate. She would close her eyes and smell the jasmine crawling over the vine, and the green lemons in the tree, ripening and swelling with each passing hour.

She sat and waited, waited even as he pulled at the gate and it swung open in front of him; she waited still as his footsteps drew nearer, and then — she knew exactly when — just as he was about to pull his hand out of his pocket and curl his fingers around to knock, she would sweep across the room, pull down the latch and throw the doors open in one liquid movement.

Every evening it was the same, and every evening a new, breathless thing.

When she woke she was angry. He owed her, she wanted to tell him; he owed her for staying behind and taking care of the mess; for getting to the end, which was never the end; for finishing it or, at least, for standing up to the struggle.

She moved through the house, her cheeks hot

166

with memory. Maya's bed was empty. Rehana had spent the evening with her, feeding her jao bhaat and running her hands over her forehead. She went to check on the Major occasionally, but otherwise the two houses were quiet, with only the swift rustle of leaves and a stretch of brief, sudden showers. Sohail said he would keep things quiet around Shona for a few days, until they decided what to do with Maya. It wasn't safe to have her at home any more; now that she knew about Sharmeen, there was no telling what she might do. And then they'd fallen asleep, Rehana more deeply than she had intended, and now here was Maya's bed, empty.

She searched the house stealthily, listening at the bathroom door, scanning the kitchen sink, the dining table. She peered out into the garden and saw a faint light coming from Shona. The light drew her in; she staggered across the garden in the darkness and hovered outside the window, where she could make out faint shadows cast by a flickering kerosene lamp.

It was Maya. She was in the Major's room.

She was circling him. Abruptly she sat down at the edge of the bed and turned up the sheet to reveal the black soles of his feet. Rehana watched silently; she couldn't bring herself to interrupt. Maya ducked under the bed and plunged her hand into a bucket of water, emerging with a wet cloth and wringing it gently, the water falling back with the sound of bare feet on a cool cement floor. She pressed the cloth against the Major's soles, first left, then right, then both together. Rehana thought she heard the Major sigh, though he kept perfectly still, and then, suddenly and awkwardly, Maya bent her head and hovered over the Major's feet, and Rehana saw she that was weeping, her tears falling on to the Major's rolled-up military trousers.

And when she looked up, Maya saw her mother watching from the window and fled, leaving the bucket where it was, the dark water rippling and gleaming, a luminous, blinking eye.

Rehana's first thought was that she should be sent away. She was guilty for thinking it; she wanted to believe her daughter should stay close, with her. Or she should go with her, wherever it was. But she couldn't leave Sohail, wouldn't leave Shona, the Major, Joy. It was not a choice; even though the whole thing sometimes felt like an accident, she was caught up; she couldn't leave now. But Maya had to go. Rehana considered, then rejected, the idea of sending her to Karachi to stay with her aunts; it would incense her, and anyway Rehana had no idea how her sisters had taken the news of the war. They hadn't written to her since the war had begun, and, while she wanted to blame it on the post, she knew they were secretly berating her, and in their hearts calling her gaddar. *Traitor.*

In the end Maya made it easy. She came to her mother the next afternoon, her eyes scratched and red.

'I'm going to Calcutta. I've arranged it with bhaiya.'

Rehana didn't know what to say; all the things she had been storing up for Maya — the soft words, the sorrys, her regret at knowing she had

168

not been able to love her as she should — crowded for her attention.

Maya misunderstood Rehana's silence. 'Please don't be angry,' she said. 'I don't want you to be angry.'

'Oh, no, I'm not angry, I'm so sorry.'

'I don't want to leave you alone.'

'It's all right.' She smiled at her daughter. 'You don't worry about me.'

'I loved her so much!' Maya said, trying to keep from crying. Her chin shook, and she kept swallowing and pressing her lips together. 'I have to do something. It's so unfair.'

Rehana nodded.

Maya looked into the distance and didn't say anything for a long time. 'They need people to write the press statements,' she said finally, the anguish gone from her voice. 'Sohail knows someone at the headquarters. Maybe I can even go into the liberated areas.'

'You be careful. I'll be worried about you. I'm always worried about you.'

'I'm always worried about you!'

Rehana was surprised to hear the words, but realized they must be true, and here it was, the thing she had been looking for, a small window into her daughter's locked heart. It was not that she was diffident but burdened. Burdened by the beloved, the disappeared. By her own widowed mother. Rehana embraced Maya, who was still so thin and brittle, but instead of telling her to be careful she found herself saying, 'Write some good stories.'

June

I loves you, Porgy

Throughout June, Tikka Khan's soldiers made their way across the summer plains of Bangladesh. They looted homes and burned roofs. They raped. They murdered. They lined up the men and shot them into ponds. They practised old and new forms of torture. They were explorers, pioneers of cruelty, every day outdoing their own brutality, every day feeling closer to divinity, because they were told they were saving Pakistan, and Islam, maybe even the Almighty himself, from the depravity of the Bengalis; in this feverish, this godly journey, their resolve could know no bounds.

The Bengali resistance was weak and sporadic. General Zia relied on the youthful spirit of his soldiers, and they had small victories. A blown-up bridge here. An army-convoy ambush there. A captured railway station. They celebrated these victories with the broadcasters of the radio, who sent up cheers in the homes of their listeners, those city dwellers spending long,

173

hot afternoons hugging their wireless radios.

After the Major came to stay and Maya left for Calcutta, Rehana's world grew smaller. She was encouraged not to leave the house too often; if she needed something, it would be brought to her. She should go to the market in Mrs Chowdhury's car, but buy only enough food for herself. She should sometimes visit her neighbours; she should appear concerned; she should talk about the war but only vaguely. It was agreed that if anyone asked she should say that she had sent Maya and Sohail to stay with her sisters in Karachi.

Things were quiet at Shona. Joy appeared occasionally to take care of the Major, and the doctor was in and out, but otherwise there was very little activity next door. It was just the three of them: Rehana, and the two men in the other house. She spent the nights with the kerosene lamp on. Every sound incited a fierce hammering in her heart. She thought she heard footsteps, soft knocks on the door; she thought she felt someone tugging at her feet as she slept. The Major next door was no consolation; he made her feel exposed.

On days when her nerves threatened to overwhelm her, Rehana tried to think back to a less turbulent time, when nothing of significance happened, when the passing of seasons, the thrill of the Eid moon-sighting, the smell of mangoes ripening on the trees, were the most spectacular events of the calendar. But their lives had never had any regularity — at least, not the sort Rehana was now sifting her memories for. There

174

was always something, some uproar, in the city, or beyond, in Islamabad, where one punishing law after another was passed; and even further afield — the death of Che Guevara, whom Sohail had mourned as though he had lost a brother. Every hiccup of the political landscape made its way to their door and, when her son was old enough, came through the door and into the bungalow, into the boy's drawn and serious face, the shadows he cast upon the corridors and over the dining table; and then into Maya, who was angrier and louder. No, there had never been any other time; their lives were populated by Lenin and Castro and Mujib and Anwar Sadaat; there was only this time, this life, this fraught and crowded era, to which they were bound without choice, without knowledge, only their passions, their loves, to lead and sustain them.

In this, as in all other things, Rehana veered between indulgence and censure. There was a part of her that wanted to allow her children anything — any whimsy, any zeal, any excess. Another part of her wanted them to have nothing to do with it all, to keep them safe, at home; in either case, she treated Maya and Sohail as though they were there to collect on an old debt, an old promise that could never be fulfilled, not in this lifetime; a yawning, cyclic, inexhaustible need. Whether the need was theirs or hers, she could not say.

Discovering herself alone in the house for the first time in many years, Rehana found she had no desire to reassemble the sewing group. She

175

didn't want to laugh with her friends any more; she wanted to stir the melancholy in the empty house, the deep sadness that was also a kind of quiet, a tranquillity, that she was reluctant to surrender.

Rehana found she took something close to pleasure in repeating the lonely rituals she had developed just after the children left for Lahore all those years ago. She scrubbed the house to a hospital shine; she shooed crows from her pickles; she took long, exaggerated baths under the bucket water; she dug up large sections of her garden and set about replanting the pumpkin, the marrow, the hibiscus, the jasmine.

The water would come on only between ten and twelve every day. Every morning she had to fill up the biryani pot and the three metal buckets and soak the clothes and the vegetables and gut the fish.

She went to the graveyard to tell Iqbal about the Major. When she got there, she felt like saying sorry, but she wasn't sure what for. Well, it was obvious what for.

You would not have liked this.

A column of ants bisected Iqbal's gravestone.

Forgive me; I haven't come in almost a month. The flowers on your plot have cracked in the heat; that bodmash caretaker promised to water them, but of course he forgot, even though I gave him an extra five annas the last time I was here.

I am harbouring a person who I don't know and who could get us all into very big trouble. No, you would not have liked it.

If you want to complain you should complain

176

to your son, he brought that man and begged me to let him stay. Could I say no? No, I could not say no.

★ ★ ★

About a fortnight after the Major's accident, Joy came to the door of the bungalow. He looked as though he'd been running: wet patches soaked through his shirt at his neck and his armpits. His cheeks glistened, and water, like tears, flowed from his forehead.

'Auntie,' he said softly, 'can I come in?'

'Of course.'

He hesitated. 'I'm not disturbing you?'

Rehana shook her head, surprised. Joy was not known for his politeness. He hovered at the edge of the sofa, bent his fingers and rubbed his knuckles together.

Rehana had just finished preparing lunch. 'Are you hungry?'

He shook his head. She saw the beams of his shoulders pressing against his shirt, which was a red-and-blue check. The collars were long and pointed towards his shoes.

She knew that shirt. Where had he got it, she wanted to ask him. There must be a perfectly innocent explanation. They had the same shirt. Simple. But Joy kept sweating and saying nothing and she started to feel panicky. 'Is something wrong?'

'Yes, I — I have to go.'

'Go where?'

His head dipped lower and closer to his hands;

177

his face swam; still he didn't move to mop his face. 'I have to go to Agartala,' he said. 'Just for a few days. I'll come back.'

'Has something happened? Is it Sohail?'

'Sohail?' he said. 'No, no, Auntie. He's in Agartala; he's fine; there was a telegram last night.'

'You got a telegram? Why didn't you tell me?' She burned to ask him about the shirt, the telegram, why he had to go. 'What's happening, beta, why don't you tell me? Here, have a glass of water.' She forced a note of tenderness into her voice. 'You sit here, and you tell me.'

'My brother is dead.' His voice was as flat as a vinyl record.

She didn't want to believe it. 'Aref?' Then there was relief flooding guiltily through her. 'Are you sure?'

'There was an operation,' he continued in the same voice. 'And they were ambushed. He was shot in the chest; he died instantly.'

Rehana compared this boy to her son. There was something wrong with his face, the thick upper lip, now shimmering with sweat, the hard, angry eyes. There was no trace of childhood.

Joy rubbed the sleeve of the red-and-blue check over his forehead, slicking his hair back until it stayed wet and stiff around the edges. 'These things happen in war,' he said. 'You know what our sector commander told us? Did Sohail tell you? He said, 'Nobody wants a live guerrilla.' '

He said *a live* guerrilla. What did he mean? He swallowed the water she gave him.

178

'We are all dead!' he said, raising his voice. 'Not just Aref, that's what I'm trying to say.' His wet face leaned close; she couldn't stop the question any more. 'Why are you wearing Sohail's shirt?'

He looked down at himself. She saw his lips rustle. 'We exchanged shirts. He wore Aref's. I took his. Aref had mine.'

★ ★ ★

Rehana picked up her gloves and her shears. She felt like attacking something.

The garden was neither pretty nor particularly ordered. The rows were messy, the colours a little chaotic, and there was too much red and white, though this was not Rehana's fault. The delta weather was punishing; it didn't support the frailer colours of the palette, only the muscular ones, the shocking whites, the brutal reds, the fuchsias and the violets. And so Rehana couldn't help overplanting the jasmine and the rojonigondha and the lilies. The dahlias and the chrysanthemums were mostly white too, and the carnations and the phlox were the crimson shade of a short, violent sunset. That was why she loved her yellow roses. Amid all the stark colours of the garden, they were the sweetest, tenderest plants.

She found a clutch of weeds growing against the eastern corner of the wall that divided the bungalow property from Shona. The weeds had spirited purple flowers, spiky and punctuated, as though they knew their time was borrowed. Rehana seized them with both hands and pulled.

They didn't budge. She planted a foot on the boundary wall, leaned back and used her weight. She strained and struggled, twisting the weed around her wrist, and finally it rushed out of the earth, trailing a long, knotted root.

Another boy dead. Rehana asked God again, as she did every day, to save Sohail. What made Him spare one and take another? She didn't know. Bless Sohail in Agartala, and my Maya in Calcutta. Maya had rung once, a few days after she'd left. She didn't say where she was calling from, or where she was staying. She said she was all right. Don't worry, she said, *I'm happy*.

★ ★ ★

Rehana devised a strict schedule for the Major: the doctor came every other afternoon, checked the stitches and adjusted the medication. Rehana brought the Major his food on a tray and left him alone to eat. Then she gave him a half bar of soap and poured a glass of water over his right hand. After lunch, he took a nap. When he woke up, she brought him tea and gave him his evening pills. The Major, who could barely speak, chose to say nothing. He always nodded thank you. He didn't smile, though, or wave to her when she said goodnight for the evening. He liked her cooking. His plate was always licked, except when she gave him fish. He would try to hide it under a pile of rice, or mix it up with the pieces of chewed-up pickle that climbed the side of his plate. What kind of Bengali doesn't like fish? She added more pickles and replaced the fish with egg curry; maybe if she found a chicken at the market she would try to get it for him.

She thought his first words to her might be 'thank you' or 'I'm so grateful to you' but instead he began with 'It won't be long now.' She assumed he meant before he was well enough to leave Shona. He couldn't mean before the war was over. In any case he was being optimistic, she thought. His leg still looked horribly twisted.

She had to lean forward to hear him, and hold her hair back so it wouldn't fall on to his face. She made a note to herself to braid her hair. She caught his breath, which smelled of watermelons. She found herself wondering how a person's breath might come to smell of watermelons. She told herself it must be because he didn't smoke cigarettes.

The next day he said abruptly, 'Why do you always wear white?' which she thought was a rude observation, but then she surprised herself by answering, 'So that you'll be convinced I'm a nurse and not just a poor widow.' At which he smiled, and Rehana was annoyed, in case she had accidentally begun some sort of banter with the man. But she needn't have worried. He hardly said a word for a week after that, only smiled briefly when she brought him lunch and dinner.

Then one day he said, 'I'm sorry about your husband,' and Rehana replied, 'It was a long time ago,' and then she said, 'Are you married?'

'Yes,' he replied, 'I was.' What kind of an answer was that? A look, a flash of something,

181

passed across the Major's face. It looked like anger. She wondered what it would be like to be close enough to the man to make him angry.

The next day he asked, 'What happened to your husband?' It occurred to her that it was none of his business, but somehow she felt the urge to answer.

'He had a heart-attack.'

'Suddenly?'

'Just like that.'

'Why did you never marry again?'

Still none of his business, but once she started, it was difficult to stop without appearing rude. 'I had children,' Rehana said; 'a reason not to marry again.'

'I thought that would be a good reason.'

'No,' she said, 'no. Children are the worst reason to marry again.'

'You didn't want someone to look after them?'

'You don't know how hard I had to fight just to keep them.' She told him about the court case. 'I had to get the children back. I needed money. A lot of money. I needed money to bribe the judge. Money for the plane ticket to Lahore. Mrs Chowdhury said, 'Build a house at the back of the property.' This is what my husband had intended as well. So that is what I decided to do. But I needed — '

'Money.'

'Yes, I needed money. I didn't have any. My father had passed away. My sisters were in Karachi. They said they wanted to come, but they couldn't. Things hadn't gone well for them, they were always struggling. I was the one who was always sending them things.' She remembered the striped aerograms with the bank drafts.

The Major looked around Mrs Sengupta's bedroom — took in the thick walls, the immaculate white plaster, the heavy double doors leading out on to the wide veranda. With his eyes he asked, *How did you do it?*

* * *

Rehana considered telling the Major about stealing the money. She told herself the thought was *practical*; after all, she had to tell someone, she couldn't keep it locked inside her for ever. A thing like that will eventually corrupt and destroy a person. And this man would be as good as any; better, in fact, because after he left she would probably never see him again. He might even die. Tobah as-tak farullah. She said Aytul Kursi in case he died. She said it again, sorry for having thought of his death.

She thought of telling him as her first selfish act in a very long time. Something just for herself. An act that would help no one, do nothing, feed no hunger, raise no children. She practised in front of the mirror inside the door of her steel almirah. She imagined the secret disappearing from her days. She lingered over it in her dreams, knowing it would soon be gone. She wondered if she would miss it.

But every day she put off telling him. She went to see him and talked about other things.

183

He listened patiently, nodding, though not frequently enough to suggest he was bored. He always looked at her mouth, not her eyes. She liked that. She didn't like being stared at in the eyes.

★ ★ ★

Whenever she intended to ask him a question, she would find herself talking instead. For instance, one day she found herself saying, 'After my husband died I lost my tongue.'

The Major tilted his head. 'Why?'

'Because I had no one to tell my sorrows to.'

And he nodded.

It appeared the conversation was over. To end it with a flourish Rehana felt it was appropriate to say, 'Iqbal was my saviour.'

'Women always say that.' He held his lips tight around his teeth, so the words struggled to get out.

Now she had to explain. 'No, it's true. We had to leave Calcutta. We — my father — had to sell everything. My sisters had moved to Karachi, but I didn't want to go. I would have married anyone.'

'You're not angry he died?'

'Yes, sometimes. He left me so suddenly.' She considered telling him about her trips to the graveyard: the negotiations, the pleas, the stubborn, embarrassing belief he might come back, that things might return to the way they had once been. But it was too soon, or perhaps too late, for such revelations. And anyway this man did not seem the type to indulge in such acts of sentiment.

'My wife died,' he said suddenly.

'Oh. I'm sorry.'

'We weren't really married. She was Hindu. But we loved each other. Does that count?'

'Yes, of course it counts,' Rehana said, thinking of Silvi's wedding.

'My father was a very religious man.'

'Mine wasn't.'

'No?'

An old image of her father flashed before her: handsome, polished, his legs crossed confidently in front of him. 'I didn't really know him. I was too young. But I remember the things he liked. Pipe tobacco. Thackeray. William Makepeace Thackeray — he used to make me say that. He played the piano — we had an enormous piano. It was always the shiniest thing in the house. Someone came to tune it every time the seasons changed.'

'You had a piano-tuner?'

'A piano-tuner. A table-setter. A horseman. Three poets.' She recited the list from memory, like multiplication tables. 'Eight cooks, two butlers, twelve cars.' She hadn't seen any of it. By the time she was old enough to know the difference, they were already poor.

'Your mother?'

'She died when the money ended. 1936. I was three.'

★ ★ ★

185

Rehana had found a chicken at New Market. From the look on the Major's face, she might have given him a trunk full of gold. He sucked on his fingers and licked the rim of the plate. When he was finished, he belched very quietly into his hand. And then he asked her about Iqbal again, and she found herself telling him about the trip he had made to London in '57, when he'd ordered the Vauxhall.

'These are the things my husband brought me from London: a black wool coat from Harrods, a gold Rolex ladies' watch, a round box of Quality Street chocolates. I kept the coat in a box with mothballs. I divided the chocolates in half. Maya ate hers in one day, and spent the next day holding her stomach and moaning. On the third day she begged Sohail for his share. He gave them up — he could never resist her — though he kept one aside, the round caramel — do you know the one? Purple foil wrap?

The Major didn't reveal whether he recognized it.

'He kept it for so long the ants got to it. But I don't think he liked the chocolates. As for the gold Rolex, well, eventually I pawned it. But it was very beautiful, a beautiful gift. And that is the story of my husband's trip to London in 1957.' Rehana piled up the dinner plates and moved to carry them away.

'Weren't there any suitors? After your husband died?' Maybe he thought he was changing the subject, but really he was coming closer to the truth about Shona. She fixed her gaze on his torn lip. She reached her hand out, as if to touch

186

it, but the hand went to the bed, smoothing the sheet, tucking it into the mattress. Time to change it, she thought.

⋆　⋆　⋆

The next day there were three sharp raps at the door. Rehana rushed to the drawing room, her heart racing, because these days it could be anything, Sohail, news of Sohail, a letter from Maya, a telegram saying they were both dead, or captured, or hurt somewhere. Or it could be the army, or a spy, or someone pretending to be a spy, or someone pretending not to be a spy. It could be anyone.

The woman was carrying a silver tray. There was a bowl on the tray, a blue porcelain bowl with a white napkin on top. The napkin had golden tulips embroidered along its edge. Something hot and fragrant was inside: Rehana caught a whiff of raisins as the woman, standing in the doorway, said hello.

'I'm Joy's mother', she said a little apologetically. 'Joy and Aref.' She had a plump, dimpled face.

'Mrs Bashir, yes, of course. Please come in.' Was she coming to ask about Aref? Rehana seated her on the sofa. She tried not to stare. *No matter how hard you look,* she told herself, *you won't be able to know if she's telling the truth.*

'May I offer you some tea?'

'No, please, I just came for this.' She pointed to the silver tray, which she had balanced on her lap. The raisin smell wafted through the room.

Mrs Bashir paused a little, then placed her palms on the tulip napkin. She had big hands and ragged fingernails.

'Can you please give this to Joy?' The words came out quickly, as though the woman was afraid her courage would suddenly leave her.

Did she know Aref was dead? If she did not know, did this mean she was telling the truth, or did it mean she was lying? 'I'm sorry, I can't do that.'

'It's nothing. Just morag polao.'

'I don't know where your son is.' *Your son is dead*. The other son, who is wearing my son's shirt, has gone to bury him.

'Yes, yes, of course you don't know.' She paused, then said, 'Perhaps Sohail can bring it to him.' Mrs Bashir looked at the doorway, and Rehana could see the anxiety, the cautious curiosity and a little jealousy, perhaps, towards another woman, another war-mother who might know something she didn't.

'Sohail is in Karachi,' Rehana said carefully, 'with his aunts.' Sohail is wearing Aref's shirt Aref is wearing Joy's shirt Joy is wearing Sohail's shirt.

'Perhaps you know someone who might pass this on. It's his favourite.'

'I know no one,' Rehana said, as though she had spoken the words a thousand times before.

'Please, Mrs Haque, you are a mother also!'

You are a mother. How many times had she repeated this very phrase to herself? I'm a mother. Above all things, a mother. Not a widow, certainly not a wife. Not a thief. A mother. But

188

now she was something else — a mother, yes, but not just of children. Mother of a different sort. This mother knew what it was to long for her children. But she also understood the dangers of such longing.

'I'm sorry. I know you miss your boys.'

'Have you seen them? How are they? How is Joy, and my Aref?'

She doesn't know her son is dead. Rehana started at the thought of Aref lying in a grave somewhere, restless and unmourned. She wanted to touch the woman's rough hand. But it could so easily be a trick. Maybe it wasn't her son. She had to pretend she didn't know anything about it. To test herself, Rehana looked straight into Mrs Bashir's eyes and said, 'I don't know. I haven't seen them since the war began.' And, as she said it, she thought of the blessing she had blown on Joy's forehead that morning when he had left for Agartala, and the needy look in his eyes as she had whispered the words, and the tender way in which he had thanked her and touched her feet. 'Mrs Bashir, please take your morag polao home.'

Rehana stood up in what she imagined was a guiltless manner and opened the front door.

'You take it,' Mrs Bashir said, thrusting the silver tray towards Rehana. 'Please, you have it. Think that I made it for you.'

'I'm sorry, Mrs Bashir, please go.'

'I know he's here, I know it. You're a liar,' she said softly. Her kajol-streaked tears fell sloppily on to her cheeks. She stepped towards the door, and for a moment Rehana thought she might fling the hot rice at her, but she didn't. She smoothed the tulip napkin and walked away, leaving Rehana in the doorway reciting the morag polao recipe to herself, wondering if she had enough chicken to prepare the dish when Joy returned.

* * *

The visit from Joy's mother was unsettling. Just after she finished the Magrib prayer, Rehana went to see the Major. She felt strangely exposed without a tray of food in front of her, a bed-sheet to change or even a vial of medicine from Dr Rajesh. 'Joy's mother was here,' she said. 'I sent her away.'

He was looking into a small mirror, examining his scar. 'You did the right thing,' he said, tucking the mirror under his pillow.

'But her son is dead.'

He struggled to lift himself up onto his elbows, dragging his broken leg, until he was sitting up and facing her. 'You have to do these things sometimes — difficult things.'

'I'm not sure I'm a nationalist,' she said. She was thinking of the well-loved volumes of Urdu poetry on her shelf, right next to the Koran.

'Well, why are you still here, in Dhaka?'

'To take care of you, of course.' She shouldn't have said that. She paused for a beat, checked herself. 'I love it here,' she said. 'It's my home, and the home of my children. I would not give it up for anything. Believe me, I've been tested.'

'Then you are a true nationalist.'

'That's kind of you to say. And you?'

'This is the greatest thing I have ever done. If I ever leave this bed!'

Her heart sank a little at the thought of his leaving.

'My life was a waste before this.'

'You were in the army?'

'I joined years ago, because I had to get away, from the village, from everything. There were too many memories.'

He looked at her, as though to ask if she knew what he meant, and she said, 'But that is precisely why I stayed.'

Three things happened at the end of June: Joy returned from Agartala, Dr Rajesh arrived with bad news, and Rehana gave the Major her gramophone. It was her idea; he'd looked so despondent when the doctor had checked his leg and said he needed at least three more weeks' rest. Rehana dusted the gramophone and dragged it across the garden to Shona. She hunted through Sohail's room and found a few records. One of them said *Help!* Another had a black-and-white photograph of Elvis Presley with his lips caressing a microphone. The gramophone needle was spiked with dust; Rehana had to spit on her finger and pluck it out. To polish the wood she dipped a rag into a little of the olive oil she sometimes used to shine her elbows.

It was as if she'd given him a month of chicken curry. He smiled so widely his scar stretched across till it touched the tuft of hair beside his ear. 'Thank you,' he whispered, closing his eyes and tilting his head to the ceiling, 'how did you know?'

In the first week he played and played again the two records she'd given him. And then one day she heard some new music. Joy must have brought the new records; or may be it was someone else; a woman, even. After all, she didn't know what happened at Shona after dark. No, he wouldn't do that. He wouldn't bring a woman into her house.

At first the records were familiar: some Tagore, a few Bengali folk songs, their lyrics changed to nationalist slogans. And then one day she heard the strangest music coming from his room. She had brought his breakfast: one scrambled egg, four triangles of toast, a glass of milk. She stood at the door, listened for what seemed like a moment but must have been much longer, because by the time she noticed the eggs they had stiffened and turned orange. What music could this be? She had never heard anything like it. She ran back to the bungalow and made new eggs, chastising herself for the waste, and retraced her steps back to Shona. But again she was rooted at the doorway.

It was a woman. In every syllable Rehana could hear the delicate intake of her breath, the tongue caressing the palette and the slow, tender piano in the background, and, as the song built, she could hear melancholy, and a low, guttural moan and stretched-out vowels. Her voice was a thousand years of sorrow. Rehana tried to make out the English words. *I loves you, Porgee.*

Who was this Porgee? The song was like the weather, a thing that was everywhere and nowhere all at once, the words falling into each other like overlapping raindrops, a dry day and then a wet one, the scale rising like a gust of wind. Sometimes it was as though the woman was holding her breath and then releasing it; she was young, almost girlish and then her voice would go deep, with the confidence of a secret masculinity. The weather filled the room; it travelled across the corridor until it rose up in Rehana.

By the time she had gathered the courage to enter the Major's room, she found herself a little out of breath. She told herself it must be the fast walking, carrying the heavy tray, trying not to spill the milk. She tried to stir up some irritation at the Major. She put the tray down in front of him harder than she meant to.

'Her name is Nina Simone,' the Major said.

Nina. Sounded like a Bengali name.

Rehana had a melting feeling in her mouth, as though she had bitten down on a pink, overripe guava.

★ ★ ★

'You like the music?' he asked, when she returned for the tray.

'It reminds me of my father,' Rehana said.

'He liked jazz?'

'There was a band once. A party in the ballroom, and dancing. And champagne. Probably one of his last.' Rehana spoke as though the memory was new to her. 'Yes. Champagne in delicate, bowl-shaped glasses, and ladies with short hair. There were lots of instruments. And it was loud, cheerful music. Not like this.'

'Nina Simone doesn't sound like anybody else,' the Major said. Rehana looked at the scattered record sleeves beside the Major's bed. A dark man with his lips pressed against a trumpet gazed out earnestly.

Then she asked, 'Where did you get this music?'

'You like it?'

'No, I don't like it,' she lied.

'OK.'

Why didn't he protest? What kind of a person wouldn't like this music?

'What do you like?' he asked.

'What sort of a question is that?'

'Simple. If you don't like this, what do you like?'

'You mean, what music do I like?'

'No, I mean, what do you like?'

'Anything?'

'Anything.'

How could she reply? No one had ever asked her that question. Why had no one ever asked her that question? It stunned her that a person could go through life without anybody ever asking them that question. She thought for a moment.

'I like the flowers in my garden,' she said

slowly. 'The yellow roses are my favourite. And I like to make dimer halwa. It's very difficult, you know. One slip and it turns into egg scramble.' She felt the weather rising up in her again, a squall, rippling and swirling. 'And the cinema. I like the cinema.' It was another lie. She loved the cinema.

* * *

It was Joy who brought the projector. It was the last day of June, and the rain had started to appear every evening just as the sun plunged crimson-shy under the horizon.

Rehana didn't know what it was at first. When she saw the hard black box she thought it might be some other thing to bury in the garden, a weapon, but then Joy opened the two buckles on the side and she saw the reel and the lens; even then she thought it must be some sort of camera, because she'd never seen one up close. It was Joy's grin that gave it away: a smile full of mischief and pride, the new face he'd acquired to mask his grief.

'Where did you get it?'

'Naz Cinema. The owner is a Hindu. They killed him in March.'

So this was what he was doing. Looting and stealing. 'So you just took the projector?' The Major hadn't said anything, and Rehana didn't know whose idea the projector was. She thought it was probably Joy's, because lately he was doing those slightly criminal things to prove there could still be pleasure, and roguishness, in the world. Or maybe he did it to forget the dead face of his brother.

'It was lying there, gathering dust.'

'You can't just take things.'

'It probably doesn't work,' Joy said, and as soon as he said it she knew they were going to keep it.

'Of course it works. Why wouldn't it work? I've seen at least a dozen films there.' She went through the films in her head: *Roman Holiday, High Society, Charade, The Maltese Falcon, The Big Sleep, Casablanca.* She was suddenly giddy. 'Shall we try it out?' She looked inside the box. *Mughal-e-Azam.* 'How did you know?'

'I just pulled this one out.'

It couldn't have been a coincidence. Sohail must have told him. 'Thank you, thank you. It's really too much.'

'Consider it a gift from the guerrillas.' Joy smiled, his face broad.

★ ★ ★

The tears welled up even before the credits began. Joy adjusted the focus and walked backwards to the door.

'You're leaving?'

'Not for me,' Joy said. 'I'll go soft!'

Rehana was already ignoring him. Akbar came on screen, praying to God for an heir. Let me not die without a trace, he was saying.

'You won't understand,' Rehana whispered; 'it's in Urdu.'

'Doesn't matter,' the Major whispered back.

'Don't you want to know the story?'

'Tell me quickly,' he said, 'before it starts.'

'It's complicated.' She had her eye on the screen, where Akbar was making his way across the desert to Nadir Shah. 'It's a love story — the Prince, Salim — Akbar's son — he falls in love with a servant girl, Anarkali. And then — '

He reached over and laid a finger on her arm. 'I understand,' he said.

Anarkali came on, posing as a statue. She flashed her tilted smile. She spoke; the throaty sugar of her voice echoed through the room. Rehana's ribs began to throb. Anarkali danced her rolling-hips dance. Prince Salim fell in love. Akbar, infuriated, jailed them both. 'Keep your precious India,' Prince Salim said. 'I will have my Anarkali.'

'She has to pretend she's betrayed him,' Rehana whispered.

'Hush.' The Major raised a finger to his lips. The film shadows moved over his face.

★ ★ ★

'You see,' Rehana said, 'it's the finest love story.'

'Right. You were right.'

'Joy really shouldn't have stolen the projector.'

'You would have taken it yourself if you'd had half the chance.'

Rehana took a deep breath. There wouldn't be a better time. The room was dark, and the projector fan was still running, a static buzz that seemed to brighten the window of white that hovered in front of the Major's bed.

Rehana turned to the Major. He made no move to turn off the projector, as though he knew she was about to tell him something. Maybe he'd planned all of this, getting Joy to steal the projector, watching *Mughal-e-Azam*, which he wouldn't understand. If so, she was willing to fall into the trap; she wanted to tell him as badly as he wanted to know.

'After the children were taken away, I thought I would die. I didn't know what to do, and the worst thing was, I actually started to think they were better off with that woman. I didn't have anything to give them, not even the money to pay off the judge. And I was such a coward, believing it was all for the best and letting Faiz take the children away from me. I will never forgive myself for that.'

Rehana looked at the Major and waited for him to say something, something like *What could you do?* or *You poor woman.* These were the things that she had grown so used to hearing, the words that followed her everywhere. But he was just waiting for her to go on.

'I closed the doors and refused to see anyone. I dismissed the servants — there was no money to keep them anyway. Mrs Chowdhury's daughter came over sometimes, and sometimes I liked that, but then she reminded me of the children, and I sent her away. I was cruel, I think, but she's a very sweet girl, she's forgotten all about it.'

Rehana paused, wondering if she should tell the Major about Sohail and Silvi.

'Mrs Chowdhury came over one day. I was

asleep, in the middle of the afternoon, wearing Iqbal's coat, and she came in through the garden — I never used to shut that gate — and she said she had an idea. That I should borrow money from the bank and build a house on the property. It was just the bungalow then, and a huge tract of land, wild grass, where I was always telling the children not to play. Iqbal and I had dreamed of building a big house some day, but it never occurred to me after he died. Mortgage the land, Mrs Chowdhury said, take a loan, build the house.'

It used to look like a field of paddy, Rehana thought, with only the tall furry grasses, and the mango tree in the middle, like a finger pointing to the sky. 'But I was just a woman. Without a male guarantor, all the banks turned me down. And then Mrs Chowdury said there was a man she knew, a Mr Qureishi, an old friend of her brother, and he had agreed to meet me. I went to the bank — Habib Bank, you know the one? The big branch, in Motijheel.

'That Qureishi man was a fraud. It wasn't Mrs Chowdhury's fault — I should have taken her with me, but I went alone, and I must have looked terrible, lost, and the man tried to take advantage.'

There he was, pressing the gristle of his cheek against her mouth, and his hand was on the sleeve of her blouse, and she could smell the curry breakfast he'd eaten that morning, and the stale old soap, and the sick, brutal need.

Still the Major didn't say anything. She saw him biting the inside of his lip, the right side, the one that wasn't torn.

'So there was no loan. Then Mrs Chowdhury decided I should find a husband. You must think I listen to everything she says, and it's true, back then it was like I was sleepwalking. And I desperately wanted someone to tell me what to do. My whole life the only decision I ever made was to marry Iqbal. And that was only because . . . well, I already told you.'

The difficult part remained ahead. Poor T. Ali, the gentle blind man with the phantom wife.

'Mrs Chowdhury suggested T. Ali. He had just moved to the neighbourhood. He was much older than me — already an old man, really — and his wife had died. And he was blind — did I say that before? Yes, he was blind. But he was rich; his father was into tea; he had inherited a fortune.' The words tumbled out of her mouth.

'The man was quiet, and the first time we met — Mrs Chowdhury invited us to dinner — he didn't speak a word to me. He ate, said a polite goodbye to Mrs Chowdhury and left. I'm sure he likes you, she said.

'I almost did it. T. Ali indicated he was willing to consider remarrying, but that I must allow him to keep the portrait of his wife in the drawing room. He invited me to his house to see the portrait. I wasn't sure I should go, but I was curious, and I thought, maybe he's just a sweet old man — a little odd, perhaps — but if we married, I was just going ask him straight out if he could give me the money to bribe the judge, the tickets to Lahore.'

T. Ali's house had been built in the traditional style, one storey with a large central courtyard and a wide veranda with rooms leading out of it. From the road it looked like a fortress, and Rehana had walked in and seen the man crouching over a chair in a dimly lit drawing room. He was wearing a chocolate-brown suit and a deep red bow tie. His hand was pressed against his chest, and at first Rehana thought he might be having a heart-attack, and she was about to curse her luck. But then he raised his hand, and in it was a small oval frame. He was holding the frame in the palm of one hand and stroking it with the other. My Rose, my sweet Rose, he kept saying. The room — the muscular wood furniture, the old carpets, the honey-toned walls, the portrait that dominated everything — smelt of crumbling plaster and damp, the colours bleeding into one another. Rose was a young woman, so pale her face foretold her death, with delicate hands folded across her lap. She wore a dress and looked like an English woman, the ones who had had worn wide, sloping hats and gloves, even in the warmest weather. Her dress, which reached down to her ankles, was a light pea-green with lace around the high collar and a tight row of buttons from chin to waist.

Rehana thought about what it would be like to have this ethereal presence staring down at her. She stepped gingerly across the threshold.

'Ali-saab,' she said softly.

'You have such a kind voice, my dear,' he said, patting the seat. 'Come, sit. Would you like some tea? Juice?'

'No, thank you,' Rehana said. And then, 'Your wife is lovely.'

'Yes, she was very beautiful. We only had a few years together.'

'I'm very sorry.'

A man in a black suit and chappals entered the room with a tray. When he reached the edge of the moss carpet, he removed the chappals and proceeded in bare feet. He set down a tray in front of Rehana. On it were two tall glasses of pink liquid each topped with a spray of froth.

'Rosewater shorbot,' T. Ali said, a hint of pride creeping into his voice. 'I have rosebushes.'

The shorbot was over-sweet and made her jaws tingle. 'Delicious,' she said, warmed by the thought of his rosebushes. She allowed herself to imagine his garden, leaning over his plants, the sun at her neck. Maybe she could marry him. The house was certainly big enough. So what about the portrait? The woman was dead, after all.

'What do you think of her?' he said lifting his cane in the direction of the portrait.

'She's lovely,' Rehana replied.

He cleared his throat. 'You see, I had tuberculosis. I was very ill — the doctor told me I didn't have much time left. And she said, 'No, I won't let him die.' She sat at my bedside and held my hands — I don't remember it; they told me afterwards. She said, 'We never had children.' I remember her saying that. She begged God not

202

to take me from her before we could have children. She prayed all the time, every day.'

Water came to T. Ali's eyes. He turned his face away from Rehana. He pulled a handkerchief from his pocket and wriggled out of his glasses.

'By the grace of God, I recovered. It was 1943. And then she died that very year. Tuberculosis. I couldn't save her.'

His voice grew faint and watery. 'She was a remarkable woman.' He nodded and worked his mouth, as though he was chewing on the memory. It made him look old. Rehana tried not to guess his age. 'Here, let me show you.'

He stood up and walked through the memorized room with his cane. His step was light and confident. Rehana felt herself relax a little as she followed him. He held the door open and invited her to pass through. As she brushed past him, she noticed the smell of mothballs, dusty and sweet. A comforting, not-so-bad smell.

He led her through an unlit corridor; then he reached for a handle and turned it. 'You see,' he said, 'I've left it just as it was.'

He moved through the room with ease, pointing to things. It was as though here, in this house, and especially in this room, he was no longer blind. In the far corner was an upright piano, the lid lifted over the keys like a curled lip. There was chair beside it, with an airy pink dress draped across the back. T. Ali touched the dress and said it was the very last thing his wife had worn. There was a dressing table with a faded velvet seat, its metal bolts black with rust. The table displayed a brush with a silver handle, a jewellery box and a plate of powder with the puff facing downwards, ready to be swept across the lovely Rose's face.

'Do you play the piano?' Rehana asked, approaching the instrument.

'Me? No,' he replied.

'The Well-tempered Clavier' was written in a curling hand above a sheet of black notes.

'It's very pretty,' Rehana managed, not knowing what else to say. The room was hot and airless. It made her want to whisper. It made her want to comb her hair and rub on some lipstick.

She turned to the mirror and examined her own face. Her cheeks were tawny with the heat. She caught the ordinariness of her looks, the starched whiteness of her dress. Mrs T. Ali, with her satin gown, her pale lips, her floating crimplene, flashed before her.

She imagined living here, in this dusty and frozen world. She forced out thoughts of the bungalow, her lemon tree, the note of bees around the jasmine. It had to be done. It had to be borne. It wasn't love, but it wasn't the worst thing that could happen.

Rehana picked up the hairbrush. It left a gleaming face in the dust, where the polished wood shone through. As she moved to set it down, she knocked it against the plate of powder.

T. Ali swivelled to face Rehana. 'Please don't touch that,' he said. He rushed to take it from her. He collided with her elbow, and then ran his hand up her arm, until he found the hairbrush. He held fast. Rehana shrank from his touch, the intimacy of his rolling, searching hands. She didn't know why, but she curled her fingers around the handle and refused to let it go. They struggled for a few seconds, until it slipped out of Rehana's hand.

At that very moment T. Ali was pulling in the opposite direction. The brush flew out of his grasp and hurtled against the mirror.

It didn't shatter at first. A swirl of cracks opened like an eye, twisted outwards and spread through the length and width of the mirror. Then the pieces began to fall, slowly, but then in a sudden, violent rush.

T. Ali flung himself at the mirror.

'What are you doing?'

'You stupid girl!'

A bead of spittle appeared on his lip as he shouted over to her. Then he was on his hands and knees, picking through the shattered glass.

'I'm so sorry, I didn't mean to upset you.'

'You've ruined everything!'

'Please, Mr Ali, you must get up.'

'Get out! Get out of here! This is my Rose's room!'

Rehana tugged at T. Ali's hands. He began to cry. 'I said get out!'

He was ignoring her, mumbling something to himself. Rehana tried again to move his hands away from the broken mirror. Then suddenly she spotted the jewellery box, its mouth open, lying on its side in a hail of glass. She picked it up without thinking, the crunch of glass under her feet masking the sound of the clasp fitting into its groove. She tucked it under her arm. Her heart was hammering in her chest. She was sure he could see her, that his map of the room would give her away.

But he was still. 'Haven't you gone yet? Leave us in peace, I say. Leave us. Oh, my poor, my poor Rose.'

Rehana made her way to the door.

He knew. He must know. She thought of leaving the box by the door; it wasn't too late; better than to be caught with it; any minute now he would climb down from the dressing table and pounce on her; he could see, she knew he could see. But a second later she was out the door and darting across the hallway; through the drawing room, where the rose-shorbot glasses had been cleared; unlatching the front door and out on the street, whose darkness instantly swallowed her; and then at home, where she crawled into her bed and sobbed, and cheered, and sobbed.

★   ★   ★

'You stole,' the Major said. It was too dark to make out his face.

'Yes,' she said. 'Yes, I stole.'

'From a blind man.'

He was about to hate her; she knew it. But it was too late. 'Yes, from a blind man.'

'And his dead wife.'

'Yes, I just told you. T. Ali's wife.'

She heard something — was he *crying?* — and then he slapped his knee, once, twice. He cleared his throat. He swallowed.

206

'I'm sorry — it's just — '

'What?'

'You kept this secret all these years?'

'Yes, I never told a soul.'

He slapped his knee again. His breath was noisy now, and she couldn't see, but she could tell his mouth was open and he was trying, with difficulty, to speak. 'I thought at the very least you'd murdered someone.'

'What kind of a thing is that to say?'

He'd given up trying to say anything, and now he was just laughing, heh heh heh — a silly, ridiculous laugh. Rehana felt a tickle at the back of her throat. She coughed it away. It came back. She took refuge in scolding him. 'You think this is funny?'

'No, no. Of course it's not funny.' And he snorted. 'Excuse me!'

'Chih! I tell you this dark, terrible thing, and all you can do is laugh.' She turned away indignantly, grateful that it was too dark for him to make out the expression on her own face. It could have been a smile, or it could have been a grimace. And the tickle in her throat could have been a chuckle or it could have been tears. It was mixed up: sad; funny; unfunny. She didn't care. And she left him there, with the projector humming in the dark afterglow of the cinema, his head tilted back gratefully, laughing as though she had just given him a prize.

July

The red-tipped bird

It was still only July, not yet August, the month of contradiction. In August, mornings were unbearably liquid, the air dense, tempers threadbare; wives and paratha-makers and jilapi-fryers laboured over breakfasts, and children woke from damp sheets and wiped their faces in limp, furry towels. And then, at some mysterious hour between noon and dusk, the sky would hold its breath and the tempers worsen, as the air stopped around people's throats, not a stir, everything still as buildings, and there was a hush, interrupted only by the whine of the city dwellers, lunching, probably, or just tossing and turning on mattresses, debating whether it was hotter to stay still or to move; women with sinking make-up fanned their faces, men with bulging chests fanned their necks. But, after the stillness, after the gathering of clouds and the darkness, there was the exultant, joyous rain, sweet water that jetted violently, and scratchy, electric thunder, and exclamations of lightning.

Altogether, a parade of weather, a feast for the hot, the tired; and every day there was one small boy, or a very old man, or even a dog, who would look up at the sky and wait for the first fat drop with his tongue out-stretched, his face full of hope, all knowledge of the morning entirely forgotten.

But this was not August; it was July, a timid, confused month that cowered under the threat of what was to come. It was only the warm-up.

It was on such an in-between day that a wail could be heard coming from Number 12, a woman calling hysterically for water, ice water for her head. When Rehana arrived at her bedside, she exclaimed, 'My poor daughter! My poor daughter!' In the garden, a dog named Juliet howled at the afternoon.

The war had finally found Mrs Chowdhury.

She was beached on the four-poster with a wet compress on her forehead. The ceiling fan was on at full speed, slicing violently through the air. Silvi was fanning her mother's face with a jute hand-fan. Between the ceiling fan and the hand-fan, Mrs Chowdhury's face was flattened, the hair plastered to her forehead.

'Faster, faster! I'm so hot!' Mrs Chowdhury said. 'Silvi, get my thermometer. I'm burning up!'

Impassively Silvi passed the hand-fan to Rehana and went to fetch the thermometer. Someone had stitched a red border around the rim of the fan, so that it looked like a seashell dipped in red paint.

'One minute hot, one minute cold,' Mrs

Chowdhury cried. Rehana worked the fan back and forth over her, watching the loose tendrils of hair float from side to side. Mrs Chowdhury's bedroom was crowded with family antiques. There was the mammoth four-poster that required a stepladder to mount, a dressing table with a heavy oval mirror and a wall of solid teak wardrobes, each with an open-mouthed keyhole the size of a baby's fist. Tucked into Mrs Chowdhury's sari was a gold chabir gocha that held the keys to the wardrobe and to the other important locks in the house: the sugar and oil store, the front gate, the back gate, the drawing room (which stayed locked and sheet-draped for special occasions), the ice-box room and, most importantly, the jewellery safe, set into the wall of Mrs Chowdhury's heaviest steel almirah.

The rest of Mrs Chowdhury's house was a museum of better times. Room after room contained haphazardly assembled family heirlooms. Some were so crowded that it was difficult to navigate among the furniture, the tarnished silver candlesticks, the clashing statues of Venus de Milo and Nataraj; others were mostly empty, a grandfather clock ticking erratically in one, a solitary birdcage in another, swaying in the breeze of an open window, its creaking echoing against damp, blistered walls. An air of accident permeated Mrs Chowdhury's house, an expectation that something would come along and stir the sad, dormant air. Only a few knew the reason for this arrangement, and Rehana was one of them: Mrs Chowdhury was still waiting for her long-lost husband to come home.

Silvi returned with the thermometer and inserted it into her mother's open mouth. She turned to Rehana and whispered, 'Sabeer has been captured.' Her voice was flat and unconcerned.

Mrs Chowdhury tried to speak through clamped lips. 'Just wait one minute,' Silvi told her. And then, 'Ammoo, there's no fever.'

'Rehana,' Mrs Chowdhury said. 'This is my poor daughter's fate. I knew she shouldn't have married that man.'

'What happened?'

'His regiment were fighting the Pak Army in Mymensingh,' Silvi began.

'Why we had to get involved in this business,' her mother interjected. 'It was you, Silvi, you just had to marry him — because he was an officer. You were so impressed. Fan harder, Rehana, I'm burning up. But I never trust military men, never. You never know what kind of trouble they're going to drag you into. What did you say my temperature was, girl? 98? That can't be. Check it again. No, not that way. You have to wash it first. Go, go and wash it and bring it back.'

Silvi turned to go, and that is when Rehana noticed her head was covered in a dupatta. At first she thought Silvi might be getting ready for the Zohr prayer, but she checked the clock above Mrs Chowdhury's bed and saw that it was only noon, still an hour before the Azaan.

'It's God's will,' Silvi said, coming back. She

put the thermometer into its leather sleeve.

'Nothing to do with God,' Mrs Chowdhury said. 'You see what's happened to her, Rehana? Covering her head? She's in pordah all of a sudden; spends all her time reading the Holy Book. Foolishness, that's what it is. Sabeer should have fled, left the country, like Sohail. Your children have some *sense*. What possessed him to join that silly army? Your husband is a fool, girl, a fool and a dead man.'

'Perhaps they'll free him,' Rehana tried to say, but Mrs Chowdhury wasn't listening.

'I've even lost my appetite,' she said. 'I can't eat, I can't sleep, I'm so hot.'

Rehana began smoothing Mrs Chowdhury's forehead with the wet compress.

'Please, apa, don't make yourself sick.'

'We don't know where he is, what's happened. We wouldn't even have known he's captured, but one of his soldier friends sent a letter to Silvi. Show her the letter, Silvi.'

Silvi nodded but didn't move to get the letter. She was massaging her mother's foot, moving her thumb in circles along the heel.

On the antique canopy bed, Mrs Chowdhury's bulk rose like freshly pressed dough.

'There's nothing to be done, Rehana, I don't even know why I called you. Nothing! And I thought he would be the one protecting us.' Mrs Chowdhury closed her eyes and waved Rehana away. She sighed deeply and turned over on to her side; in a few minutes she was snoring lightly. Silvi glanced at Rehana and whispered, 'Thank you for coming, khala-moni.'

'I'll bring some food over this evening,' was all Rehana could manage. How had Sabeer been captured? How did they know? And what was it about Silvi's look, her calm self-assurance, pressing her mother's feet instead of wailing and beating her chest like any other wife? Rehana felt slightly queasy, as though she hadn't eaten all day.

★ ★ ★

After lunch, Silvi appeared at the front door carrying a small cloth shopping bag. She was panting and worked up, as though she had leaped across the street, and she gave off that summer body smell: sweat masked by a heap of perfumed talc. She was wearing a loose, long-sleeved salwaar-kameez, her face framed tightly in the dupatta.

'Ammoo's asleep,' she explained, unwrapping her head.

Rehana watched her hair coming loose. 'Here,' she said, pouring a glass of water. 'Drink.'

Silvi drank the water in one gulp. She set the glass down with an emphatic 'Sobhan Allah!' Then she said, as though they were already in the middle of a conversation, 'It would be arrogant to say that God had found me, or that I had found God. Who are we to find Him, that holiest, most exalted of beings? For He is everywhere, in every breath, every heart. One has only to look.' Her eyes shone healthily. 'All this is but an illusion — do you not see that, khala-moni? This bodily life, this suffering.' Her

216

hands were restless, playing with the dupatta, smoothing the sleeves of the kameez. 'You were the one who taught me the prayers, remember? Ammoo didn't have the patience. It was you. You will be blessed for ever for that deed.'

Rehana gave Silvi a surprised nod of thanks, remembering the thin bones of the girl's hands as she raised them, once, twice, three times, to her forehead.

'God forgives everything, but only if we atone. Every day I beg for forgiveness.'

'What could you possibly have to atone for?'

Silvi's face was vigorously scrubbed, and she looked transparent, undifferentiated, all the colours blurred into a pale pink heat, except her cheeks, which pulsed, red and alive. She took a breath, hesitating, and Rehana could see the girl's entire past in one instant: the stifling but strangely indifferent love of her mother; the vast, crowded house; the burden of losing her father, knowing that if she had been a boy, he might have stayed. Rehana had always imagined she could see into Silvi; the guilt she carried around with her had reminded her of her own guilt, her own burden. But now, in her simplicity, Silvi was predatory, fierce.

Silvi was clutching her bag and trying to say something. When she finally opened her mouth, her speech was formal, more like a recitation. 'I wanted to give these to you. I would have burned them but I wanted you to bear witness to me, giving these to you, giving them up. So that you would know. I wanted someone — you, I wanted you. To know.' Now the words were rushing out

217

of her mouth. 'God sees everything, so it should have been enough that He was witnessing it, but I'm ashamed to say it wasn't.' Silvi put her hand to her forehead and smoothed the middle part in her hair.

'I'm sorry about Sabeer, beti,' Rehana finally said. 'Are you sure it isn't just a rumour?'

'It's not a rumour.'

'How do you know?'

'Sohail,' Silvi said, as though it was his fault, or even Rehana's, but that she forgave them both.

Rehana felt her heart stop. 'You've seen him?' she asked, trying not to raise her voice, 'Where is he?'

'No. I haven't seen him. I'm in pordah. I don't appear before strangers.'

Strangers? What had happened to Silvi? What religion had possessed her? Certainly not the familiar kind. Rehana was not irreligious herself. She prayed every day, at least once, at Magreb, the most important prayer-time of the day. When Iqbal died, she had used the prayer to give her something to do, something that didn't immediately remind her of the cruel hand she'd just been dealt, and she was unashamed about the solace it had given her. Life had punished her enough; the God she prayed to was not a punishing, not a vengeful, brutal God; He was a God of comfort, a God of consolation. She accepted the relief with entitlement, with confidence, and in turn she demanded very little from Him — no absolution, no change of destiny. She knew, from experience, that this could not be achieved.

Now Silvi riffled through her bag and took out a square packet. It was tied together with a length of deep red silk. As Silvi untied the knot, a few flattened flower petals tumbled out, their edges brown and brittle. She unwrapped the package, and inside was a stack of folded pieces of paper. They were of different shapes and sizes, some of them lined, like school notebooks, others plain, with a small but confident hand. Rehana glimpsed English, Bengali, a snatch of Urdu — and then she knew.

'From Sohail,' Silvi said. When Rehana didn't answer, she continued, 'I wanted to burn them. And then I thought, perhaps you would want to have them. In case.'

'In case of what?'

'In case something happens to him.' She said the words with deep sigh. 'I can't keep them any more.'

Rehana wondered if she should feel wounded, for Sohail's sake. 'But they're yours.'

'At first I was worried Sabeer would find them. But now I just don't want to have them. It's not right.'

'You're sure?'

Though her face betrayed no signs of a struggle, Silvi was still holding tightly to the stack of letters.

'Yes, yes, of course I'm sure. You can read them. There's nothing — just poetry, a lot of poetry. I thought you might want it.'

'All right. Give them to me. I'll keep them.'

Still she clutched the letters, 'Or burn them. I

219

was going to burn them.'

A few seconds passed. Then Silvi carefully picked up the petals and retied the bundle, her fingers smoothing the fabric, stretching it tightly, mask-like, over the letters.

When she finally held out the package, Rehana was struck with a presentiment, as though her son had already died and the letters were like a gift, an exchange — a life for a stack of letters. She promised herself she wouldn't open them.

'I'm sorry about Sabeer,' Rehana repeated, in an effort to change the subject. Thank God, Rehana was thinking, thank God my son is alive. 'So, Sohail told you about Sabeer?' And again she thought that her son was alive. It sang in her chest. Just being able to ask was a relief. 'You spoke to him?'

'He came to the house. 'I'm in pordah,' I said, but he insisted. So I opened the window, but I stayed behind the curtain. And he said, 'Sabeer's been captured. They're holding him somewhere. I'm going to find out.' And he said, 'Don't worry, I'll bring him back to you.' '

Foolish, foolish boy.

How much did the girl know? Rehana clutched the letters. Her poor, foolish boy.

★ ★ ★

She went straight to the Major. 'I want to see Sohail,' she said, keeping her eyes on his broken leg. 'Did you know he was in Dhaka?' She knew the answer. 'You knew he was here but you didn't tell me?'

220

As usual, he offered no explanation. 'It's too risky.'

'I don't care. Just do it. I haven't asked you for anything. I've taken care of you. Now you have to do this for me.'

He seemed to hesitate, his skin glowing a dark, sickly amber. His fingers fluttered and landed on the buttons of his grey-green uniform. Rehana ignored the small stab of guilt she felt at reminding him of his debt to her.

Three days later she got her instructions.

She was to leave in the morning as usual, with Mrs Chowdhury's driver. She would instruct him to take her to New Market. On the way there she would complain about all the shopping she had to do, that the tailor had mismatched her green petticoat, that she needed mutton bones to make haleem for Mrs Chowdhury, and where would she find mutton bones at a time like this. When she arrived in New Market, she would get out of the car and ask the driver to collect her in two hours. She would walk straight to the fabric section of the market and stop at the petticoat shop called Miss Pretty. She would ask for a green petticoat — the colour of a tia-pakhi feather, she should say. And the petticoat man would give her a package. It would contain the green petticoat and a kilo of mutton bones. The petticoat man would walk out of the store and lead her to Sohail's hideout.

* * *

221

The petticoat man led her to a squalid block of flats in Nilkhet. He pointed to a four-storey building, told her to climb the stairs to the top floor and left her with a brief 'Khoda Hafez, Joy Bangla!'

At some time in its history the building had been painted yellow. Now it was a rainbow of decay: the outside walls were streaked with bright green moss where the rainwater had collected; the paint had peeled in places and the cement showed pale grey underneath; and the remnants of the yellow paint were orange in some spots, coffee in others. The verandas were covered in wet laundry, lungis and blouses and soggy pyjama bottoms. Rehana saw a grey pair of men's underwear, next to which was an equally tired brassiere, and beside that a small child's nightie. She felt an old swell of longing for the unit, the family: man, woman, child. This was the formula for happiness, the proper order of things. All other equations suffered in its shadow.

As she approached the building the smell of shutki suddenly assaulted her. Some people considered the dried fish a delicacy, but in all her years in Dhaka Rehana had never been able to stomach it. She saw another clothes line dotted with a row of tiny fish. The smell followed her up the stairs and to the flat on the top floor, where she had been promised her son would be waiting. She knocked impatiently.

'Ammi,' her son said, as soon as she entered. The Urdu word was the secret language of long ago; it meant he was a boy, her boy, again.

'My son,' she said, 'my poor Sohail.' She was

so relieved to be in his presence. Everything, the war, the Major, Silvi, all seemed so distant, so much smaller than this moment. She pushed him away and searched his face. She saw the bright, earnest gaze, the serious forehead. 'Ammi,' he said again. Through the grate of hardness she could still hear the sound of her son, who was never meant to be a soldier. It was him. She was always checking to make sure he was still there.

'You heard about Sabeer,' he said. Rehana looked around the room before she replied. A man's whole life seemed to have been crammed into the tiny space, like a too-short novel. There was a bed in the centre, overpowering the room, the mosquito net still draped over it, like a giant, elephantine ghost. The windows were shut, and the only light came from a single bulb strung crudely from the ceiling, casting a tired mustard halo.

'Silvi came to see me on Saturday,' she said sharply, suddenly reminded of the danger Sohail had put himself in. 'Why, beta, why did you tell her?'

'I thought she should know.'

'But she could find out more. About you, the guerrillas, Shona.'

'She already knows.'

'You told her? When?'

'She's always known. I saw her when we were setting up Shona. And then later, a few other times.'

'You went to see her?' Rehana tried to keep the tension out of her voice.

'Only a few times.'

She couldn't stop repeating the question. 'You went to Mrs Chowdhury's?'

'Ammi, I'm sorry. I had to see her. After she was married, I just had to make sure.'

Rehana felt her eyes burning. 'I can't believe you would do such a thing.'

'I thought . . . but something's happened to her. Have you noticed? I didn't see her for a few weeks and when I came back she said she wanted me to stop coming. She said we'd be punished, God would punish us. She said we had sinned.'

'You went to see her? How many times?' She wanted to hear the details, the dates, the number of times.

'Not that many.'

'How many?'

'I don't remember.'

'I'm so angry, Sohail, I can't speak to you.' For an instant she thought of leaving him there in his shadowy gloom. She began pacing the small room. She found a pile of his clothes next to the bed and began folding. She counted two shirts, three vests, one kurta, one pyjama, two pairs of trousers.

'I thought, if I told her, she would begin to trust me again.'

One lungi, one pair of socks.

'Ammi.'

'Promise me you'll never do it again.'

'I can't do that. I just need a little more time.'

Rehana put down the lungi in her hand. 'She wants it to end.'

Sohail shook his head. When he turned, she saw the flattened curl on his forehead. 'That can't be true. She says it but she doesn't mean it.'

'She's returned your letters.'

'What?' Sohail came over to the pile of clothes and stood above Rehana.

'I have them at home.'

'I don't believe you.'

'I'm telling you, I have them.' Rehana paused, and then she guessed: 'You quoted Rumi, Amir Khusro.'

'You read them?'

'Only a little.' It wasn't true. She hadn't dared break her resolve. But if she'd had love letters to write, those were the poets she would have chosen. Then she saw an opportunity and took it. 'Sohail, listen to me. The Major says there's nothing to be done anyway. Silvi doesn't need to know. The important thing is to keep quiet from now on.'

'You told the Major?'

'Of course I told him. Who else can I turn to?' And suddenly she wanted this meeting to be over, so she could tell the Major about it, about the painful love for her son, about the dirty flat, the girl that was no longer a girl but a curse, and she knew that it wouldn't be until she told him that the day would have any meaning.

'There's nothing to be done, Sohail. Just let it go — Sabeer, God willing, will survive.' For a second she was almost glad Sabeer was captured. She could trace back the start of all this madness to the day he'd walked into her

225

drawing room with Mrs Chowdhury flushed and cooing with pride.

'Nei, Ma, there is something. Something you can do.'

Rehana thought she had misheard. 'Me?'

'That's why I came back to Dhaka. It's you. You can save Sabeer.'

'I don't understand.'

'He's been brought to jail. We know he's somewhere in the city.'

The light outside was fading. Sohail was kneeling in front of her. His hands were on her knees but she couldn't feel them. His voice was coming from far away, under water, and hers was unnaturally loud when she said, 'You want me to offer to take Sabeer's place? Should they torture me instead of him? That's what you want?' Rehana could barely see Sohail any more; he was a blur of hair and mouth.

'Faiz Chacha can get Sabeer out,' said the under-water voice.

'Faiz? Your uncle Faiz? No.'

'I'm telling you.' A wave, a roar.

'Why?'

'He's got something to do with the army — we're not sure exactly what. But he has a lot of influence.' Sohail's red-rimmed eyes widened.

The words sank in, and the room grew quiet. 'You're going to send me begging to him?' Rehana whispered.

'It's the only way Silvi will trust me again.'

'You're serious.'

'Yes.'

Rehana waited for the words to settle. Go

begging to Faiz and Parveen. Rescue Sabeer. When she pictured it in her mind, she felt strangely relieved. It was the most distasteful, gruesome task. But it was also an opportunity. Her son was giving her another chance to atone. The years of slavish devotion, the mothering, the theft — she had always known they would not be enough. She could not help welcoming the prospect of some new sacrifice.

Still, the feeling of injustice did not vanish. 'You can ask me to do this?'

'He'll think you're doing it for Mrs Chowdhury. You can say she begged you to come to him. Say how fond you are of her daughter.'

'You've thought of everything.'

'Ammi, please do this for me. This is the only thing I care about.'

'This is the only thing? What about the war, the country, the refugees, all of that? Suddenly none of it matters? What do you think will happen if I bring Sabeer back? You think Silvi will fall into your arms?' Before he said anything she already knew the answer.

'Yes, I do.'

'She's married to him. Not to you.'

'She'll know how far I'm willing to go.'

'What have you been doing all these months? Fighting a war or throwing sand at Silvi's window?'

'Ammi, I was there when Aref died. He looked at me and he said, 'If I had a hundred lives I would lose them all.' How can it be the greatest and the very worst thing we have ever done? Everything, everything is upside down. Wrong is right. My mind is full of the filthiest, most brutal things — and I just need her. I can't explain it. When I see her, at the window, I just need her.' Sohail's eyes were swimming. 'Please, Ma, for me, just once, I'll never ask you for anything, just please, go and get Sabeer, get him out of there. Ammi, amar jaan, please.'

'Enough. Stop begging.'

Sohail was sobbing now, his face collapsed, his palms pressed against his eyes. 'It has always been Silvi, ever since I can remember.'

'All right.'

'You'll do it?'

'I'm as much a slave to you as you are to her.'

He looked up, and she knew he was thinking he would someday make it up to her, pass the debt back. Neither said anything for a few minutes. Sohail was still kneeling in front of her. She passed him a rag from the pile of clothes, and he wiped his nose. And then he smiled and said, 'How do you like my palace?'

'It's disgusting. They couldn't find you somewhere decent?'

'I've been teasing Joy. He has your cooking, and I have to stay here.'

'Why don't you let me bring you something?' It seemed such a pathetic question. What could she possibly bring him?

'You can't come back here,' he said.

'I can send someone with food, clothes.'

'It's too dangerous.'

Something snapped inside Rehana. 'Dangerous! There are enough explosives buried under the rosebushes to flatten all of Dhanmondi.

You're worried about putting me in danger?'

Sohail wrapped his long arms around her and whispered, 'Thank you, thank you, Ammi, you are saving my life.'

My life is your life, she thought. 'Will you be here long?'

'No. As soon as Sabeer is released I'll go back across the border.'

'There's no guarantee Faiz will release him. Or even if he can.'

'He can. I know he can. You just have to convince him.'

★ ★ ★

The first thing Rehana did when she got home was take a bath to get the fish stench out of her skin. She changed her sari and put the rice on the stove for dinner. Dusk was settling in the sky, its purple light gently grazing Shona and the bungalow.

Then she went to the Major's room.

The record player was silent, and his hands were folded together on his lap. He appeared to have shaved, his chin and cheeks gleaming. He was sitting up and doing nothing, just staring at the opposite wall, which was bare except for a framed, garlanded photograph of Mrs Sengupta's parents.

'Was it far away?' he asked without saying hello. 'Did you get lost?'

'No.'

'You just got back?'

'Yes.'

'Why is your hair wet?'

'I bathed.'

'I thought you said you just got back.'

'Are you worried or just nosy?'

He didn't say anything after that. It was obvious he wanted to know what had happened, but for some reason she was irritated at him, and the events of the afternoon refused to assemble themselves into any sensible order. Now that she had finally seen Sohail, she could no longer imagine they were using him for some exclusive, important task. He was just a beast like the rest of them, useful only for his body, his strength, like any other body, any other strength. If it was the same to them, why did they have to have him?

'He thinks I can get Sabeer out,' Rehana finally said.

'You? Get a soldier out of jail? How?'

'My husband's brother. He has some connection with the army.'

The Major's face closed up.

'The thing is — Sohail is in love with Sabeer's wife.' It came out accidentally. Why did the words just fall out of her mouth in this man's presence? Again he said nothing, and again she was grateful — probably because he appeared never to be shocked. To make herself feel better she told him to get up so she could change the sheet.

'You told him you'd do it?' he asked, not moving.

'Of course I did.'

'I'll come with you.'

The suggestion irritated her further. 'How can you?' she said cruelly. 'You can't even walk to the gate.'

'You could get caught.'

'He's my brother-in-law, he wouldn't turn me in,' she said, knowing it wasn't true. 'I can just be concerned for a neighbour. There doesn't have to be anything suspicious about it.'

'And when he asks you where you stand, with the war, if you believe in Bangladesh or Pakistan, what will you say?'

'Whatever I have to.'

'You shouldn't do it.'

'You don't have children.' She felt her neck burning, and she smelled the wheel soap she had scrubbed into her face, and the remnants of the jobakusum oil in her hair, and the astringent sharpness of the talcum powder under her arms.

The Major's ceiling fan was switched off. In the afternoon, though it was always hot, his fever rose and he would shiver under his blanket until the sun travelled low and dipped beneath the horizon.

Rehana, wiping the dampness above her lip, said, 'Why don't you play a record?'

'This is a bad, a terrible idea.'

'I've already sent a message to Parveen. They're expecting me for lunch on Friday.'

★   ★   ★

I won't tell Iqbal, she said to herself that night, watching a mosquito trying to break into the net. If I tell him I'll end up talking myself out of it. I

231

know it's dangerous, and it probably won't work. And imagine the smug look on Parveen's face. Those stupid, bulging eyes. No, it probably won't work. Who is Sabeer to me anyway? Would he save my Sohail if he had the chance? Nothing doing. Phat-afat he would run the other way. Mrs Chowdhury? We both know the answer to that. And that girl, Silvi, she's the cause of all this hangama.

By the end, she would have talked herself out of it. No, she would not visit Iqbal.

A black Mercedes-Benz came to collect Rehana. The driver was a man in a white shirt and a skinny black tie. He sat rigidly in his seat, blowing cigarette smoke out of the window. When he saw Rehana close the gate and turn to fasten the padlock, he shot out of the car and stood stiffly against it. He was dark and very thin. He crushed the cigarette with the heel of his shoe and waited for her to approach.

When she was within a few feet of the car, the man's arm scissored into a clean salute.

'Mrs Rehana Haque?' he asked.

Rehana's tongue glued itself to the roof of her mouth. 'Ji,' she managed.

'Quasem driver. Accompanying you to the Haque residence.'

'Thank you,' Rehana replied.

The door slammed shut behind her. The inside of the car was enormous and smelled of kerosene. Quasem jammed his foot on the accelerator, and they sped away. Rehana felt herself slide uncomfortably on the leather seat, her sari getting crumpled as she was dragged from side to side. She had dressed carefully for her meeting with Parveen. She wore the most unflattering sari she owned — a starched, grey organza that would puff out at the pleats and make her look thick-waisted. She didn't try to iron out the creases; she didn't even smooth them down with her hand. She didn't wear any make-up; she tied her hair into a flat, severe bun and fastened it with plain black bun-clips. Parveen always needed to be the more beautiful one.

They went through Mirpur Road and turned on to Kolabagan. They sped past the open fields of Second Capital and approached the airport. Rehana sank further into the inky space and tried not to panic.

The car took a turn and suddenly she didn't recognize the street. It was a wide road, like a highway, and it stretched into a foggy, unfamiliar distance. Her thoughts turned to the torture centre Sohail had described. She craned her neck, to see if any of the low-lying buildings looked like places that held dirty secrets.

'Where are we going?'

'Not to worry, madam.' Quasem found Rehana in his rear-view mirror and gave her a small wave. 'We'll be there soon.'

A few minutes later, after crossing a set of railroad tracks, they turned and stopped beside a small booth. A man in an army uniform peered through the blackened window.

'Window down!' he barked, spraying spit on to the glass.

Rehana was struggling with the handle when Quasem interrupted.

'Don't you see the fucking plate!' he called out from his side.

The soldier stepped in front of the car and examined the number plates. Then he returned to Rehana's window and continued to peer in. 'Who is the passenger?'

'Sister of Barrister Haque.'

'Who? I have to check the register,' he said.

'Don't you know our own people, sister-fucker! We pass this checkpoint every day. Suddenly you don't know the car? You want me to get out and teach you a lesson?'

The soldier paused for a moment; then he shrugged, as though it hadn't mattered to him in the first place. 'OK, go. But we have to report.' And he rapped on the black windscreen with the wooden handle of his gun.

'Don't worry, madam,' Quasem said as they sped away, 'there's no problem.'

Faiz and Parveen lived in Gulshan. It was at the opposite end of town, edging across the northern periphery of the city, past the airport and the army cantonment. Gulshan was newer and even less settled than Dhanmondi; the plots were bigger, the fields between them vast and waterlogged. There was a lake. Faiz's house was off the main road on a street lined with old trees. The house itself was invisible behind a high gate and solid brick fencing. A darwaan opened the gate, and then they were in the half-circle of the driveway, which led them to the front door, a wide, dark purple teak against a black-and-white chequered patio.

Rehana rang the doorbell. A tinny, fake-bird sound echoed through the house. Then the clatter of shoes on an expensive floor. A few seconds later the door swung open, and Parveen appeared, presenting Rehana with a warm, open-mouthed smile.

'As-Salaam Alaikum,' she crooned. She wore a gauzy, canary-yellow chiffon. Around her neck was a string of fat, rolling pearls. Her lips were shiny and parted with lipstick. With a start Rehana realized that she had pulled up the achol of her sari so that it covered her head. The chiffon headdress made her look like Grace Kelly. Has there been some sort of decree, Rehana wondered, no more bare-headed ladies in Dhaka?

'Walaikum As-Salaam,' she replied.

'Please,' Parveen said with excessive tenderness, 'come in. I'm just so happy to see you.' They began to walk through a brilliant white corridor. 'It's been — so busy — I've been meaning to call, and when you did I was just thinking of you and wondering why you sent the children to Karachi — they're perfectly safe, with Faiz's influence, no one would ever harm them — and anyway, this will blow over in no time — tea? Abdul! Abdul!'

Abdul, the old servant, wore a pair of smudged gloves and a hand-me-down suit. The trousers were rolled up to reveal the twin

235

twigs of his bare feet.

'My bhabi is here,' Parveen announced when Abdul appeared. He nodded with his eyes fixed on the floor. 'Bring some tea — the English tea — and the biscuits in the round tin — not the crackers, the *biscuits* — he always confuses them.' She led Rehana into a sunny sitting room and sat her on a large, sinking armchair. At the back of the room a wall of windows overlooked the garden, a tangle of trees and bushes that stretched back into the distance, blocking out the city.

'I knew you'd like the view,' Parveen said, pleased with her own forethought.

'It's a beautiful garden,' Rehana replied.

'I can't take any credit. The trees must have been here since the British. I didn't think I'd like living so far from town, but it's very peaceful here. And lots of new houses going up. This one was just finished.'

Rehana registered the astringent smell and the bluish tinge of the walls. Aside from the armchair she sat in and its matching sofa, on which Parveen was birdily perched, there was just a round brass-topped table.

'We're still moving in,' Parveen said, noting the swivel of Rehana's gaze, 'it's still in such a state.'

'It's lovely. Very spacious.'

The empty walls reverberated with Abdul's scattered foot-steps.

'Have you had any news of Sohail?'

'Yes, he's well mahshallah.'

'Is he staying with one of your sisters?'

236

'No.' Rehana had rehearsed this. 'No, he's with a school-friend. You know how children are — always preferring their friends. A friend from Shaheen School. They haven't seen each other in years but always exchanged letters.'

'Yes, of course,' Parveen said. 'That Sohail. Such a popular young man. Always surrounded by people. Who would have thought, na, he was such a quiet little boy.'

It was always a dangerous thing, their shared past, but Rehana wanted to sweeten Parveen. 'Yes, you're right. He was very quiet. He's changed — once he discovered books, suddenly he couldn't stop talking.'

'I've heard he gave some pukkah speeches at the university!'

Rehana was wary of being baited. Sohail's speeches had titles like 'Peking or Moscow? Third World Socialisms' and 'Jinnah: Statesman or Imperialist Demagogue?'

'And his poetry!' Parveen gushed.

'Yes,' she said, 'he does have a knack for recitation.'

'What was that Ghalib he did for us? *Na tha kutch tho Khuda tha . . .* ' she began in broken Urdu. She proceeded with a blundered rendition of the poem.

'Excellent. What a wonderful voice you have.'

Parveen's gaze descended from the distance and landed on Rehana. 'Thank you. People often say that — it was all those years of acting study.' Rehana was always amazed by people who managed to multiply, rather than deny, compliments to themselves.

'And what about Maya?' she asked, and again Rehana conjured the speech she had practised.

'Maya is in Calcutta,' she began.

'Oh? Why?'

'I still have some relatives there — my father's people. And they were eager to see her.'

'I thought you'd sent her to Karachi.'

'No — well, it was closer,' Rehana grimaced a little to indicate it also had something to do with money, which Parveen pounced upon.

'But you should have told us — '

'I couldn't impose.'

'We're always here to help.'

'Actually, there was something — '

'Abdul — the tea, what's keeping you?'

Abdul entered the room sleekly and set the tray down on the brass table-top without a rattle, for which he was rewarded with a nod from Parveen.

'Pour,' she said, handing the biscuits to Rehana. Rehana chose one from the proffered tin and admired, through crumby lips, the buttery crunch.

'Now that your brother is . . . in a *position*, we are allowed these small indulgences. And well deserved, wouldn't you say? In times like these?'

Rehana realized that in this house, the war would be referred to with phrases such as 'times like these' and 'troubled times', as though God had sent these times to them without warning and through no fault of their own.

'Yes, difficult times, I know.'

Footsteps. Rehana's stomach lurched as Faiz paraded into the room with his arms wide, a

238

deep, satisfied smile illuminating the lower half of his face. The top was obscured by a pair of enormous dark glasses.

'Sister!' he boomed festively. 'How wonderful to see you!' Rehana stood up to receive his embrace. He was wearing a stiff white kurta and a matching cap, and he had the faint rosewater and dirty-feet smell of the mosque.

'This is a sight,' Parveen exclaimed, not getting up from her chair. 'You don't know, bhabi, how long it's been since your brother has been home for lunch. It's impossible to get him, even on a Friday.'

'I'm grateful,' Rehana whispered, as Faiz sighed into a chair.

'I wouldn't miss lunch with my bhabi.' He pulled off the glasses and pointed them at Rehana. 'Mahshallah, you're looking very fresh.' He rubbed the bridge of his nose, where the glasses had left their indentations.

Rehana, not sure what to do with the compliment, looked around at Parveen, who had arranged herself on the armrest of the sofa.

'Isn't she looking lovely?' Faiz continued.

'Yes, of course,' Parveen said.

'You know what I admire about you, bhabi. You manage to remain so cheerful despite all your hardships. Being a widow — no fate worse for a woman — and yet here you are, two children, almost grown up — '

'Of course,' Parveen interjected, 'everyone has their suffering. For instance, I was not blessed with children, but you don't see me complaining.'

At once Rehana was reminded of the day she had taken the children from Parveen. Parveen had sobbed and wailed and beaten her chest. She had fallen at Rehana's feet and begged her to let her keep them. *One*, she had said, please, let me have one. Sohail, she said, I want a son. I want the boy. And Rehana had left her there, rolling back and forth on the pink marble floor as though putting out a fire, and all Rehana could think was, poor girl, she'll catch cold. And Abdul was there, and he had opened the door for her and she had marched through it, a child in each hand, holding on for dear life.

Rehana pulled self-consciously at her grey organza. Faiz combed his moustache with his thumb and forefinger.

'Well,' he said finally, 'how are my niece and nephew?'

Rehana repeated the stories, careful to add a few new details. Schoolfriend from Shaheen Secondary. Nice boy, studies accounting in Karachi.

'Mahshallah!' Faiz said. 'Thank God the boy has the sense to stay out of trouble. It's not safe for the young men.'

Because you kidnap and mutilate them, Rehana thought. 'Yes, that is why I insisted,' she said.

Faiz raised one hand, palm upturned. 'Bad influences.' Repeating the gesture with his other hand, he said, 'Impressionable youth — and you have what we have now.'

Genocide?

'Gondogol!' Troubled times. Parveen's arm

240

snaked into her husband's kurta pocket and emerged with a square silver case. Faiz ignored her as she pressed a switch and snapped the case open. Then she pulled out a cigarette, holding it up between two loudly manicured fingers.

As she raised her hand to her lips, Rehana found herself gawking.

'Really, bhabi, don't look so shocked.'

Faiz, ignoring Parveen, continued his speech. 'The integrity of Pakistan is at stake.' He leaned towards Rehana and the hot steam of his breath passed over her.

'National integrity, religious integrity, this is what we are fighting for. We are the freedom fighters.'

'Lunch, sir,' Abdul interrupted.

'Ah, lunch. Come, Rehana, let's eat together.'

As they moved to the dining room, Faiz gripped Parveen tightly at the elbow. Rehana, walking behind them, pretended not to notice the pink patches Faiz was leaving on his wife's arm. 'Put it out,' he muttered.

'I have nothing better to do,' she replied, louder than she needed to. Her hollow womb shouted its presence.

★ ★ ★

The table, an enormous teak plank, was set for three.

'You shouldn't have gone to such trouble,' Rehana said to Parveen, taking in the row of dishes.

'I didn't make a thing — didn't even plan the

241

menu. It's the cook that comes with this place. Making me fat.' And she patted her slate-like belly.

'Please, sit,' Faiz said, waving to his left.

Rehana examined the spread. There was an oily eelish curry and an even oilier rui. There were two preparations of chicken: mussalam and korma. And, stretching to the end of the table, polao, a steaming bowl of dal, several bhortas, salad and a dish of pickles.

'Start with the fish, Rehana, it's fresh — caught today,' Faiz said.

There had been no fish — certainly no eelish — in the market for months. Rehana's teeth ached.

'These youths,' Faiz said, after Abdul had served the rice, 'young Turks — are fighting for what? A useless battle. You think Mujib cares about them? He is just getting fat on his paycheck from India. The point is, Pakistan must not be divided! What do you say, sister?'

The bite of eelish Rehana had taken stuck drily in her throat. She asked God to forgive her. She nodded. 'Yes,' she managed, 'you're right.'

'Pakistan Zindabad!' Parveen proclaimed, the Grace Kelly veil falling to her shoulders.

While Faiz's fingers were still dipping into the sludge of dal on his plate, Rehana decided to take her chance.

She cleared her throat. Her own plate was still crowded with food. She pushed the rice and fish to the side, to make it look as though she had finished eating. 'Faiz, bhaiya, I've actually come to ask you for a favour.'

'Of course!' Faiz said, pulling the napkin from his collar. 'What's mine is yours,' he said, as though there could be no other reason for her visit. 'Let's wash our hands and have some sweets, and you'll have whatever you wish.' He waved in the direction of the kitchen. Abdul appeared with a brass bowl of water and a cake of soap.

★   ★   ★

As they rearranged themselves in the drawing room, Rehana began again. 'The thing is, my neighbour has fallen into some trouble.'

Faiz frowned with his forehead. 'Your neighbour? The Hindus?'

'No, not the Senguptas. They've left.'

'Parveen told me you had Hindu tenants.' Faiz said. 'Now they've gone and what are you supposed to do? No chance you'll find tenants in the middle of this mess. I suppose they didn't even pay you the rent?'

'They were in such a hurry — '

'That is what I always say! Haven't I said this a thousand times, wife, haven't I said it? They don't treat it like their own country. Leaving at the drop of a hat, going off to India — they were never a part of Pakistan. Good riddance to them, I say, let them go back to where they came from. So, you need money, is it?'

'It's my neighbour Mrs Chowdhury.'

'Oh, the famous Mrs Chowdhury,' Parveen said. 'Jaanoo, remember Mrs Chowdhury?' She didn't wait for him to remember. 'You know.'

243

'Yes,' Rehana said.

'And how is dear Mrs Chowdhury?'

It was not going well. 'Mrs Chowdhury has been extremely kind to me over the years,' Rehana said.

'Yes, we know all about that, don't we, jaanoo?'

Faiz patted his wife's knee. 'What's the problem?' he asked, already slightly bored.

'It's her son-in-law.'

'That slip of a girl is married?' Parveen asked.

'She married an officer,' Rehana began.

This elicited a look of mild interest. 'An officer? Who? Do I know him?'

Rehana decided to tell the whole story all at once. 'He was in the Pakistan Army, bhaiya, but he joined the rebellion along with all the other Bengali regiments. He's been fighting. And he's been captured. They've heard he's in Dhaka and I've come to ask you for his release.'

Before the words could settle, Parveen draped a protective arm around her husband. 'You shouldn't have asked, Rehana. This is not something your bhaiya can do for you. Something for you, for the children, of course, but not this.'

'She's right,' Faiz said tersely. 'You shouldn't have asked.'

'This is why you came here? This is why you've come to see us after all this time?' Parveen blew air out of her nose.

'I just — I wanted to help.'

'This woman has been giving you bad advice

244

all these years, and still you prefer to take her side?'

'The poor girl — Silvi — she's desperate — '

'She shouldn't have married a Bengali rebel, then, should she?'

'She didn't know he was going to join the resistance before she met him. Mrs Chowdhury thought she was marrying her daughter to an army officer.'

Something in Faiz's face told Rehana to press on. 'He just got swept up in the thing. What could he do? His entire regiment was rebelling. The boy is weak, actually. He was in the army before the' — she was going to say massacre — 'before *March*, and then he just got swept up.'

'Swept up?'

'Oh, you know, young boys, they don't know what they're doing — you said so yourself, they just go along with whatever everyone else is saying. He's no leader, that boy, he just follows, and now he's gone and got himself into this mess; in fact, you'd really be saving him, you know, you'd be saving him from himself. He would come out of it so grateful to you, and he would know that you, I mean, the army, were here to put things right, to restore order, not to punish anyone. You would be doing us — your country — a great service.' The words were tumbling out of Rehana's mouth; she didn't stop to think or even breathe, just read Faiz's growing interest and mowed forward. 'Perhaps the boy can be saved,' she finished breathlessly.

'Saved?'

'You can save him.'

Faiz considered this for a moment. Parveen rearranged the sari around her head and tried to look righteous.

'How do I know he won't return to the mukti bahini? Isn't it safer to keep the boy in custody?'

'That's true,' Parveen said, her voice raised high. 'Listen to my husband, Rehana, he understands people.'

'Be quiet, wife, let me think.'

After a suitable pause, Rehana said, 'Have faith, bhaiya. If you save the boy he will be changed. Changed by your generous act. When he sees you opening those gates, he will never want to join that dirty rebellion again.' How easily the treacherous words slid out of her mouth.

★ ★ ★

This time he was waiting for her in Shona's drawing room. He sat on the sofa facing the door with his leg propped up on a cushion. He was wearing a new shirt.

'What happened?' he asked.

'He said yes!'

He shifted his leg so that it pointed to her; his heel was scrubbed clean, pinkish and smooth. 'He could still change his mind. It could be a trap.'

'I'm telling you I fooled them,' Rehana said. 'They had no idea!'

'I don't think it's safe.'

He was beginning to sound like Iqbal. Here she was, triumphant — over Faiz and Parveen, how sweet! — and all he could talk about was safety. She felt her face warming up. 'You said joining the rebellion was the greatest thing you've ever done — well, this is the greatest thing I've ever done. Something for my son. Can't you understand that?'

He seemed to consider it. Then he said, 'Risk is too great. Aren't you doing enough?' He moved his arm to indicate Shona, the guerrillas she had harboured, himself.

'No,' she said, angry now, 'I'm not doing enough. I want to do my part. Maybe it's not for my son — maybe it's something else. What, you don't think I can love something other than my children? I can. I can love other things.'

'But not as much.'

She was startled by this wisdom. Peering into her as though she were a pool of water. 'No, not as much.'

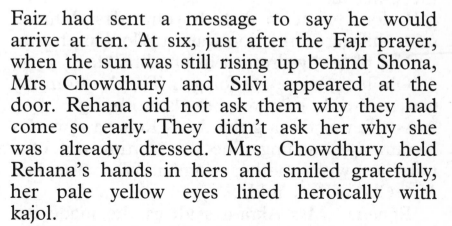

Faiz had sent a message to say he would arrive at ten. At six, just after the Fajr prayer, when the sun was still rising up behind Shona, Mrs Chowdhury and Silvi appeared at the door. Rehana did not ask them why they had come so early. They didn't ask her why she was already dressed. Mrs Chowdhury held Rehana's hands in hers and smiled gratefully, her pale yellow eyes lined heroically with kajol.

'Let's have breakfast.' Rehana said.

'Yes, what a good idea. Silvi, help your khala-moni in the kitchen.'

'What shall we have? Egg paratha?' Rehana knew how to crack an egg in the middle of a paratha without breaking it.

They had just settled themselves around the table when there was a hesitant knock at the door. Rehana went to answer and found Mrs Rahman, wearing a pink cotton sari and holding a few stems of rojonigondha in her hands. The flowers smelled innocent. The grey at Mrs Rahman's temples stood out like steel wings. All this time she's been dyeing her hair, I didn't know! Rehana smiled at the new knowledge. It all felt like such a long time ago.

'Why didn't you tell me?' Mrs Rahman asked. She looked wounded. 'I didn't know you were so involved.'

Rehana didn't know what to say.

'I could have helped.'

'I rang them,' Mrs Chowdhury said, approaching from behind Rehana. 'Aren't you going to invite her in?'

'I don't want to disturb you,' Mrs Rahman said, shifting in the doorway, still looking hurt.

'No, please, we're just having breakfast.'

'Oh, here, these are for you. They're from my garden. I didn't know what else to bring.'

As she was closing the door, Rehana saw Mrs Akram approaching. She was getting out of a rickshaw with another woman. Who else had Mrs Chowdhury told?

'Rehana,' Mrs Akram said, as she made her way up the driveway, 'Mrs Chowdhury told us

248

you were going to rescue Sabeer. This is Mrs Imam. Her husband was also taken.'

★ ★ ★

Rehana taught Silvi how to plunge the paratha in the hot oil, wait until it was almost crisp, then tip the egg into its centre. Mrs Imam was bringing the egg paratha in batches from the kitchen. The guests sat in a circle in the drawing room and said very little. After serving the tea, Rehana realized they were waiting for her to say something. Something brave and defiant, something to temper the images of horror stored in their hearts — the deaths of strangers, the sounds of tanks rattling through the city, the rap at the door, the rap of the bullet, the dull, heavy sound of a lover, a son, falling to the ground.

'I can only hope,' she said, 'that if my son were in danger, someone — perhaps one of you — would come to his rescue.'

★ ★ ★

The egg-paratha finished, Rehana passed around a plate of wrapped betel. The party quieted down into a lazy mid-morning hush. Now would be a good time to make her escape.

'Time to go, I think,' she said to no one in particular. Mrs Chowdhury, red-lipped and drowsy from the betel, was sprawled across the sofa. Eggy plates and empty glasses were scattered around the room.

Rehana was about to bid them all farewell

when a car sounded in the distance and fired its horn.

Mrs Chowdhury was suddenly galvanized into action. 'He's here!' she cried. 'Hurry up, your brother is here. You should go now. Get ready and stand by the gate so you don't keep him waiting.'

The women roused themselves and shuffled towards the door. Rehana waited for them to say their goodbyes, but they just moved into the driveway and stood looking at her.

'Please,' she said, feigning politeness, 'don't wait for me.'

'Nothing doing,' Mrs Chowdhury said, 'we'll see you off.' The others nodded in assent.

'We'll wait,' Mrs Rahman said. 'It's the least we can do.'

'But I — please, don't trouble yourselves.'

'We're staying,' Mrs Chowdhury said, relishing her own magnanimity, 'don't argue, girl.'

'All right; I just, I just have to change my shoes.'

'Go, go! Hurry up!'

Rehana hesitated. 'I'll just be a minute.'

In the bedroom she regarded the shoes absurdly, finally settling on a brown pair with a short, square heel. She had put on a navy-blue cotton sari and, at the last minute, a pair of gold jhumka earrings.

'All right,' she announced brightly, 'I'm ready.'

'Go on, then, you don't want to be late,' Mrs Chowdhury said, a heavy hand upon her wrist.

Rehana made her way to the gate, the small

party trundling behind her. Silvi took Rehana's arm and began to mutter softly in her ear:

La te huzuhu sinetun wala nawmun,
Lahu ma fissemawati wa ma fil'ardi.
(No slumber can seize Him, nor sleep,
All things in heaven and earth are His.)

They were at the gate. 'I've — I've forgotten something.'

Rehana slid past their surprised faces; she heard Mrs Chowdhury say, 'Poor thing must be nervous,' and she thought she heard Mrs Akram ask, 'Has she changed her mind?' And then she was too far away to hear the answer. She fled, past the driveway and through the drawing room, unlatching the small veranda gate, hurtling through the wet sheets hanging like surrender flags. She fumbled with her keychain, cursing her slow fingers, and finally pushed open the lock of Shona's back door.

* * *

The Major was waiting, dressed in the uniform in which he had arrived; she had stitched the trousers back together with bottle-green thread. He stood up, his gaze fixed on her as though she had been there before she arrived.

She had rarely seen him standing. She had always hovered above him. She had known the top of his head, the dense thickness of his hair, the meandering seam of his hairline. She had known his face — at least, as far as she

251

had dared to know it.

But, since that first day when they had met and he had taken her palm in his big hand, she had not been confronted with the full, standing presence of him.

The grey flints of his eyes.

The horizon of his chest.

If he had been sitting, she could have pretended he was still her patient, her charge. Standing up, he was a stranger.

The stranger said, 'Don't look anyone in the face.'

She nodded at the stretched-tight fabric of his shirt.

'In fact,' he said, raising his voice, making a little space between them, 'don't say anything. Don't speak at all.'

'All right,' Rehana said.

'Doctor sent a message,' the Major began.

'What?'

'I'm cured. Leg is healed. Time for me to go.'

She felt the weather stirring. She pressed it down. 'Goodbye, then.'

He shook his head. 'I'll stay till you return.'

She shrugged, a show of bravery.

'If you're not back in three hours I'm coming for you.'

'I'm late,' she said, 'everyone is waiting.'

'Khoda Hafez.'

'Khoda Hafez.'

'Fiamanullah.' Godspeed.

★ ★ ★

Quasem did not get out of the car this time. Nor did Faiz. The black Mercedes swallowed Rehana. 'Good morning,' Faiz said solemnly. He wore a coal-coloured suit with a shiny handkerchief tucked into the breast pocket. A lemony scent whispered from the suit. The slicked black hair, thinning at the temple, revealed the rake of a thin comb.

Don't look anyone in the face. Rehana averted her gaze, so that it landed on the back of Quasem's head, square and coconut-oily.

Faiz remained silent. He wore his dark glasses and sat close to the window, holding a newspaper. Rehana was relieved; she didn't feel like talking. She concentrated on what she would find at the police station. Mrs Imam had said her husband's body had never been returned. She tried to school her thoughts.

I'll come for you.

Minutes passed, the city sailing by, washed by the morning's rain. Faiz sat so still and quiet Rehana forgot he was there. Instead she tried to think of old film tunes she used to sing with her father. She couldn't remember any. For some reason 'God Save the King' was circulating in her head, and *Send him victo — rious!*

Faiz was still reading the newspaper. He must have been reading very slowly, because he didn't turn the page.

Hap-py and glo — rious!

At the Tongi light Faiz turned to Rehana and said quietly, 'You lied to me.' His voice was a reedy tremble. She could feel him frowning behind the glasses.

There were so many things he could mean.

'You lied to me. You're a liar.'

'There must be some sort of misunderstanding.'

'You're a liar and a traitor.'

Rehana straightened to face him. He knew something. She ran through the list of possibilities in her head. She determined which would be worst (knowing about Shona), which best (nothing, nothing would be best).

'You're a traitor and your children are traitors. What do you have to say for yourself — do you deny it?'

Rehana didn't deny it.

'You come to *my* house . . . '

It wasn't what's mine is yours any more.

' . . . you nod your head when I talk about Pakistan and inside you're stabbing your country in the back!' There were two white points of spittle gathering at the corners of his mouth.

'I don't know what you're talking about,' Rehana said.

'You're going to deny it? To my face?'

'What I mean is, there must be some sort of misunderstanding,' she repeated.

'Misunderstanding?' He shook his hand at her. The newspaper flapped in his fist. 'I'm reading the paper this morning. I'm reading this traitorous rubbish, about how brave, how valiant, are the muktis, and how corrupt the Pakistan Army is — then the heading catches my eye — and what do I see — what? My niece — that girl of yours — it's her! Sheherezade Haque Maya, that ridiculous name my brother gave her

— the name of a *storyteller*, you said. Well she certainly has made up a story — lies, full of lies — '

The hand with the newspaper continued to shake.

Rehana pressed her back against the seat and resisted the urge to close her eyes.

'LIAR!' He hurled the newspaper so that it landed at her feet.

She thought he meant to throw it, but when she left it there he said, 'READ!'

She picked up the newspaper and read. 'Chronicles of a Young Woman in Wartime. By Sheherezade Haque Maya.' It isn't her, Rehana wanted to say, but a smile, unbidden, crawled into her lips. She covered her mouth with the back of her hand.

'I shouldn't have lied to you,' she said.

'I won't begin to count the things you *shouldn't* have done. You should have controlled your daughter.'

'It's not her fault.'

'How do you explain this? You let Maya join the resistance? At least your son had more sense.'

So he didn't know about Sohail.

'What have you done with my brother's children? We should never have let you take them. You ruined them.' He leaned into her, so that she could see her own reflection, her forehead bulging in the sunglasses.

Rehana felt guilty at the mention of Iqbal; she realized she hadn't thought of him in some time. A long time. It's been so busy, and so strange, she told herself. And then she wondered if there wasn't something more to it. Would she be here if Iqbal were alive? Would she be here, asking Faiz to release Sabeer? Would she be allowed to want something dangerous? Or would she have learned to want what her husband wanted?

She was relieved she didn't have to know. She wouldn't have to know if Iqbal would have had the strength to stay in Dhaka, or if the children would have inherited his small, anxious world. Her head began to spin with the thought of all the things that might have been different. Now she was remembering the cloud of his fears, the orbit of worry, the nervous, scared man who had tried his best not to upset fate, to live without danger, without risk. Had she ever wondered what life would have been like without him, and had she rejoiced, even a little, when he had died? Despite the bone-breaking grief, had there also been release?

She wanted to pretend it wasn't true, but it was.

'Now see what you've done,' Faiz was saying.

What could it be that moved Faiz to believe the opposite of what she believed? How could he be on the other side of her black-and-white? She could imagine herself believing nothing else; it was as plain to her as God.

He was not a bad man.

It was time to tell the truth.

'I sent her there. To Calcutta, to join the muktis.'

The spittle points grew. 'You *sent* her there?' He let out an angry breath. 'You tell me everything. Right now.'

256

Quasem's shoulders were hunched up against his ears, as though he was trying not to hear.

Rehana saw Faiz's chin quiver in anger. Time to tell the truth.

'I'm sorry I lied. I shouldn't have lied — '

'You should be ashamed of yourself.'

'But I'm not ashamed.' Rehana swallowed a few times to steady herself. 'She had a friend who was captured by the army in March. The girl's name was Sharmeen.'

'What does that have to do with anything?'

'You listen to me. Her name was Sharmeen. They took her and they kept her at the cantonment — not a mile from your house. And the girl was tortured until she died. They did things — unspeakable things — to her. She was the same age as Maya. How do you explain that?'

'I don't have to explain these things to you.'

'How? You think I could look my daughter in the eye and tell her it was all right?'

'So you sent her to the muktis?'

'I should not be ashamed; you should be ashamed.'

'You don't know anything.' He turned his face away from her. She saw the square chin, the one that marked him as the older, more confident brother. 'It's nonsense.' And then: 'The girl was a casualty of war. When you believe in something, certain things have to be sacrificed.'

'Children?'

'There are always casualties.'

'I thought there was a chance you didn't know what the army was doing. But now I'm telling you. You can wash your hands of it. Surely you don't want this on your conscience?'

With his index finger Faiz loosened the knot at his neck. Rehana thought she saw a flicker of doubt.

The car slowed to a halt. 'Sir,' Quasem said, 'Mirpur Thana.'

Faiz seemed to consider something. He paused while Rehana gathered her handbag. Then he said, 'Go.'

'Where?'

'The police station is over there.' He pointed to a low building across a field.

'You're not coming with me?'

'I'm not a cruel man, bhabi. You remember that. Now you go and rescue the man yourself. I can't risk having anything to do with you — if I hadn't already sent the release order, I would send you home right now.' He dipped his hand into his jacket and pulled out an envelope. 'Show them this.'

'But I — you want me to go there alone?'

'I'm not making this my business any more.' And he swivelled his face so that she was left looking at the thinning blackness of his hair.

She turned to leave. Suddenly all the possible consequences of his knowing collapsed upon her. 'Are you going to tell anyone? About Maya?'

'You should have thought of that when you let her print this garbage,' he said roughly, still looking away.

He hadn't answered the question. He could do anything, now that he knew. It would be easy to find out Sohail wasn't really in Karachi. And all

258

he had to do was arrive at Shona in the middle of the day to discover the Major. 'Don't forget she's your niece. Your blood,' Rehana said. She wanted him to turn around, so she could read something in his face. But he had dismissed her.

Rehana stumbled out of the car. The door slammed shut behind her. Quasem gave her a brief, apologetic smile, and then the car careened away, leaving her in its choking, dusty wake.

Rehana clutched the envelope in one hand and straightened her sari. She considered hailing a rickshaw and going home. Mrs Chowdhury would understand. She looked down the road, towards Dhanmondi, but she couldn't get Sohail's pleading face out of her head. So she made her way across the washed field, stopping occasionally to readjust her ankle strap.

★   ★   ★

High above, the sky thickened and the air swirled in a leisurely trance. It was an hour, maybe two, before the noon shower. As she approached the entrance to the thana, Rehana realized she had forgotten to rehearse what she would say. She paused outside the door, which had a rusted metal handle dulled by the press of palm prints. The field had soaked her shoes. As she opened her handbag to check for the bundle Mrs Chowdhury had given her, she shifted on her feet and tried to shake away the crawling damp. The sight of the bundle, rolled up comfortably in its rubber band, reassured her. She took a deep breath and prepared to enter. She was about to reach for the handle when the door swung open. A tall, bearded man in a military uniform stood there. He gave her a look of mild bemusement and brushed past her with a brief 'Excuse me' in Urdu. And he stepped aside to let her pass.

Rehana crossed a dark corridor and arrived at a large, windowless room. At one end of the room was a bald man behind an enormous glass-topped table. Metal chairs were arranged in rows in front of the desk. Anxious, silent people sat in the chairs. She felt their eyes on her as she made her way to the glass-topped desk. The whirr of the ceiling fan above the desk was accompanied occasionally by the creak of the bald man's chair as he shifted his weight this way and that. As she approached him, he looked up from under a pair of heavy eyebrows.

'I need to speak with someone,' Rehana said. Her voice came out louder than she had intended.

'Take your form and wait over there,' the man said absently, pointing with his chin.

'Form?'

'Prisoner Visit Form — here.' He handed her a soggy sheet of paper.

'I'm — I'm not here to visit.'

His head snapped up. 'Then what?' Betel juice had stained his lips a sunrise orange.

'I'm here — to release a prisoner.'

'*You're* here' — he laughed an orange saliva laugh — 'to release a prisoner?' Tiny orange dots of spittle fell on to the Prisoner Visit Form. 'Who are you, Police Commissioner? *You* don't release prisoners, *we* release prisoners — understand?'

260

He wore a police-blue uniform, tight at the armpits and the collar. Over the back of his chair, where his head would usually rest, was a pink-and-white striped towel. The man turned to the towel and wiped the betel spittle from his mouth.

Rehana held out the envelope Faiz had given her. 'I have a release order,' she said.

'Let me see that.' He pulled it roughly from her hand. 'Sabbeer Mus-tafa,' he said. He turned to an enormous notebook and began to shuffle through the curling pages. Rehana leaned as closely as she dared. The book gave off a sweaty smell. He ran his finger down a list of printed names.

'He isn't here.'

'What? Are you sure?'

The man turned the register around impatiently. 'Do you see his name?' he said, before snapping it shut with a clap.

'Please,' Rehana said, 'check again.'

The book remained closed. 'I said he's not here. You're wasting your time.'

Rehana pulled out the bundle of Mrs Chowdhury's sugar money. She unwrapped it slowly, making sure the man could see the rupee notes. She pulled out fifty. 'Check again,' she said, mustering her courage.

He grabbed the money with five fingers, shoving it into a gaping breast pocket, and reopened the notebook. After a brief pause he said, 'Yes. Mustafa. Released — no, transferred.' He raised an eyebrow. 'To Muslim Bazaar.'

'Muslim Bazaar? Another thana?'

He smiled, revealing a set of stripy teeth. 'No. It's not a thana.'

'What is it? How will I find it?'

'I can't help you any more.' He shook his head and waved her away. Rehana didn't budge. She felt the row of chairs shift behind her. The man opened a drawer and pulled out what looked like a folded handkerchief. He unwrapped it, revealing a stack of heart-shaped leaves. He peeled one off the stack and placed it lovingly on the glass counter. Rehana watched him unscrew the lid from a small round tin. He snapped off the stem of the betel leaf and plunged it into the tin, emerging with a glob of white paste. This he smeared on the leaf. Then he added a pinch of shredded betel nut and a pinch of chewing tobacco, finishing the job with a few folds of the leaf and popping the triangular packet into his mouth.

Rehana let him chew the paan until it settled into a round bulge in his cheek. Then she said, reaching into her bag again, 'Perhaps you can telephone someone at Muslim Bazaar and ask them.'

The door opened behind Rehana. The man quickly swallowed his paan and tented his fingers on the desk. He cleared his throat. 'As I was saying, the prisoner is not here.'

'Kuddus?' Rehana heard. She turned around to see the man she had passed on her way inside. 'Ei Kuddus,' he said in rough Bengali, 'cha do.'

Kuddus disappeared for a few minutes, came back and squeezed into his chair.

'Boss likes the Chinese tea,' he said, sounding

a little embarrassed. He rubbed his hands on his trousers.

Rehana was ready with another fifty. 'Can you ask someone to bring him here?' She pressed the note on to the glass.

The Chinese tea had made allies of them. 'I'll see,' he said. He picked up the heavy black telephone and turned the dial. 'Hullo? Inspector Kuddus. Mirpur Thana. There's a woman here. Says she has a release order. Sabeer Mustafa. Was here — he's been transferred to you. Hold on? OK. Who's this? Oh, yes, sorry, sir. Sir, the woman is asking — yes, yes of course. I'll tell her. Ji. Khoda Hafez, sir. Ji, sir, Pakistan Zindabad.' He turned slowly to Rehana.

'You'll have to go over there yourself,' he said, almost regretfully. 'They have to see the paperwork. I'll send word. They'll be expecting you. You can catch a rickshaw — tell them Muslim Bazaar, the pump house. They all know it.'

'Thank you,' Rehana said.

'No problem. Best of luck.' Kuddus looked her over and nodded. Then his face changed as he pointed over Rehana's shoulder. 'Sen?' he said, 'Mr and Mrs Sen?'

An elderly couple approached the desk, their heads tilted towards one another, the woman holding a tiffin carrier. Rehana heard the slosh of something liquid inside the tiffin carrier and conjured up an image of this woman's son, sinking his grateful hands into his mother's dal.

'You can go in now.' Kuddus stood up and unhooked a circle of keys from his belt. 'Come with me.' They left together. Rehana heard the clang of the gate as he locked it behind him.

★ ★ ★

Outside, it was raining. Thick sheets of water fell heavily from the sky, hardened by a bellowing, circular wind. The sucking sound of her feet accompanied Rehana as she made her way back across the field and on to the main road. An uneven line of tea stalls greeted her at the roadside, surrounded by a cluster of rickshaws. Rehana tried her best to cover her head with her achol, but it was no use; the wind attacked from all sides, knocking the achol out of her hand and sending her flailing to gather her sari together.

She ducked under the slim awning of the nearest stall, where she saw a group of men sitting cross-legged on the raised floor, their faces lit red by a flickering kerosene lamp.

'Muslim Bazaar? Keo jabe? Anyone?' The stall smelled of biscuits and petrol.

They were saying something to one another. Rehana couldn't hear through the drumming rain on the tin roof. One of them, the youngest and smallest, uncrossed his legs and rose. 'Bokul will take you,' a man at the back said, motioning towards the boy with the burning point of his biri. Bokul packed and tucked his lungi between his legs. He looked like he was down to his underwear, but Rehana was beyond embarrassment; her sari was moulded to her body, and she didn't let herself look down to see what had happened to the colour. At least

264

the rickshaw-men had the decency to gaze into the kerosene lamp rather than to look at her directly.

'Wait here,' the boy said, darting out of the shop. Rehana watched him struggle with the hood of a rickshaw; once he had secured it, he pulled a sheet of plastic from under the seat. 'Ashen! Come quick!'

Rehana clung to the scalloped rim of the rickshaw hood as Bokul pumped mechanically through the rain. He stopped just once, to yank the front wheel out of a flooded ditch. She couldn't see anything, she was only aware of the driving, unceasing rain, of the sari clinging to her and the violent wind, which made her shiver and wish desperately for a change of clothes. She ignored the street names and stopped looking for familiar landmarks. The trees glistened in the wet.

Bokul stopped in front of a square concrete building. The building had a high, triangular roof made of wavy sheets of tin. A faded sign painted on the tin read INDIA GYMNASIUM. As she made her way out of the rickshaw, Rehana gave Bokul twenty rupees. 'I'll have another twenty for you when I come out. You wait here for me,' she said, shouting above the roar of the rain. 'You wait here, no matter how long it takes. An hour, two hours — anything — you wait, you hear me?'

Bokul nodded. 'Ji, apa!' he said.

* * *

265

In the third hour of her vigil, Rehana began to worry about food. She had no idea what time it was. She was hungry; it must be after lunch. She berated herself for not packing a biscuit in her bag. She couldn't be seen fainting. The rain made it difficult to determine the hour; the sun was blotted out by the grey mass of clouds that sat low on the horizon. Through a narrow, barred window pitched close to the ceiling, Rehana could see it was still pouring steadily. By the time her sari was dry, her eyes were stinging, and there was a dull throbbing in her joints. She folded her knees under her and thought of closing her eyes, just for a moment, just until they stopped burning.

When the guard finally brought Sabeer out, Rehana thought she might be dreaming. She jerked herself upright, ignoring the ache in her arms from where her head had rested. The thana was a dim memory. She wasn't sure how long she'd been asleep. It had stopped raining. The tube light buzzed steadily; it smelled of evening.

There was something black covering his head. A mask — no, a hood. It was pulled tight over his face. She could see his nose, his square chin. He shook his head back and forth, breathing noisily through the gaps in the weave.

He wore no shoes. His soles made sliding tracks in the dirt.

Rehana turned to the man who had brought Sabeer. She saw a sleek black beard. Her gaze travelled upwards. He was very tall. Had she seen this man before? She checked again. *Don't look*. The man smiled briefly. Stop panicking. She held hands with herself to stop from trembling.

'You can take him,' the man said. 'Sign here.' He handed her a form and a pen.

Rehana didn't read the form. 'Can you remove — the hood, please?' she said, scribbling on the sheet. 'And untie him.'

'Of course,' the man said politely.

He undid the knots at Sabeer's wrists. The sleeve of Sabeer's shirt flapped over his hands. The man lifted the hood with a flourish.

Rehana kept looking at Sabeer's face to see if it was him. It was. She recognized the bulge of his Adam's apple, the thickness of his neck. His lips were blistered; a white crust had formed around them, like a ring of coral.

'This woman has brought a release order,' the guard said. 'You can go.'

Sabeer stared blankly at Rehana. 'I'm Rehana — Mrs Haque.'

★   ★   ★

The rain had left the leaves shiny and the air smelling of rust. Rehana and Sabeer said nothing to one another, and she could hear only the movement of his breath, the clouds invisible above, the stars beginning to flicker, the delta beneath them churning and swimming.

'Bokul!' Rehana called out. 'Bokul!' The road was empty and slick. No sign of the rickshaw-boy. She couldn't remember where the main road was. There were no shops here, just an empty stretch of road flanked by dipping telephone wires.

'Sabeer, beta, can you walk a little?'

Sabeer was squatting on the edge of the road like a stray dog, his arms hanging loosely at his sides.

'We have to walk,' she said a little louder.

His head was between his knees.

'Sabeer?'

Rehana heard a sound like a siren coming from his bent head. 'Sabeer?' she repeated. No answer. She pulled at his shoulder. The wailing grew louder; it was high-pitched and alien; a cry with no mouth.

She wasn't sure what to do. He looked so small and insignificant, folded up as though the earth might swallow him; and no one would care that he was gone because he was just a wailing, rocking speck. She crouched awkwardly beside him, wondering whether he could hear her, if he even knew who she was. She felt a sudden, hysterical urge to leave him there and run away.

In the distance she heard the keening of the evening curfew.

'We have to go, Sabeer, please try,' she said. He didn't move. She saw the dirt around his collar, and his neck, grey and tired. Perhaps he was asleep.

'OK. You wait here,' she said finally. 'I'll find something.' She continued to speak to him as if he would answer. It made her feel less alone. 'Stay here. Don't move. You hear me? Don't move. I'll be back.' He didn't shift when she stood up and began to trudge up the broken path.

Rehana walked away from the gymnasium, clutching her handbag, feeling for Mrs Chowdhury's bundle of money. I'll throw this at the next person I see and beg them to take me home. Or anywhere, anywhere away from here.

She turned a wide corner and continued to walk until the gymnasium was out of sight. It was getting darker; without streetlights or a moon it would soon be impossible to see the road in front of her. I should turn around, she thought. Stay with Sabeer, at least I'll have him with me. She was about to go back when she slammed into something.

'Who's there?' she shouted into the gloom. She reached her fingers out in front of her and found the ridge of a rickshaw frame, fanning out like a ribcage.

'Apa, it's me,' someone whispered. It was Bokul.

'Bokul!' Thank God. Rehana wanted to let out a cheer, but instead she said angrily, 'Where in God's name have you been? I told you to wait! I've been walking for miles.'

'They wouldn't let me stay. A man came out of the building with a stick.' She could make out his face now. 'I've been here, waiting.'

Rehana climbed into the seat. 'We have to go back.'

★   ★   ★

Sabeer was not where she had left him.

'Half an hour till the curfew, apa,' Bokul said.

Rehana scanned the area for Sabeer. It was too dark to see anything. 'Sabeer!' she called out, 'Sabeer!' Then she heard a clanging sound coming from the gymnasium. Hands slapping against the door.

Rehana ran towards the gymnasium. She could barely make out his shape; she tried to reach around to his hands. 'Sabeer, quiet! I have a rickshaw. We're going home.'

She grabbed hold of his hand and pulled him towards the rickshaw. Suddenly he let out a scream. 'No, please!' he cried.

Rehana held on, trying to soothe him, stroking the softness of his fingers. 'Beta, cholo, let's go, I'll take you home.' But Sabeer kept screaming and twisting away from her. The sleeve of his shirt peeled away, and she saw that the hand she was holding was dark at the tips. Someone had painted his fingers. Sabeer grunted his animal grunt and said, 'No, please, I didn't do it!' His voice was thick and gummy. Finally Rehana released him, and he sank to his knees and began to sob. 'No, no, no,' he whispered, holding his hands against his chest, 'please.' Rehana bent down and looked closer. The nails were soft and pulpy. Closer. Not nails, just red-tipped fingers. There were no nails. No nails; only red-tipped fingers.

'Oh, God,' Rehana whispered. She was afraid to touch him now, afraid to know what else lay hidden beneath his clothes.

'Apa, I can carry him to the rickshaw.' Bokul

had come up behind her. He squatted in front of Sabeer and cradled his head. He dragged his other arm under Sabeer's knees and rose with a grunt. He was stronger than he looked. Sabeer's head flopped back. Bokul trundled to the rickshaw. 'Can you hold him up?'

Rehana climbed in from the other side and pulled on Sabeer's collar. 'Sit up, please, son, try to sit up.' She felt the tears falling from her eyes. Sabeer's body stiffened a little, and, with both arms around his shoulders, she managed to keep him upright. 'Go, hurry,' she said to Bokul.

'Where do you live?'

'Dhanmondi. Road 5.'

★ ★ ★

All she could think was, I have to see him, just once, just look a little at him. The black hood will disappear, Sabeer will not die, Sabeer is a red-fingered bird, oh, God, just one more time, even if he doesn't say a word, not a word, I won't have to tell him, he'll already know, he'll know before I step through the gate, he'll know before I open my mouth to tell him. I won't tell him about the hood, I won't say it, I won't hope he's still there. I'll imagine he's already left; I'll go home and unroll my prayer mat. I'll ask God to do it. God will do it. I won't ask for anything after that. Just take the man away. Take the man away.

Sabeer is a bird, a red-tipped bird.

He wasn't there. Shona was empty. When her

271

sister Marzia had malaria, Rehana's mother had sat beside the sickbed and said, please, God, take the sickness from her and give it to me. Not my daughter. Give it to me. Now Rehana wanted someone to look after her in the same way. Take it from me. Take his blistered lips. Take his milky, dead eyes. Take his tired breath. Please, oh, God, take his bleeding hands. Take his red-tipped wings. I don't want them. Not me. Take my relief. Take my relief it wasn't Sohail. Take my want, take my want. Take the missed beat when he wasn't there.

She lay down on the pillow, dipped into his scent.

God, she said, the tears flowing freely from her eyes, take my want.

The room spun around. Mrs Sengupta's parents stared down at her from the wall. She closed her eyes and dreamed of a man kneading her shoulder with a rough, callused hand. His hand travelled to her neck, pressing the tendons, pressing until she almost choked; and then the hand was on her shoulder again, and then travelling down the length of her arm, slipping through the hollow between her elbow and her waist.

'Rehana.' She was startled by the sound of her name. Her name was a stranger. 'You were dreaming.'

'No — it was all there — Sabeer — '

'I know.' *I knew you would know!*

The Major's breath was in her hair. She felt the warmth of his belly against her back. She saw his hand, its tense vein, snaking across her waist and holding her down, as if she might float away without its weight.

The burned-rubber scent flooded her nose.

She pressed wet eyes against the pillow. She opened her mouth and swallowed the sob. She felt him knowing everything. This was his gift. Speaking little and knowing more.

His hand tightened, and she tilted backwards, feeling the hard weight of his chest. Brick and breath. The breath burned into her ear.

Her fist closed around the pillowcase.

'Sleep,' he said, 'you can sleep.'

Miraculously, her eyes closed, and she felt her limbs relaxing, and, though her breath was still quick, she drifted into a hard, dreamless sleep.

August,
September,
October

Salt Lake

The sky over Bengal is empty. No mountains interrupt it; no valleys, no hills, no dimples in the landscape. It is flat, like a swamp, or a river that has nowhere to go. The eye longs for some blister on the horizon, some marker of distance, but finds none. Occasionally there are clouds; often there is rain, but these are only colours: the laundry-white of the cumulus, the black mantle of the monsoon.

Beyond the city there are no beautiful buildings that might sink in the heat or wilt under generations of rain. The promise of the land is not in the cities — their sky-touching glamour, the tragedy of their ruin — but in the vast unfolding plains, this empty sky, this stretching horizon. Every year the land will turn to sea as it disappears under the spell of water, and then prevail again, as if by magic, and this refrain, this looping repetition, is the archive of its long, flood-turned history.

It was through this simple, spectacular

landscape that Rehana's train, the 2.55 from Agartala to Calcutta, clattered westwards, chasing the sun. Rehana was in an empty compartment, the open window whipping her hair until it haloed around her face. The long shadows of trees fell across her and moved away, light and dark, back and forth, like piano keys.

She'd had to get out of Dhaka. *It's not safe.* Faiz knew about Maya. Joy and the Major thought she might have been followed. Perhaps the house was being watched. No choice. Make sure it looks as though you'll be gone a long time. So she had locked up the two houses and draped sheets over the furniture — she had seen her father do the same, a long time ago, when they had lost Wellington Square. She wondered if it made her a refugee, this train, this distance, the sheets on the furniture.

She had to take a roundabout route, first travelling east and crossing the border into India, then catching the train to Calcutta. The train journeyed north, passing the remaining stretch of Bengal — the mustard fields, the rice fields, the chilli fields; then the land curved and dimpled as they went west and entered Assam. In the morning she woke to a rolling, jostled landscape painted in the sunwash of early light. The air was crisp and smelled of apples. Hill air.

This semicircular track, now called the Chicken Neck, had been laid by the British, a holiday route carrying memsahibs to their winter destinations: Silchar, Shilliguri, Shillong — hill stations with names like rustled leaves, where clothes did not flap, exhausted, in the humidity, where the air was dry, the lips chapped, the hats possible. It smelled of home.

The light was different here. Without the wet air to temper it, it fell directly from the sky in a brilliant, eye-aching shade, illuminating the hills below, falling on the green that covered everything and the licked, glistening dew.

Rehana turned the words around in her mouth. *I'll come for you.*

She was not a refugee. The bungalow was waiting for her, a padlock on its front door. The kerosene lamps were full. The water pump was hungry. The windows were shut. The curtains were up. The beds were dressed. She had neighbours. Dirty plates. A leg of mutton in the ice-box.

She had taken Sabeer to Mrs Chowdhury's. She had seen Silvi come out to the gate and look at her husband, her grey calf eyes dominating her face, and tiny lines appearing at the corners of her mouth, dragging it downwards.

She had left without saying goodbye.

She had done her duty. She hadn't waited for them to realize what exactly she had brought back from Muslim Bazaar.

★   ★   ★

Rehana put her feet on the bench opposite and took out the stack of letters. They smelled of mothballs. She wondered where Silvi had kept them; perhaps folded between her clothes, between a matching salwaar and kameez, or among her jewellery, or her old schoolbooks. At the last moment, when she'd had to decide what to take and what to leave behind, Rehana could not bear to leave the letters. They were her only concession to nostalgia. The rest of her packing was purely pragmatic: three saris, three blouses, three petticoats, a nightgown, a plastic comb, a thin towel. A blanket. And a plate. Joy had told her to pack a plate.

After she had finished, the Major told her he was not going with her. He would go back to Agartala on his own. 'It's safer for you that way. Maya will meet you in Calcutta. Everything's been arranged.' She saw the slight tremble of his eyelids; battling feeling; winning.

Rehana unscrewed the cap and took a sip from her flask. How very close it is to illness. The loose, restless limbs. The feverish cheeks. The burning salt of the heart. The prickle of sweat. *Love*.

She remembered a line from Ghalib. *Zindagi yun bhi guzar hi jaati*. Life would have gone on; somehow it would have passed, unstirred, predictable, and without this, the weather in her kicked up.

As the train turned south towards Calcutta, the monsoon fields returned. Rehana gazed out on to the waterlogged landscape. The land was divided into rectangular plots of rice, framed by a raised mud bank the width of a footprint. Different stages of growth were segregated in the plots: there were the pale, tiny shoots the colour of limes, which would be pulled and replanted when they grew waist high; and then the established shoots, denser and slightly darker;

280

and finally the milk-toned paddy, ready to be harvested. The plots were miniature islands, each in its own flooded pool; together they were a chequered palette of green and gold.

The weather changed, and suddenly the sky was the colour of washed slate. Slanted sheets of rain began to pour through Rehana's open window. She stood up and struggled with the latch, until the window fell down with a clap upon its groove. And then there was only the sound of the train itself, the looping wheels on the track, the water falling onto the window like tapping fingers, and everything blue-black: the wood of the bench, the low-hanging clouds outside, the rattle of the window in its frame.

★   ★   ★

The train approached Shialdah Station, grunting to a halt. When the doors opened, Rehana tumbled out with her bag. It was like being thrown into a roiling human sea. People were everywhere, choked together in a dense blur. She pushed through and made her way to the end of the platform, tiptoeing to see over the mass of faces. How would Maya ever find her? She found a few inches of space in front of a bench and sat down on her bags. After a few minutes she began to distinguish the different categories of traveller. There were the just-arrived ones, wearing the same ragged, anxious expression as herself; and the recently arrived, still hanging around the station, waiting for something to happen, for someone to pick

281

them up, or to tell them what to do now that they had made it to Calcutta; and those who had arrived weeks, months, ago, who realized that there was nowhere beyond the station, no other possible home, and so had remained there, lying down on the platform in jagged, uneven rows. Their blankets covered their faces; they had lost hope of being picked up and taken anywhere else. Whether it was day or night, time for sleep or not, they lay there, in masks of death, carving out their shroud-like places on the platform.

'Mrs Haque?' A young man with a friendly gap between his teeth called out to Rehana. He shuffled towards her on squat legs. 'You're Mrs Haque?'

Rehana wasn't sure whether to answer. She managed a hesitant 'Yes?'

'Remarkable resemblance! Even in this crowd I recognized you.' He grinned, incongruous in this mess of lost bodies.

'You are . . . ?'

'Mukul, Auntie, I'm here to collect you. Maya-di couldn't come; she's very sorry, she sent me. I'll take you straight to the office — she's waiting.'

Rehana was too tired to question the boy further; and here he was, wrestling the bag out of her hands, pushing cheerfully through the crowd, leading her outside, where the heat pulsed through the open mouth of the station entrance.

Mukul's car was a yellow Volkswagen Beetle. Someone had thought of painting the bumper to match. Through the opening of doors and lifting of bags, he began a monologue that lasted until he'd pulled down the brake and jerked the car into motion. 'Please, sit comfortably at the back — front seat is full of rubbish — well, not rubbish exactly, pamphlets — I was supposed to deliver them before I came to collect you but the roads were chock-a-block and I didn't want to be late!'

'Thank you for coming,' Rehana said.

'It's an honour, Auntie. I've heard all about you from Maya,' he said, catching Rehana's eye in the rear-view.

'Oh, really?' Rehana muttered, trying to shield her eyes from the afternoon glare.

'Yes, of course,' he answered. 'Why not? You are an example to all of us. A hero!' The car sped past a flooded pavement and splashed a huddle of schoolboys.

'Your first time in Calcutta?' Mukul asked, swivelling around to face her.

'Um, no actually, I used to live here.'

'Really?' Mukul asked. 'Where? Which neighbourhood?'

Rehana was too taken aback to give him a fake address. 'Wellington Square.'

'Wellington Square? My goodness, your people must be rich.'

The Volkswagen hiccuped down the narrow city roads. Rehana kept the window rolled up, but even through the glass she could make out the mud-and-rotten-vegetable smell of Calcutta. She heard the clatter of the tongas, the shuffle of roasting peanuts. She fixed her eyes on her lap and resisted the temptation to look at her old home.

I have not returned to Calcutta, she told herself, I have not returned to Calcutta.

By the time her marriage to Iqbal had been arranged, she was desperate to leave. One by one her sisters had been married and shipped to Karachi. The house in Wellington Square was long gone, and they had rented a flat above a dusty bookshop on College Street. Every morning her father would go down into the bookstore and announce the names of the titles he used to own. '*Great Expectations!*' he would shout. '*Akbar-nama. Tales of the Alhambra.*'

Mukul's car shuddered to a halt in front of a two-storey house. A rectangular patch of garden was laid out in front like a welcome mat. The sign above the gate read NUMBER 8, THEATRE ROAD.

'Auntie,' Mukul said, 'please go ahead. I'll park the car and bring your jeeneesh-potro.'

'It's all right — just a small bag — I'll bring it in myself.' Rehana climbed gratefully out of the car.

The office door was open, and she could hear the clatter of typewriters inside, and the screech of a radio being tuned. She stepped over the threshold and entered a high-ceilinged room that smelled of cobwebs and newsprint. A bright strip of tubelights gave the room its official, fluorescent-wash feeling.

'Ma!' Maya ploughed into Rehana's chest, knocking the breath out of her. Then she grabbed her by the shoulders, pushed her away

284

and scanned her face with a giant smile. 'Ammoo!' Then she was pulling her close again, and Rehana thought she heard a sniffle as Maya buried her face in Rehana's sari. 'I'm so sorry I couldn't come to the station — the Soviets signed the treaty, can you believe it? How are you, Ma, I've missed you' — she waved her arms around — 'everyone, amar Ma!' A few people looked up from their desks and salaamed and nomoshkared Rehana. 'You'll meet everyone later. Was it all right, the train?'

'Yes, yes, it was.' Rehana took a moment to note the change in her daughter. She had exchanged her white sari for a brilliant red cotton. Her lips were chapped and bitten, and her hair was a mess, overgrown and forced into a braid that ended in a thin, weak tangle, but there was a rough health about her. On one of her fingers she wore a ring made of a cheap brown metal. Everything about her was different. Her eyes were bright, and Rehana could feel their warmth as they summed each other up. 'I was worried,' Maya was saying.

'No, it was nothing, just a little tiring.'

'Well, I've arranged the place — you want to go, sleep a little?' Maya pulled the bag from Rehana's arm.

Rehana felt her way around the new mood between them. 'I'm a little hungry — and maybe a bath — if that's all right — you're not busy?'

'No, Ma, today I'm all yours.' She flung her arm around Rehana's shoulders and laughed easily. 'Where d'you want to go? Victoria Park? Wellington Square? Oooh, College Street?'

'First let's — '

'Yes, sorry — home — yes, first home. Just a few minutes, Ammoo. Here, you sit behind the desk, I'll just finish this paragraph.'

Rehana was so tired her arms were starting to grow cold.

'Let me bring you some tea first.' Maya ran off.

Rehana took the opportunity to examine the office more closely. There wasn't much to see. Stacks of paper columned up the desks and covered every inch of spare floorspace. Young men in spectacles frowned over typewriters. A few posters were strung on the wall. Above a doorway leading to a back room was a framed photograph of Mujib in his black coat. Already the picture looked out of date.

Rehana pressed her head against the worn leather seat, hypnotized by the clack-clack-clack of the typewriters.

In the back room the radio squealed into focus.

'Ammoo,' Maya said, bearing a cup of tea and a pair of biscuits, 'the BBC broadcast, then we'll go.'

Rehana heard snatches of the radio programme, interrupted by comments from the people at the office. *This is the BBC World Service . . . a historic Indo-Soviet treaty . . . if Indira Gandhi intervenes, the war will surely be won for the people of Bangladesh . . .*

A loud cheer went up in the room. Three telephones rang at once.

'Joy Bangla! Joy Bangobandhu!'

The cheer was repeated several times, followed by scattered backslapping.

Rehana devoured the salty, cumin-studded biscuits and felt her knees turning to stone.

'Beta,' she said to Maya, 'why don't you just take me to — the flat?'

'Ma, I'm so sorry — we'll go now.' She hesitated. 'It's not a flat, really.'

'No matter. I just want to put my feet up.' Rehana gathered her things and began to walk towards the front door.

'No, Ammoo, this way.' Maya led her to the back of the building, where there were yet more serious-looking workers hunched over their desks. They squeezed through a small cluster of people who were still huddled over the radio. A young woman dressed like a man in a pair of grey trousers waved to them as they brushed past.

'Your mother?'

'Yes — Ammoo, this is Sultana.'

The girl-boy beamed at Rehana. She had shiny, black eyes. 'We've heard all about you, Auntie. You need anything, you ask me.'

They passed through a narrow doorway and into a dim stairwell. 'It's just upstairs,' Maya said, climbing the stairs two at a time. Rehana followed Maya along the betel-stained corridor, stepping to avoid the crumpled bits of newspaper, the spit-globs, the smeared streaks of mud on the walls.

The stairwell opened on to a wide, flat roof. A low railing surrounded it, and beyond Rehana could see the other rooftops on Theatre Road. In the building next door a fat woman was pinning a yellow sari to a clothes line. 'This way,' Maya said. They crossed the roof. At the far end was a small shed topped with a sheet of tin. A set of narrow double doors was held together with a padlock.

Maya slipped a key into the lock. The doors swung open to reveal a tiny room with a sagging cot against one wall and a heavy wooden desk against the other. Between the cot and the desk was a sliver of window criss-crossed with crude metal bars. A tired gamcha hung from the bars, its chequered red-and-green pattern casting weak Christmas shadows on the concrete floor.

'Ammoo, this was the best I could do.'

Rehana pushed aside her surprise.

'I cleaned it!' A tattered mop was angled against the wall.

'It's all right, jaan. It's not for long.'

'It's a promotion! All this time I've been sleeping downstairs.'

'In the office?'

'There's no other place,' Maya said, shrugging, 'and anyway it's been rather fun.' Maya was unwrapping herself from her sari, and Rehana followed, her back to the window. She pulled her head through her nightgown and began to pick the pins out of her hair.

Maya was already sprawled out on the cot when she said, 'Ammoo, I heard about Sabeer.'

She didn't really want to talk about Sabeer, but she told Maya about Sohail, the flat in Nilkhet, how he'd begged her to help.

'Mrs Chowdhury was hysterical.'

'And Silvi?'

'Sohail thought . . . well, he wanted to do it for Silvi. He thought she might love him again if he — I — brought Sabeer back.'

'And?'

'Jani na. Sabeer was in very bad shape.'

'You persuaded them to let him go?'

'I had to ask your Faiz Chacha.'

'How did you do it?'

'I honestly don't know.' She realized she was telling the truth; that day was a blur, as though it had happened to someone else and she had just borrowed the memory.

'You're braver than you thought.'

'Or perhaps I'm just foolish.' Rehana rifled through her bag. She pulled out the blanket and held it to her face, breathing in the scent of the sun on her clothes line.

'You look different,' Maya said, 'something . . . I don't know.'

Rehana wrapped the blanket around her shoulders and wedged herself between the wall and her daughter. She looked up at the dimpled ceiling. Damp patches shaped like clouds dotted the whitewash. 'I was thinking the same about you.'

Maya flipped on to her back. 'I needed to leave, Ammoo, I hope you can understand that. I felt so bad leaving you all alone . . . '

She hadn't been all alone. She'd watched *Mughal-e-Azam* and fallen in love with a stranger and uttered words she'd kept hidden for more than a decade.

Maya was still speaking: ' . . . and it's been so

289

busy here, I hardly have time to think.' With a start she sat up and parted her hair in the middle, grabbing the left side and twisting it into a braid. The mattress pitched and wobbled. Rehana swallowed a groan. She had forgotten how restless the girl could be.

'Was he — Sabeer — what did they do to him?'

Rehana didn't move her eyes from the ceiling. She considered which version of the truth Maya would not immediately reject.

'We've been getting reports about the prisoners,' Maya said. 'I already know.'

'Then I don't need to tell you.'

'I still want to know.' She was working on the second braid now and climbing into her younger, schoolgirl face.

'He was tortured.'

'How? What did they do?'

'I don't know.'

'Of course you know.'

'I don't really want — '

'For God's sake, Ammoo, I'm not a child!'

Rehana sighed, resigned. 'All right.' Keep your eyes on the clouds, she told herself. 'They beat him, broke his ribs.

'They made him stare at the sun for hours, days.

'They burned cigarette holes on his back.

'They hung him upside down.

'They made him drink salt water until his lips cracked.

'And they tore out his fingernails.' The tears travelled across her cheeks and pooled in her ears. She closed her eyes and saw the blood pulsing through her eyelids. When she opened them, Maya was at the window, folding and unfolding the torn gamcha. Then she turned around and said in a hospital voice, 'He's lucky you came for him. They would have made him dig his own grave and buried him in it.'

Rehana turned and pressed her forehead to the wall. It was rough and spiked with dust.

'Ma, you were so brave,' Maya said, collapsing heavily on to the cot. 'So brave.' She stroked Rehana's back. 'Let's sleep, now, OK?' She turned and curled herself around her mother. Rehana felt her daughter's restless warmth at her back. 'Tomorrow we'll visit the camp.'

She lay awake and thought about the Major, his blue-threaded arm, the weight of his breath.

It wasn't like the love for children.

It wasn't like the love of home.

Or the accidental love of her husband.

It was a swallowing, hungry love. Already she wanted more. Not one day had passed and she wanted more. There was pain in it, but not a pain she knew. Not the pain of losing fathermotherhusband. Not the grinding pain of waving goodbye from a foggy airport window.

'Ammoo, utho, wake up!' A lock of hair tickled Rehana's cheek. She opened a clammy eye to find her daughter bent over the cot, a steaming mug of tea in one hand, a toothbrush in the other. She tried to remember where she was. 'We have to hurry,' Maya said, handing the toothbrush to Rehana and swallowing a gulp of tea. Yesterday's softness was gone, replaced by a charmless efficiency.

'What time is it?' Rehana turned on to her back, wincing at the stiffness in her neck. 'It's still dark.'

'Five thirty. We have to get ready and meet Sultana.' She waved the mug in the direction of the door. 'She's waiting downstairs.'

'Where are we going?'

'I told you, today is my day at the camp.'

Rehana's stomach was hot and empty. 'What about breakfast?'

'There's a canteen — the food's not bad — just hurry up and we might have time for a little aloo paratha before we go.'

'All right,' Rehana said, heaving herself out of the bowl of the mattress, 'I'll just change and get ready. Go downstairs, I'm just coming.'

★　★　★

Half an hour later, after Rehana had dressed, brushed her teeth in a downstairs toilet that smelled of sweat and wolfed down a few potatoes rolled in a greasy paratha, she found herself wedged between Sultana and Maya in the front of a shabby truck. Sultana was behind the wheel, wearing the same grey trousers and an open-necked white kurta. *She's driving a truck,* Rehana mouthed to Maya, who carried a box labelled ORAL REHYDRATION THERAPY on her

292

lap. Maya turned to Rehana and smiled inscrutably. 'It's a war, Ammoo,' she whispered; 'we can do whatever we want.'

They stopped in front of a battered coffee house. Mukul, smelling like eggs and toothpaste, stuck his head through the open window and shouted, 'Nomoshkar! Good morning, Auntie.' Then he jumped into the back of the trunk and settled among the medical boxes and tins of dried milk.

An hour later the sky was not even yellow and the heavy night-time dew still clung to the trees and the windscreen. Maya and Sultana picked up a song. Sultana said something about a Pakistani soldier and a jackfruit that made Maya hold her stomach and laugh. Rehana willed the journey to pass quickly.

'Halfway!' Maya called out cheerfully. And then it started to rain. Criss-crossing sheets made baby rattles on the windscreen. The road stretched ahead, vague and muddy.

Once they had crossed Howrah Bridge and left the perimeter of Calcutta, the landscape was barren and yellow with fields of drying hay. They passed a jute factory, with its smell of grass and dung, and a leather factory, spilling its fishy odour on to the road, and a cement factory, with black towers of smoke and a piercing, staccato clatter. Half an hour later Mukul rapped on the glass. 'Almost there!' he shouted, pointing ahead to a hand-written sign that read SALT LAKE 2 KILOMETERS. The wind flattened his hair and ears.

Sultana swung the steering wheel to the right,

and they passed on to a narrow, rough track. In the distance Rehana saw an enormous tent, and beside it an expanse of makeshift shacks and hutments. The fields beyond were stacked with oversized cement pipes.

'Is this it?'

'Ji, Auntie,' Sultana said, 'this is it.'

As they approached the tent, Rehana saw a giant banner painted with a Red Cross sign.

'Ammoo,' Maya said, 'this is it. Salt Lake Refugee Camp.'

'What's that tent?'

'It's a hospital.'

Long wooden boards made a path from the car to the tent. The field that lay between was littered with the detritus of people who had hastily abandoned their homes. Shoes, combs, fragments of clothing, broken cooking pots were sinking into the mud like swirls of confetti.

Maya and Sultana skipped over the boards, manoeuvring though the oily puddles and smudged footprints. Maya had pinned the red sari a little high, so that it just skimmed her ankles; she wore closed, sturdy shoes. No one had told Rehana what to expect. She hitched up her sari so that it wouldn't trail in the mud, and with the other hand she covered her head with a copy of the *Calcutta Statesman*, because the sun had begun to force itself through the clouds, trapping the air in a hazy, thick heat. She kept her head down and concentrated on navigating the tilting, uneven boards.

Inside the Red Cross tent Maya and Sultana were greeted with cheers and handshakes. A tall man in a white coat came striding towards them. 'Ah, my Tuesday angels,' he bellowed.

'Dr Rao, this is my mother,' Maya said.

He had glittering olive eyes. 'Welcome to Calcutta. Why don't you join me later, when I do the rounds?' He put a hand on Maya's elbow.

'Sure,' Maya said, colouring, 'we'll just unpack the supplies.'

'OK then, see you later,' he said, sailing away on long, quick legs.

Sultana was already unpacking the supplies and giving instructions to the half-dozen volunteers who had gathered around her. Maya joined her in an assembly line, cracking the boxes open with a blade, pointing to the different shelves that made up the medicine stores. Rehana wedged herself into a corner and watched, shifting her weight from one foot to another. It was like being with her sisters again, disappearing while they went on with important, grown-up tasks.

'Ammoo,' Maya said, unwrapping a package of syringes, 'do you want to have a look around?'

'Yes, sure,' Rehana replied, relieved.

'Sultana, we'll just be back.'

'I'll catch up with you later.' And she raised a teasing eyebrow. 'We can meet Dr Rao.'

When they stepped outside the tent, Rehana saw a ragged line of families snaking out to one side.

'What are they waiting for?'

'Vaccinations,' Maya said. She checked her watch. 'They do them every morning at ten.' At the head of the queue, on a foldout table, a sandy-haired man in a coat plunged needles into spindly baby arms.

Maya was leading her to the field of shanties, where the beehives of discarded cement pipes were stacked three or four high.

'This is where they bring the newcomers,' Maya said, pointing to the pipes.

'Where?'

'Over there.'

There weren't any buildings, only the pipes. 'I can't see anything.'

'*Inside* the pipes, Ma, look.'

Rehana put her hand to her forehead and looked. The scene came into focus.

It was true. The pipes, each just wide enough for a grown man's stretched arms, had people huddled inside them. Lungis hung across some for privacy. Saris lay drying on top. Inside, their backs bent against the curve of the pipes, men and women pitched against the sloping walls.

Maya and Rehana walked on, drawing closer to the pipes. The ground grew more sodden as they approached, and boards were laid down again. The stench of human waste suddenly assaulted Rehana, and she stopped in her tracks.

'Maya,' Rehana said, covering her mouth with her sari, 'how long do you think we'll be here?'

'At the camp?'

'No, in Calcutta.'

'Why?'

'I just want to know — how long before we go home?'

'Dhaka isn't safe any more. They've been raiding houses, and if even one person tells the

296

authorities you've been harbouring freedom fighters, we could all end up in custody. Especially you. Sohail's very worried.'

'But I knew all of this when I decided to do it.'

'Things have changed. The army is nervous; they're cracking down.'

Rehana knew it was childish to indulge in feeling homesick, but she couldn't help it. Everything had happened so quickly, she hadn't even had time to consider what would happen next, after she arrived. She hadn't bargained on feeling so *lost*. She shouldn't have come.

'Don't worry, Ma. You'll soon settle in.'

They marched on.

The pipes were no bigger at close range. Children dangled from their edges, while women hung back inside, their faces covered with the limp ends of their saris.

They found a boy, no more than six or seven, squatting beside his pipe. 'You arrive today?' Maya asked, crouching down herself and looking him up and down. 'I haven't seen you before.'

The boy was braiding two flat lengths of jute. When he looked up, Rehana saw the skin stretched over his face. On his neck, where his pulse should have been, was a pink millipede scar.

He kept his eyes on his hands and mumbled something incoherent.

'Speak up, boy,' Maya said roughly, taking his chin in her hands.

'Ji, apa.' He finished his braid and began another one.

'Where are you from?'

'Pabna,' he whispered.

'Where?'

'Pabna,' he said, even more softly, holding the first braid in his mouth.

'Which village?' Maya asked.

'I don't know.'

'You don't know the village?'

'Dulal, tara tari koro.' A woman with a fist on each hip crawled out of her pipe and looked Rehana up and down. 'I need that basket.' She had something — a chicken — tucked into the crook of her elbow. She twisted it around and held it by its wing.

'Who's this?' she asked, looking at the boy and pointing to Maya. The chicken flapped its free wing against the woman's leg.

Maya stood up. 'My name is Maya. I work here.' Maya didn't introduce Rehana. 'Is this your boy?'

'No. He's from my village.'

'Where are his people?'

'Dead,' the woman said stiffly.

'See that tent?' Maya said, pointing, 'go and register there. Him too. You can get food, medicine. Bujlen?'

The woman nodded. She passed the chicken to Dulal, who had tied his jute braids together into a loose net. Rehana wanted to ask her a few more questions, how old she was, how she had arrived at the camp, did she have parents, a husband, children of her own, but Maya was already moving on, waving her hands at an old man with a lungi hitched up around his knees.

Rehana rifled through her handbag and pulled

298

out a few notes. 'I can give you some taka — '

The woman gave Rehana a parched, blinkless stare. 'I don't need money,' she said.

Rehana reached out a hand to touch the woman's arm, but she shifted slightly and her fingers grazed the sari instead. She ran to catch up with Maya.

They went deeper into the camp. It was getting unbearably hot and the stench was even worse there; the stacks of cement pipes had given way to shacks and makeshift shelters built out of plastic and scraps of wood. The lucky ones had a few pieces of tin sheeting to keep off the rain. Rehana pulled her sari around her ankles, and with the other hand she tried to swat away a family of flies that were following her. Everywhere she looked she saw the haunted faces of the refugees. They held out their hands, and she thought they might grab her, drag her into the muck. She had an image of them forcing her into one of their pipes, making her weave those jute strings all day. You're one of us, they would say, you're one of us. She imagined Maya leaving her there, going back in the truck with Sultana and Mukul, laughing all the way to Theatre Road.

'Maya,' Rehana said finally, 'I can't go on.'

'It's just a bit further,' Maya said, pointing ahead. 'There's someone I want to see on that side.'

'Really,' Rehana said, feeling her stomach twist, 'you go ahead, I'll stay here and wait for you.'

'Where will you wait?'

Rehana glanced around. There was no place to sit. 'I'll go back to the tent.'

'Will you be able to find it?'

'Yes — just go ahead.' Rehana couldn't wait to get rid of her; she could stop pretending to be interested and run back to the tent. She thought about the truck. Maybe she could go back to the truck with a cold glass of water and listen to the radio. Or sit beside those volunteers and their medicine boxes. Anything, anything but this stink.

She picked her way to the tent. Slipping quietly through the flaps, she found herself in the hospital ward. All the beds were pushed up against each other, so that it looked like an unbroken stretch of bodies. She walked through the aisle, stepping over people. It was the women who made the breath catch in her throat. It was the way they squatted next to the children, holding up empty breasts to their mouths, their hair matted with the road.

'Mrs Haque?' A man approached: it was the doctor, coming towards her with a quizzical wave. A pair of white rubber gloves were stretched across his hands. Rehana saw dark spots on the fingertips, and, as he drew nearer, a smattering of red above the pocket of his white coat. 'Chachi? What are you doing here?'

She wanted to hug him. 'I — I came to look around a little.'

'Well, this is it. We have a small operating theatre at the back, and a dispensary. Shall I take you around?'

'No — it's all right. I just — I wanted to see.'

300

'There are so many,' Dr Rao said, fixing his gaze on her. 'From all over the country. They've left everything, walked for days, only to arrive at this place.'

Rehana couldn't keep her eyes from the red smudges on his gloves.

'There's a register — I can show it to you.'

They turned a corner and entered another room. There were more crowds, echoes of wailing children. A grating mechanical hum shrouded all of the other sounds.

'What is that noise?'

'Generator,' the doctor replied. 'We get power for the OT, and a few hours of light in the evening.'

'Do you stay here?'

'Yes,' he sighed, smiling. 'There's another small tent in a far corner of the field.'

'Where are you from?'

'Kashmir.'

'You came to Calcutta to study?'

'No,' he said. 'No. I came for this.'

★ ★ ★

'Ammoo,' Maya said that night, 'Dr Rao suggested that you might want to help at the camp.'

I knew. I knew she wanted to leave me there. 'Me? What can I do?'

'They really need help. You could do what you did at Shona — just talk to the refugees.'

Rehana did not want to talk to the refugees. Why was it always her? Rescue this one, save that

301

one. 'If I'm in the way I should just go back to Dhaka.'

'Ammoo,' Maya said, 'you know you can't do that.'

'I should never have come.'

'It's very serious, they could have arrested you.'

The thought of spending months there, in the shed, or worse, at the camp, was suddenly unbearable. 'So what? I deserve to be arrested.'

'Stop talking nonsense.'

'I don't want to go back to that camp.'

'Fine. Stay here.' Maya turned her back and folded her hands under her cheek. Just like her father slept, Rehana thought. As though she were praying.

★ ★ ★

The stifling heat in the shed woke Rehana. The bed was empty; Maya's clothes were strewn across the floor. Rehana started picking up the clothes and folding them. There was a smell coming from Maya's kameez. It needed a wash. The rest of her clothes were no better: the hems of all her saris and petticoats were streaked with mud.

Rehana stepped out of the shed to see if there was a tap. She circled the perimeter of the roof, holding a hand against the sun. She followed a copper pipe, and in a far corner she found what she was looking for, fastened to the wall. Below it was a hole where the water would run off.

There wasn't any laundry soap. She took out

the cream-coloured bar of soap she had brought to wash her face. She turned the tap, and a weak trickle made its way out. The water was warm and comfortable; she soon felt herself relax as she kneaded Maya's salwaar-kameez in a familiar double beat: clap-clap, clap-clap, clap-clap.

She hung the clothes over the railing, pleased with the sight of them sizzling under the sun. The fat woman from the other day was on the next-door roof again, pinning up the same yellow sari. She waved. Rehana waved back.

Downstairs, Maya was attacking the typewriter with a pen in her mouth. The pen had leaked a little; on one corner of her lip was a growing patch of indigo.

'Ma, where've you been?'

'Just tidying a little upstairs.' Rehana pointed to her mouth. 'You have a little — '

Maya had already turned back to her typewriter. 'Isn't it hot up there?' she said distractedly.

'I'll go out and see if I can get us a few things,' Rehana said. 'We need soap, and maybe a few snacks.'

'All right,' Maya said, her eyes on her punching fingers. 'You go ahead.'

On her way out, Rehana passed Mukul pasting a flyer on to the wall. He wore a blue cap that was pulled down to hide his eyes.

'Auntie, hello,' he said, raising his chin so he could see her. 'You going out in this heat?'

'Just down the road for a few things.'

'It's burning up!'

'I'll only be gone a few minutes.'

'Here, why don't you take my cap?' he said, peeling it off his head. His hair was plastered wetly to his forehead. She saw the ring of sweat around the rim.

'No, really.'

'Please, I insist.'

'No, no, don't worry, I'll just be back.'

It was furiously hot outside. Within seconds Rehana's cheeks began to burn. She considered turning back, but the thought of Mukul in his sweaty cap kept her moving ahead; she continued down the street until she came to a junction. Tram tracks bisected the road, and on either side there were shops with open doors and loud, clashing hoardings. Rehana didn't remember this part of Calcutta, but the tonga-wallahs, skipping barefoot through the traffic with their elbows pointed up and out, and the shapes of the buildings, the wide avenues, the trams — she recognized all of these, despite the years of wilful forgetting.

Now everything was louder and more crowded. People choked the streets and tilted the tram carriages. They perched on the edge of the sidewalk and left barely a sliver of pavement through which Rehana could push her way. She ducked into the nearest shop, blinking against the change in light. It was a dark, narrow room with a row of shelves lining one wall, a counter running alongside. The shelves held a confused and mismatched assortment of things — chocolates, baby formula, shampoo, pomade, pickles. A man stood in front of the display with his palms on the countertop.

Rehana pointed to a blue bar of washing soap. 'That one please, how much?'

'Six annas,' the man said, chewing his gums.

'Give me one. And a pao of moori. And a — do you have scissors?'

'Scissors?'

'Yes, I need a pair of scissors.'

The man pulled out a drawer and showed Rehana several samples. After inspecting the blade and putting her thumb through the handle of each one, she chose the smallest pair.

'Total comes to three rupees, twelve annas.'

Rehana was about to pay the man when he said, 'Have I seen you before?'

She took a closer look at him. He was old; her father's age. Could she know him? Trust me to find the one person in Calcutta who remembers me. But no, she hadn't seen him before. 'I don't think so.'

'I'm sure I know you,' he insisted.

'But I don't live here.'

'Where are you from — are you Joy Bangla?'

'Sorry?'

'Are you from Dhaka? Bangladesh? Joy Bangla?'

No, actually, she thought, I'm from Calcutta. But she said, 'Yes, I'm Joy Bangla.'

'Ten per cent discount,' he said, smiling. 'Ten per cent refugee discount.' He passed her the shopping bag with a freckled hand. 'I was a refugee also, in '47. That's why I recognize you.' And then he looked at her with such fatherly tenderness. 'You come back here when you need anything. Anything at all.'

Suddenly the man was a blur. He waved his hand at her. 'Please, don't cry! You want a choc bar? Milon, get my daughter here a choc bar. Don't cry, Ma, don't cry.'

Rehana tugged at the paper with wet fingers. Her teeth broke into the chocolate and through the ice-cream.

'Go on, Ma. You go on.'

She stepped back into the noon heat with the ice-cream turning to milk on her tongue. She walked a little further, passing a tobacco shop and a Chinese restaurant. On the corner of the next street she found a bench, shaded by the shadow of a three-storeyed State Bank of India. The two women who had already collapsed on the bench wriggled together to make room for Rehana. There was a tram stop across the road, and Rehana watched the passengers emptying and filling the compartments.

She saw that they were the same as the people from the train station, and from Shona's garden, and from the camps, refugees now trawling through the streets.

There were some that seemed less desperate, almost ordinary. But, despite their attempts to blend in, she could tell they were also refugees. They kept their hands in their pockets and a grateful smile stitched to their lips. They had unwashed hair and dirty shoes. Clothes that looked decent, but, looking closely she could see the ragged hems, the worn pleats. And everywhere they went their memories argued for space, so that they forgot to cross the road when the lights were red, or over-milked their tea, or

306

whispered into their newspapers as they scanned hungrily for news of home. Rehana found she could not bear to look at them; she was afraid she would see herself; she was afraid she wouldn't see herself; she wanted to be different and the same as them all at once, neither option offering relief from the rasping feeling of loss, and the swallowing, hungry love.

★   ★   ★

'I'm going to cut your hair, Maya,' Rehana said. It was night again, and they were getting ready for bed. Rehana had tidied and swept the shed. Maya's clothes, smelling of afternoon sun, were folded and stacked on the desk. The window was open, and there was just the hint of a breeze.

'There's nothing wrong with my hair,' Maya said. Her first instinct was always to say no to everything. 'What's wrong with my hair?'

'Nothing. I just want to trim the edges. Look at this,' Rehana said, showing Maya the tatty end of her braid. 'I'll just make it straight.'

'How do you know how to cut hair?'

'I've always known. My sisters made me cut theirs.' Right here, in Calcutta. And she used to cut her father's, when they were poor and there was no more credit at the barber's.

'Really? How is it you never cut mine?'

'You never let me get near your hair! I used to cut Sohail's.'

Maya smiled wryly. 'Yes, I think I remember now. I always thought it was because he was your favourite.'

'Na, it was because you were so stubborn.'

'Go ahead, then, let's see what you can do.'

Rehana was ready with the scissors and a small mug of water. She dipped the end of Maya's raggedy braid into the water, then she undid it and began to comb.

'Full of knots!' she said. 'It's a mess.'

'No commentary from the haircutter, please.'

Rehana pushed Maya's head forward and started to work the scissors. 'Stop moving,' she said, 'or it'll be uneven.'

The curling half-moons fell to the ground. 'Maya, I was thinking about what the doctor said — perhaps it is a good idea.'

'Really, Ma, you don't have to.' She twisted around to face Rehana.

'Hold still.' Rehana pushed Maya's head back into position. 'There's really nothing much for me to do here.'

'I'm sorry, I know I've been busy.'

'You have your work. It'll be good for me to have something to do. There must be some reason why I came here.' Rehana pulled two ends of Maya's hair together to see if she'd cut a straight line. 'All right,' she said, patting Maya's shoulder, 'all done.'

'The war will be over soon,' Maya said; 'we won't be here for ever.'

It wasn't until September that Rehana got her reason. She was trailing Dr Rao through the

308

ward, taking notes on the new patients, writing down their medications and prescriptions. They came to the end of the row of cots, and on the last bed was a woman Rehana hadn't seen before. A blanket covered most of her face, but her forehead and her long hair were visible, and one arm, on which she wore a red-and-gold glass bangle.

'Who's this?' Rehana asked. There was something about her, lying there on the cot, that made Rehana want to see her face.

'I'm not sure,' Dr Rao said. 'I don't think I've seen her before.'

Rehana peeled back the katha and saw a pair of closed eyes, framed by long, ropy strands of hair. She looked closer. She knew this woman. 'Supriya.' It couldn't be her. Could it? She looked again. Of course, of course it was her. It was the kind of thing that happened so easily these days. 'This is my friend, Mrs Sengupta,' Rehana said, 'from Dhaka.'

Dr Rao lifted the bangled arm with his thumb and forefinger, his eyes on his wristwatch. 'Why don't you stay here, Chachi? I'll see if I can find out who's been treating her.'

'Her husband must have brought her. See if you can find him. Mr Sengupta.'

Rehana pulled off the katha. Mrs Sengupta's sari was bunched around her knees. Her calves were grey and papery. Rehana dragged the sari down and covered her legs. She looked like a felled tree.

'What happened to you?' Rehana whispered. She lifted Mrs Sengupta's head and pulled the

309

soggy hair away from her neck. She saw her friend's eyelids shift, as though she were dreaming, and then she opened them slowly, turning first to the ceiling and then slowly focusing on Rehana.

'Supriya?'

Mrs Sengupta stared emptily at Rehana. She opened her mouth. Her lips were black.

'What happened to you? Where's Mithun?' But she had already turned away, her face shut.

The doctor returned a few minutes later. He carried a blood-pressure cuff and a bag of saline. 'I'm afraid she's here alone, Mrs Haque. No one has seen any family.'

'That can't be right. She has a husband, and a son. She wouldn't have come without them.'

When Rehana went to the ward the next day, Mrs Sengupta was exactly as she had left her, smeared across the cot with the sari around her knees. But she was awake. Rehana stroked her forehead. There was no fiery teep, no sindoor.

Rehana began to make a habit of spending her afternoons at Mrs Sengupta's bedside. She poured coconut oil into her hair and picked out the dirt. Then she washed it with a small square of soap she had bought from the old man on Theatre Road. She cut Mrs Sengupta's nails and creamed her elbows. Her friend followed her with her eyes, but still she said nothing. Aside from a small bamboo pipe she kept under her pillow, she appeared to have no possessions.

It was not unlike sitting at Iqbal's grave. There was never any answer, but she imagined somehow Mrs Sengupta could hear her.

'After you left a lot of other people left also. The club shut down and the markets were mostly deserted. And a lot of boys ran off to join the army. Sohail wanted to go but I said no.'

Sometimes, as with Iqbal, she was tempted to lie, or exaggerate.

'But he went anyway. You would not believe the change in him. And Silvi. She looks nothing like the girl we knew. We should never have let her marry that boy. I met him again, you know, but under very different circumstances.'

She kept certain things from Mrs Sengupta. The details of Sabeer's capture, for instance. She didn't want to upset her. And she didn't talk about the Major. She didn't know how she could put it. *I fell in love with a stranger.* Having to explain would mean giving some reason. Which it did not have. It was an unreasonable thing. She hardly even knew him. Sometimes it occurred to her how very little she did know. For instance, if he had any brothers or sisters. Or what he planned to do once the war was over. She had never even asked him when, or if, she would see him again.

In the afternoons, when Mrs Sengupta slept, Rehana walked around the hospital with Dr Rao. She befriended a few other women, stopping beside their cots and holding their hands while they told her how they had come to be there. They started to recognize her. They called her apa. Every day they told her new stories about the war. She waited for a letter from Sohail. She waited for a letter from the Major. Neither came.

Rehana got used to the rides in the truck with

311

Mukul, and by October the rooftop was almost pleasant. She kept the doors of the shed open and sat on the threshold, watching the evening descend and the city slide easily into dusk. The fat woman was there every few days, flapping and pinning her yellow sari.

★ ★ ★

Every day it was the same. Mrs Sengupta had still not uttered a word. 'Won't you say anything, Supriya? Tell me what happened? Maybe I can help.'

One night on the roof Rehana was patching up the torn hem of her white petticoat. She hadn't brought enough clothes for such a long stay, and the ones she had brought were starting to wear out. She was threading a needle when the thought suddenly occurred to her that, even though Mrs Sengupta didn't want to speak, perhaps she would agree to write. She remembered the day Mrs Sengupta had asked her about *Sultana's Dream*. She put down her petticoat and went downstairs to ask Maya for a notebook or a few scraps of paper. The next day at the camp Rehana presented these to Mrs Sengupta, along with a sharpened pencil.

Mrs Sengupta lifted her head. She shook it.

Rehana pointed to the notebook. 'That's for you.'

A few days before this, Rehana had said, 'Did you know the story of how I lost the children?' She told Mrs Sengupta about the courthouse and the judge, and how she had allowed her grief

312

to betray her. 'But I got them back. You can find Mithun too. And Mr Sengupta.'

Rehana was convinced it was just a matter of being lost. Maybe they were rushing to get somewhere and Mrs Sengupta got separated from the others. Mr Sengupta must be looking for her right now; that's why Rehana kept checking the register to see who had arrived at the camp. Rehana had visions of Mr Sengupta hunting through every refugee camp, every train station, every hospital, for news of his wife. Surely if they were patient, they would find each other again.

The next morning, when Rehana went back, Mrs Sengupta held up the notebook. She had written a few lines. *I went into the reeds*, it said. *In the pond.* She pulled the bamboo pipe from under her pillow and put it to her mouth. *I left him*, she wrote.

'I don't know what you mean, Mrs Sengupta,' Rehana said. An image came, unbidden, of Mrs Sengupta sinking into a grey-brown silt.

Mrs Sengupta's hand moved slowly over the page. She finished a sentence, crossed it out, then wrote again. After what felt like a long time, she handed the notebook back to Rehana. *I left him and ran into the pond.*

It couldn't be right. It couldn't have happened that way.

'You got separated?'

Again she began her slow scrawl, her fingers knotting together. *I didn't think about him, I just ran.*

'Mr Sengupta?' Rehana asked. She had already

313

written something down and was pointing to it now. *They shot him.*

She couldn't bear to see any more. 'Supriya, get some rest now, I'll be back with some lunch.'

Mrs Sengupta gripped her notebook.

True, she wrote, *true true true.* She closed her eyes.

Rehana left her that way, black-lipped and shaking her head back and forth.

★ ★ ★

Rehana didn't know what to say. She was afraid some accusation might slip from her lips, even if she said it was all right, that she understood. No matter how she tried to picture it, she still could not help feeling disgusted by the thought of Mrs Sengupta abandoning her son. There must have been some other way. There was always another way. She could have taken him with her. Or stood between him and those soldiers. And how could she bear to be alive, not knowing, imagining he might be somewhere, lost, with strangers, or worse?

The next day Rehana avoided Mrs Sengupta. She did not visit her the day after that. A week passed, and she tried to put it out of her mind. Then she found the telegram. It was early in the morning, and she was looking for a safety pin among Maya's things when she found it, dated 16 October 1971. Two days ago.

SABEER DEAD STOP TRIED OUR BEST STOP
COULDN'T SAVE STOP GOD BLESS MRS C

314

Rehana folded the telegram, neatly, making sure the edges lined up. She felt weak and shaky and her fingers trembled, but she continued to fold, until it was a tiny sliver of paper that she could tuck into her blouse, like loose change. All the way to Salt Lake she felt her heart beating against it. She remembered that terrible night, lashing herself to Sabeer as they travelled through the dark, his chipped hands hugged to his breast. Then her thoughts lingered on Silvi, and Mrs Chowdhury, and Romeo turning to dust under a coconut tree, and her whole body burned with the need to go home, back to the neighbourhood, to the bungalow, and to Shona.

Home made her think of Mrs Sengupta. Where would Supriya go, when this was all over? Rehana decided to approach her, to tell her the truth. That she didn't understand how a mother could abandon her son to save her own life, but that it was not, in the end, her place to understand. That was between her and her maker. She was only her friend.

★ ★ ★

At the ward Rehana waited for her daily appointment with Dr Rao. The trembling in her fingers spread to her arms, a cold travelling shiver.

The doctor approached, making his hurried, long-legged strides. He was right on time, as usual.

'Did you check the list today?' Rehana asked.

'Yes, Chachi, I checked the list.'

315

'And?'

'Nothing, I'm sorry.' He sighed. They went through this every day. 'Chachi, I know she's your friend, but there's really not much more we can do.'

'But her son is lost — now we know exactly where he was last seen. We have to keep looking. Promise me you'll keep looking.' She stood up to go. The floor tilted towards her. She lunged forward, leaning heavily on the doctor's arm.

'Chachi? Are you all right?'

'Nothing. I should probably have some breakfast — haven't eaten all morning.'

'There must be something in the kitchen. Shall I take you?'

'No, please don't worry. The list — you'll keep checking? Sabeer Mustafa. I mean, no — Mithun. Mithun Sengupta. You got the name?'

'Yes, Chachi.'

The spinning went on as Rehana made her way to the canteen. The din of the hospital was by now familiar to her, and she had learned to ignore it, just as she could ignore the pressing mass of people with urgent faces who lined the corridors. But now there was a roar in her head like rushing water. She put her hand to her mouth and felt the flame of her breath. I need to sit down, she said to herself. Just for a moment. She was scanning the room, looking for an empty chair, when Maya intercepted her.

'Ammoo, are you all right?'

'Nothing, jaan, just a little weakness.' A feathery shiver passed through her body. 'The telegram — why didn't you tell me?'

'Ammoo, let's sit down somewhere.'

'OK.' Maya grabbed hold of Rehana's hand. They made their way though the beds. Some of the women waved to Rehana as they passed and cried out, 'Apa!' Rehana heard them as a warbled, rippling echo.

'Maya-jaan, I'm not feeling well,' she whispered. Maya was in front of her now, pushing people aside. 'Make way, please!' she was saying.

Rehana slipped out of Maya's grip. The people rushing into the hospital overcame her, and she let go, falling into the throng, strange, icy hands gripping her shoulders, raising her up, her arms flopping like fish fins, and then darkness.

Rehana drifted in and out of a heavy-lidded sleep, her throat thick with questions. She dreamed of Sabeer, his cracked lips mouthing something incoherent, and Mithun, with a face like Sohail's, under water, wailing for his mother.

'Ma,' she heard Sohail say, 'I'm here, Ma.'

When she woke, she patted herself; her face was still hot, but the shivering had stopped, and now there was just an aching heaviness in her limbs and a hard throbbing in her head. She rubbed her feet together; they were buttery, even the heels. Someone had been tending to them. She turned and caught a whiff of jobakusum.

'My hair . . .'

'Mrs Sengupta's been washing it,' she heard a man's voice say. 'Doesn't speak to anybody, just does it. And your feet.' The voice had a weathered rasp.

She wondered if she was dreaming. 'Sohail?'

He leaned over her so she could see it was really him.

'When did you come?'

'I was coming anyway — you didn't get my letter. Just a few days. You've been in and out.'

'What happened?'

'Jaundice. Rao said you've probably had it for weeks, you just didn't know. It's very contagious — they had to check everyone.'

'Maya?'

'She's fine.'

Rehana had so many questions, but she was too tired to form the words. 'Hold my hand,' was all she managed to say. Before she drifted away, she saw Sohail's arm, caramel and shiny with sun, moving across the bed.

★ ★ ★

'I have an assignment, Ammoo,' she heard him say the next day. He had brought her a green coconut with a triangular hole cut into the top, which she was tipping slowly into her mouth. 'We're going to take out the grid.'

The coconut water was milky and sweet. She dipped her finger into it and pulled out a strip of the flesh. Sohail smiled through his beard-cloud. Rehana couldn't help noticing how beautiful he was, and so alive, his eyes electric as he told her the news.

'Whole city will be in total darkness. We're going to dig up the stash in the garden, Ammoo. I have to go back to Dhaka.'

'What about us?'

318

'You too. I've come to take you home. And Maya.'

Home. She wanted to throw her hands in the air and send up a cheer.

'Is it safe?'

'It's been two months since you left and we've kept a close watch on the house — it doesn't look like they know anything.'

'Sabeer died.'

'I know.' His face betrayed nothing — no relief, no shame.

'He didn't die for nothing, Ma. We've made some major gains. Just last week we took the Pak Army out of one of their major supply routes in Comilla.'

'Are we going to win?' It was the first time she had asked him the question.

Sohail was about to say, Yes, of course. But she gave him a weak squeeze of the wrist that meant she wanted to know the truth, and he paused for a minute before saying, 'It's not impossible.' He waited another moment, and then said, 'We're outnumbered, outgunned, outmanned. But sometimes we can beat the hell out of them.' And again he smiled his cloudy smile and said, 'I can taste the end. The modhu-roshogolla-honey end.'

★   ★   ★

When she opened her eyes again, Mrs Sengupta was at the foot of her cot. She looked like a dark apparition, the washed planes of her face muted and still. She wore a clean sari and flat

319

sandals. Her hair was oiled and tied into a glossy braid.

'Now I'm the one in the sickbed,' Rehana said.

The barest smile touched Mrs Sengupta's lips.

What happened to you, Rehana wanted to ask. Instead she said, 'You washed my hair?'

Mrs Sengupta bent her head but didn't open her mouth. She waited stiffly at the foot of the bed. A few moments struggled by. 'I'm going back to Dhaka,' Rehana said finally. 'Why don't you come? The war will be over soon. It'll be like it was before. You can stay at Shona — we'll be neighbours again. Or come and stay at the bungalow with me. Remember Road 5? And Mrs Chowdhury, and our card-friends — they'll all want to see you.' Rehana's throat was sandy. 'It's your home too. Come with us.'

Mrs Sengupta showed no hint of understanding. She kept her eyes on Rehana's face and fingered her glass bangle, moving it up and down her forearm. Then she walked around to the side of the cot. Rehana reached a hand to her hand. She felt the blood leaping under Mrs Sengupta's skin. At that very moment she was convinced the glass bangle had kept her friend alive, like a pulse at her wrist.

Mrs Sengupta dipped her face to the cot. Rehana thought she might be trying to tell her something; she struggled to lift her head. It was the barest, faintest touch as Mrs Sengupta's lips brushed Rehana's cheek. Then she rose and turned to go.

Rehana made one last attempt. 'Please, Supriya — come home with me.'

320

But she was already gone, pulling the sari over her shoulder and moving with that slow grace Rehana had envied since the first day she had arrived at Shona, perched on her high heels with a book under her arm.

November

Take my affliction

They decided to take a long ferry route, crossing the border in Rajshahi and floating downstream on the Padma, past Kushtia, Pabna, Faridpur. It would take two days, and they would arrive late at night on Wednesday after transferring to a train in Faridpur. Sohail would stay at Shona. On Thursday, Joy would come, and they would dig up the rifles buried beside the rosebushes. On Friday, after sunset, they would take out the power grid.

Sohail, Maya and Rehana spent most of the journey on the ferry deck, spread out on a bench that hugged the left side of the boat. The air roared past their ears, making it hard to breathe or to say much of anything. When they spoke, their words were sent up to the air, where the clouds curdled together, or into the water that swirled confidently below. The Padma spread out before them like the sea, its banks so far apart they were visible only as grey lines on the horizon, and in hints offered by the distant shore

— a clutch of seagulls, the dotted wave of a fisherman.

They swayed in silence, narrowing their eyes against the sun and the warm needles of wind.

★ ★ ★

The ferry stopped in Pabna, and Maya bolted across the gangplank for a snack.

'What do you think she'll do?'

Silvi. So he hadn't forgotten. 'I don't know, beta.'

'Sometimes you can love someone more when they're dead,' he said, tracing the slanting metal floor of the ferry with the toe of his sandal.

'Yes.'

'But then you can also forget them.' He looked at her as though she should know which direction Silvi's affections would take.

'Sometimes. Sometimes they just grow with each memory. You can't know.'

He gripped the railing with white fingers. 'She was acting so strangely — I just, I felt her slipping away.'

'You have to wait.'

'Bhaiya!' Maya called out, running across the deck. 'They have the best jhaal moori.' She thrust her hand out, holding a newspaper cone.

Sohail plopped a handful into his mouth. 'Ouch! How can you bear it so spicy?' He hung his tongue out of his mouth. 'Quick, get me some water, I'm dying.'

Maya darted into their cabin for the flask. The huts and tenements that ribboned along the river bank were tilting towards the water, as though aware of their fate; for every monsoon the rivers ate into the floodplain, stealing vast chunks of land, entire houses with their contents, cooking pots and holey mosquito nets and gas stoves and a bridal trunk in which three generations of women have carted their possessions and next year's rice store and dried chillies and babies and doorframes and tin roofs. And every year they were rebuilt, new tin roofs cobbled together with the remnants of the old; new mud walls; the new year's baby — hopeful little shacks bowed by the knowledge of what would always, inevitably, happen again.

Maya returned with the flask, flushed from the effort. 'Eesh,' she teased, 'still can't bear a little morich.' The ferry horn sounded its animal blare.

'You have a stomach like a steel tank,' Sohail said, tipping the flask and gulping greedily. The ferry pushed away, swaying left to right with the effort, its egg-white wake trailing behind like a signature.

'What do you eat out there?' Maya asked.

'Whatever I'm given. You wouldn't believe some of it. But I can always talk the mess cook into something extra.'

'Still using your charms to ill ends,' Maya said.

He smiled a young smile, which she returned, and Rehana was suddenly jolted back to the past, when their faces were fresh, unmarked by grief or history.

★ ★ ★

327

When they descended from the ferry in Faridpur, Sohail crouched on all fours and kissed the silty shore.

★ ★ ★

'Will you talk to her?' he asked Rehana.

They were at the Faridpur Station, waiting for their train to Dhaka.

'I'll go to see her tomorrow.'

He stalked away and returned with a box of shondesh. The sweetmaker, a lean man with an improbably protruding belly, had tied it with a pink string that matched the lettering on the box. Alauddin Sweetmeat. In Faridpur, as everywhere else in the country, only the Muslim sweetmakers were left.

'She likes shondesh,' Sohail said. 'She likes the molasses ones better, but you can't get those till winter.'

As soon as she woke on Thursday she could feel the difference. It was there, even though the house was thankfully familiar — the old teak wedding bed, the shapes of the night-time shadows, the mothball scent of the cupboard, from which last night she had pulled out sheets, pillows, kathas, for them to collapse on after the long train journey home. She had kissed Sohail on the cheek and sent him to Shona, where he had curled up on the Major's bed and fallen asleep with his chappals still dangling from his toes.

Rehana heard her daughter's long breathing beside her. She rose, pulling her hair into a knot, crossed to the kitchen, poured herself a glass of water. As she sipped, she leaned out of the kitchen doorway and into the small side porch. It was always at this time of the day that she allowed herself a selfish moment, when the house, the world, was hers, and there was no one to love, no one to save. It lasted only a few minutes. A few minutes was all the time she would grant it.

The air was grey and heavy with night. She ducked into the bathroom, splashed water on her hands, her eyes. The backs of her ears. She bent her knees on the prayer mat. Every day she asked for the same thing. Protect my children. Forgive me. Save that man. She could not bear to utter his name. She dared to have a hope she might see him today.

She hurried to the kitchen and thought about breakfast. It was the last breakfast for a few weeks. Tomorrow was the start of Ramzaan. For one month they would eat before dawn and not again until sunset. She mixed flour and water and worked the dough with her fingers. She rolled out flat disks, enjoying the quick, steady movement. The kitchen was orange with the coming sun; she stacked the chapattis on the edge of the counter and covered them with a damp square of muslin.

★   ★   ★

329

She went back to the bedroom and tried to wake her daughter.

'Ammoo, it's so good to be home.' Maya burrowed deeper under her katha. 'Come,' she said, patting the bed, 'give me an ador.'

'I'm already up.'

'Come on' — she peeled back the blanket — 'please.'

'All right,' Rehana sighed. She sank into the mattress, which smelled of sleep and talcum powder.

'It's a big day,' Maya said.

'I know.'

Maya ran her fingers across Rehana's forehead. 'You feeling OK?'

'Yes. Your doctor fixed me up!' She searched Maya's face for a clue. In the two months they had been in Calcutta, she hadn't given anything away.

'Ammoo — I want to tell you something,' Maya said seriously. 'The year we were in Lahore — we never talk about it.'

Immediately Rehana's eyes began to water.

'I want you to know — it was all right.'

'How could it be all right?'

'It was.'

'You didn't miss — '

'Of course we missed you. We missed everything. But we were children. And it was only a year.'

'It was a lifetime to me.'

'You should forgive yourself, Ammoo.'

'I thought — I keep thinking — it must have been very bad.'

330

Maya shook her head. 'It wasn't so bad.'

'Was it very good?' This was the other thing she worried about.

'No — of course not.'

'What's the worst thing?'

'Parveen Chachi made me wear frilly dresses — I looked like a cake every time we went anywhere.'

'No, seriously. Tell me the worst thing. I want to know.'

'I don't know . . . ' Maya began slowly. 'I think it was — oh, I know — I couldn't remember your face. I kept asking Sohail, and he would say, Ammoo has the prettiest eyes, and I would nod, but I'd forgotten.' Maya dropped her gaze and looked down at her fingernails. 'It was a long time ago.'

'I would have given anything — my life — '

'I know, Ammoo. I always knew.'

At eleven, after they had both bathed and Rehana had washed her clothes and Maya had strung them up in front of the lemon tree and Rehana had picked the grit out of the lunch rice, they stepped across the street to Mrs Chowdhury's house.

Mrs Chowdhury and Silvi met them at the gate.

'You're back! I thought I saw some lights on last night — beti, didn't I say, that must be Rehana, but she wouldn't come back without telling me, so I wasn't sure.' She turned to her daughter, but Silvi had disappeared into the kitchen. 'Rehana, my goodness, you're so thin! What happened?'

'I haven't been well. I brought you these — a little mishti.'

Mrs Chowdhury peeked into the box. 'You shouldn't have bothered,' she said, lifting the lid and examining the shondesh. 'Now tell me, what's happened to my poor friend? I hardly recognize you!'

'Oh, nothing to worry about. Just a touch of jaundice.'

'Jaundice! Ya'allah! How did you get that?'

'We were at the refugee camps,' Rehana began.

'What, you went to the camps?'

'Mrs Sengupta is there,' Maya interjected.

'Ki bolo! What are you saying? Mrs Sengupta? Our Supriya?'

'Yes, the very one.'

'And?' Mrs Chowdhury's hips were at the edge of her armchair.

Rehana shook her head. 'Poor girl. She didn't even recognize me at first, and even after weeks together she said nothing.' She wouldn't tell Mrs Chowdhury about the note, the bamboo pipe.

'What happened to her mia?'

'We don't know. Something terrible.'

'Where is she now?'

'I tried to bring her back with me, but she refused. And anyway I wasn't sure how things would be for her here.'

'Aharey,' Mrs Chowdhury said, sighing deeply, 'we have all lost so much already.'

★ ★ ★

Silvi came in carrying a tray with tea and salty nimki in an empty Horlicks jar. A scarf was pulled around her head and knotted tightly around her chin. Stray strands of hair had been disciplined and tucked away. She worked neatly, setting down the tray, arranging the cups on their saucers, stirring the teapot.

'Sabeer — we got your telegram — I'm so sorry.'

'It's God's will,' Silvi whispered, kneeling in front of the tray. 'Sugar?' she asked Rehana.

Silvi had been making tea for Rehana since she was old enough to boil water. 'Yes, two. And a little milk,' Rehana said, unsteady in the face of this new formality.

'Maya?'

'One chini. No dood.'

'Hai Allah!' Mrs Chowdhury groaned, heaving herself backwards and piling her feet on an ottoman. 'We tried our best. In the beginning the boy just lay there, staring up at the ceiling. He hardly spoke. And his fingers!' She bit her tongue. 'His fingers turned blue, and then his whole hand. Doctor said it was gangrene — they had to go. Both hands. Imagine, a young boy like that.' She held up her own thick fingers.

Silvi was passing the tea around steadily.

'And then one day — one night, he came out of the bed and sat here, in the drawing room, and he smiled — so beautifully, na, Silvi? As though he was looking into God's own eyes.' She pointed to the sofa where Maya was sitting. 'And he was gone.'

Rehana felt her stomach lurch, as Maya,

333

shifting with a teacup in her hand, said, 'Did you ever find out what happened? How he was captured?' She directed her question at Silvi.

Silvi was unscrewing the Horlicks jar and arranging the nimki on a plate. She pursed her lips together and appeared not to hear the question.

'Silvi, do you know what happened?' Maya repeated, a little louder. Without a word, Silvi passed the plate of nimki to her mother. 'Did you even bother to ask?' Maya said.

'These are unspeakable things,' Mrs Chowdhury began.

'Things which need to be known.' Maya slammed her cup down with a porcelain clatter. 'Silvi, your husband was a hero.'

'That was his business,' Silvi said finally, 'nothing to do with me.'

'But it's your country!'

'Not everyone believes what you believe,' Silvi said simply.

'You don't believe in Bangladesh?' The name of the country, still a new word, fell out of Maya's mouth like a jewel.

Silvi was still crouching next to the tray. Now she lifted it and slid smoothly out of the room.

'I don't know what's become of her,' Mrs Chowdhury sighed.

'You have to do something,' Maya said; 'she sounds so strange.'

Rehana found herself agreeing with her daughter for once, and feeling a stab of envy at how easily Maya could speak her mind.

'Your problem,' Silvi said, returning with a

334

plate for the shondesh, 'is that you can't tolerate a difference of opinion. I happen to think this war — all this fighting — is a pointless waste of human life.'

'When the army came and massacred us and drove us out of the country, we should have rolled over?'

'They were restoring order,' Silvi said, tugging at the knot under her chin. 'Making things safe.'

'Have you been anywhere beyond your drawing room lately? People are being massacred . . . ' Maya's hands were in the air, the breath whistling out of her mouth.

'Pakistan should stay together,' Silvi said, as though reciting from a textbook. 'That's why it was conceived. To keep the Ummah united. To separate the wings is a sin against your religion.'

'The sin is being committed against us — look outside your window!'

'I'm not ignorant, Maya. Sometimes you have to make sacrifices. And I'm not the only person — '

'You and the army, thinking alike. What a relief!' Maya's voice was beginning to crack.

Her hysteria appeared to have a calming effect on Silvi. Mrs Chowdhury had given up and was leaning her head against her chair, looking at the ceiling like a martyr.

'I want to believe in something greater than myself,' Silvi said serenely.

'So do I,' Maya spat. 'Ammoo, please let's go.' She tugged at Rehana's elbow.

'Silvi,' Rehana said as she turned to the door, 'the important thing is for you to look after your mother and for all of us to survive the war.'

'Ji, khala-moni, thank you.' She relaxed her forehead and her eyebrows separated, revealing her old, reverent face.

★ ★ ★

Sohail was waiting for them at the bungalow.

'I can't believe — I've known her my whole life!' Maya was shouting at the walls, ignoring her brother.

'She's shocked — her husband dying like that.'

'What's going on?' Sohail asked, moving his eyes from mother to sister.

'But how?' Maya's cheeks were wet, and she was swallowing large gulps of air. 'How could this happen?'

'You want so badly for everyone to believe.'

'Of course I do.' Maya rubbed her nose violently against the sleeve of her blouse. She looked angrily at Sohail and bolted out of the room.

'She's upset,' Rehana said slowly, 'because Silvi wouldn't — '

'Wouldn't what?'

'She wouldn't acknowledge the war in any way, beta.'

'What do you mean?'

'She doesn't think we're doing the right thing.'

'That can't be true. You must have misunderstood.'

'She said she thought it was a sin, the country splitting.' Rehana put a hand against Sohail's back, where his shoulder blades were stretched apart.

'Someone must have done this to her. A bad influence.'

'Doesn't matter how. She's turned against it, for whatever reason.'

'Religion?'

'Maybe,' Rehana said, trying not to put the blame on God, 'but she's so young, who can know why?'

Maya came back into the room. She had tried to compose herself, and failed. Her face was wet and her lips a dark, angry bruise.

'So you heard what happened?' she said to Sohail.

He nodded silently, his eyes avoiding hers.

'It's a disgrace,' she continued, brushing away the tears with the back of her hand.

Sohail pressed his palms against his face.

'Are you still in love with her?'

'Maya — ' Rehana warned.

'You're still in love with her. You're bloody still in love with her!'

'No,' Sohail said, shaking his head weakly, 'of course not.'

'Look,' Maya said in a thick, fierce voice, 'this is the moment when you decide what is more important to you. Understand? This moment, right now. That girl is over there with her stupid, twisted politics and she's not even thinking about you, and you've risked everything — everything — to get her. Now you let her go, bhaiya, please, I'm begging you, for all of us, let her go.'

'Don't question my loyalty,' Sohail whispered.

'I'm not questioning your loyalty, I'm questioning your judgement.'

He moved his hands away from his face, and for a moment it looked as though he was going to get into a fight with her, shout things about devotion and love and the country, but instead he strode over to her and put his arms around her. 'You're right,' he said, his shoulders shaking, 'you're right.'

★ ★ ★

It was getting late. Sohail was waiting for Joy at Shona; they were going to dig up the guns. 'We have to make Sehri,' Rehana said to Maya. 'What do you want to eat?'

'I don't know.' The tears were still falling heavily on to Maya's cheeks. 'Do we have to fast?'

'Of course we do. Tomorrow of all days.'

For once Maya didn't argue. She took the glass of water Rehana offered. 'I want dalpuri,' she said with a sniff.

'Good idea. I'll put the dal on.'

Maya brought the glass to her lips. As she began to drink, a fresh wave of tears overcame her.

'Maya,' Rehana said, chiding her, 'we have more important things to worry about today.'

'I know, I'm sorry — I just can't help it.' She blew her nose thunderously. 'It's just that it wounds me' — she prodded herself with a finger — 'here.'

'The boys will be here in a few hours.'

Rehana parted the curtains and watched from the drawing-room window.

Joy and Sohail filed in through the back gate and circled the rosebush. It was hard to see through the moonless black. She recognized Joy's bulk, and beside him was Sohail, slighter, carrying a shovel and a hurricane lamp. She allowed herself only a brief moment of disappointment. There was no reason to expect the Major.

Joy lit the lamp, and Sohail began to dig. After a few minutes they exchanged places, Sohail holding the weak light while Joy squatted down and pulled at the earth, the silt piling up beside them. Finally they paused, and Joy leaned over the hole they had dug. He shifted, laying flat on his stomach, and started to tug at something. Rehana could barely make out his face, twisting with the effort.

Just as Joy had pulled the object — a rectangular wooden box, discoloured by its long burial — they heard a scattered, staccato drumroll. Gunfire. The sound grew suddenly, filling the air. The boys crouched on the ground, dipping their heads. It was Joy who raised the box above his shoulders and stood upright and scurried out of the garden. He slipped behind the mango tree and waited for Sohail, who was shimmying towards him on his elbows. They became shadows, rustling through the branches of the tree. And then they were gone.

Rehana became aware of her heart pounding

against her chest, and her breath making circles that grew and retreated on the closed window.

The drumming grew louder and Rehana froze, fixed in her place facing the empty garden, the hole they had left like a shout under the rosebush.

'Ammoo?' Maya came into the room, her hands white with flour. 'What's going on?'

They moved to the other side of the room, where the windows faced the road. Rehana parted the curtain in time to see a convoy of trucks hurtling down their street. A pillar of soldiers in green stood on the back of a truck, waving their guns in the air. Passing through the street they shouted, 'Pakistan Zindabad! Pakistan Zindabad!' As the last truck ambled away, one of the soldiers, a young boy with a thick mop of raven hair, pointed his gun at the bungalow. I could kill you right now, his face said.

Rehana snapped her head back and yanked the curtain closed.

'Did you see that?'

Maya circled an arm around Rehana's shoulder. 'It's just a show of force, Ma. It doesn't mean anything.'

'But why here? It's just a small road. That shipahi was pointing right at us.'

'They're getting hints India's going to come down on our side. And then it'll be over.'

They had started saying things like 'when the war is over'. Rehana thought it was too soon, but people, especially the young ones, were confident the freedom fighters would save them. A rescue by the world. It had to end soon. *I can taste the*

340

end, Sohail had said, and Rehana had thought of it as the kind of thing a child says to his mother when the lines between them become blurry and he no longer wants to be the child, and she no longer the mother. She had relaxed into the phrase, and his cool hand on her forehead. But she hadn't believed him.

Without the diversion of meals, Friday spooled out slowly ahead of them. There were still things to be done. Pretend it's any other day. Do the washing. The preparations for Sehri, for Iftar. Air out the house. Collect water from the taps. Boil it for drinking. Drag down the cobwebs.

All day she ignored the cold fear at her back. Sohail left in the afternoon, his face unmoved as she kissed his forehead and said Aytul Kursi and blew the blessing on his eyes. The fear breathed on her neck and sent the hair upright, electric. It caught her in the double-beat of her heart, the pulse she could feel at her temple, the tremor of her hand as she fried the Iftar food. Beguni, the crunchy strips of eggplant. Chickpeas and tomatoes. The dalpuri Maya had rolled out and stuffed. Orange juice. Tamarind juice. Lassi. It was not elaborate enough for a special occasion, not simple enough to indicate want. A meal for an ordinary day. A meal for a day without war.

Rehana brought the food to the table. They ate in silence, their fingers working the pooris with small wet slaps.

Afterwards Maya crawled under the bed and pulled out the kerosene lamp.

'Put that away!' Rehana said.

'Why? When the current goes out — '

'We don't know the current is going to go out.'

'Of course it will.'

Rehana shot Maya a warning look. 'Put the lamp away and say Isha with me.'

With Shona's long shadows edging towards the bungalow, they tried to pick up the radio transmission. Maya fiddled with the knob, but all they heard was static.

'Do you want a song, Ma?'

Rehana was taken aback by the offer. 'Really? I would love that. Sing 'Amar Shonar Bangla'.'

At nine o'clock, when only blackness and the nail-shaped crescent moon remained, they held their breaths and waited.

★ ★ ★

Rehana began to think of what she would like to be doing when the lights went out. She could go into Sohail's room and count the medicines and blankets that still needed to be distributed. She could start a letter to her sisters. But what would she say? The letter would have to be full of lies. And she wouldn't end up sending it anyway, or she would have to contend with a reply. *Thank Allah you're alive — we've been worried sick — why don't you leave that godforsaken place and come to Karachi — we've been telling you for years.* No, she wouldn't write a letter.

342

Maya was fidgeting with the dinner plates, stacking them carelessly.

'Just leave those.'

'I want to make sure — ' Maya bit her tongue.

'Leave them.'

'Oh, for God's sake, Ma.' But she left them anyway and threw herself on the sofa beside Rehana.

'What now?'

'We wait.'

Maya had never been good at waiting for anything.

'But there's nothing to do.'

'Do you want to play rummy?'

Her face brightened. 'Shotti? We haven't played since — '

'Since Sohail started beating you and you refused to play.'

'No — no, that's not how it happened. He discovered poetry that year, and everything else was forgotten.'

'That was a year later. There was a period in between, for about eight months, when you wouldn't play anything with him — not cards, or chess, or badminton.'

'You can't blame me for the badminton. He was so tall, it wasn't fair.'

'True. But poor Silvi — she persevered.'

'That's because he always let her win.'

They grew silent, collecting their memories together.

'OK,' Maya said, slapping the armrest, 'I'll get the cards.'

But Rehana had changed her mind. 'Do you

mind if we skip the cards? I want to read a little.'

Maya nodded. 'OK.'

'What do you want?' Rehana asked, but Maya was already in Sohail's room, fingering his bookshelf.

'Let's have some tea.' Maya pulled out a slim volume. 'I'll make it,' she said, tucking the book under her arm.

A few minutes later she emerged from the kitchen with a tray.

'I think I'll read Iqbal,' Rehana said, 'it's been a while.'

'Which one?'

'*Baal-e-Jibreel.*'

Maya pulled out her own choice with a flourish. '*Gitanjali!*' she said mischievously. Tagore had been banned, and, though the poetry was all about love and God and the monsoon, there was still an incendiary thrill in reading it. His white beard triangled down the cover, matching the shock of white hair that framed a long, serious face.

They climbed into bed with their tea and their books. Rehana forced herself to read hers from the beginning. Perhaps once she reached her favourite, 'Chamak Teri Ayaan', the house would be in darkness. By an unspoken consent they kept the overhead tubelight buzzing and the fan rotating at full speed. The circulating air kept their pages rustling.

'Chamak Teri Ayaan' came and went. Maya was flipping her own pages slowly, reading out the title of each poem before she began it. She made her way through 'Alo Amar Alo' and lingered at 'Amar E Gaan', which Rehana knew was her favourite.

Rehana was at 'Kya Kahun Apne Chaman', with three poems to go, when they heard something in the distance, like passing thunder. 'Was that it?' Maya leaped to the window and peered out into the street. 'All the lights are still on. Maybe they couldn't do it — maybe they tried, and they just couldn't.'

Rehana ignored her, and eventually Maya crawled back under her katha. She sighed heavily and picked up her book again. Rehana could tell she was beginning to regret not having chosen a longer volume.

Iqbal was finished and the lights were still blazing. Rehana checked her watch. 12.20. Her eyes were beginning to sting. Maya had slipped *Gitanjali* under her pillow and was unbraiding her hair. 'I'll brush my teeth,' she said in a joyless voice.

She was stepping over the threshold with the empty teacups, sighing heavily, when it happened: a scratching thud, unmistakable, a flicker of the light, an electric blink, and they were sunk into darkness.

'Maya?' Rehana felt under the bed. 'Come back and take the hurricane.'

'*THEY DID IT THEY DID IT THEY DID IT!*'

They fell asleep in their clothes, Maya laughing into her pillow.

★   ★   ★

'Rehana.'

'Who's there?'

'Shhh.' A finger on her lip. A lip on her lip. Hands tunnelling under her, lifting her up, swinging her out of the room. Three long strides to the garden gate, kicking it open, navigating the steps. Ashes in her nostrils, measured breath in her ear; her body was a feather, a wisp of cotton, a gust of wind in his arms. Swivelling past the gate, through Shona's front door, her bare feet brushing the frame.

She didn't think to worry until she was sure it was him. There wasn't enough light to see; she reached out, felt the scar on his cheek. Then she said, 'What happened? Is everything all right? What are you doing here? Where's Sohail?'

'They did it.'

He put her down on the bed in Mithun's room and stepped away, sitting on the rattan chair, his hands just beyond her reach.

'You were supposed to go,' she said.

'I know,' he replied, his eyes piercing the black.

'Why?' she asked, knowing the answer and wanting to hear it anyway.

'I had to see you. Suddenly you were gone — '

'So were you — and no letters.'

She heard him rustling through his bag and shaking something. Then there was a small scratching sound, and he held up a match. She saw his eyes, and the tightly curled hair on his head. He held the match steady, until it burned down to the nub. He let it drop. He struck

346

another. She felt its passing heat, the dusty sulphur as it flickered away; he shook his wrist and put it out.

'So pale,' he said.

'I was — I had jaundice.'

'I know.' He was whispering, his breath on her eyes.

A sob, hard as salt, welled up in her throat. She caught it, and the tears fell freely, but before they could drop from her chin his hands were there to catch them, spread them thinly on her cheek, like butter.

She heard his tongue moving around inside his mouth. Tonguing the teeth. Caressing the roof. She heard it so clearly it seemed like her own tongue, teeth, roof.

He kissed her. His lips were softer than she had imagined. She felt his tongue; reaching, knowing. Like a conjuring trick, he unfastened her blouse. He dipped his head. He ran his tongue across the width of her. Up one breast, down. Across the bone, up again. Like an aqueduct.

The lick-track burned.

He placed his thumb on her face. A heartbeat pulsed inside the thumb. She turned her face and met his lip, which she had the urge to bite, but did not.

★ ★ ★

Moments, an eternity, passed. A tiktiki cackled from the ceiling. The poor slice of moon offered only the dimmest light, through which she could just make out his square face and the dense, wiry hair.

She wanted to tell him how foolish he was to have come, but she was afraid if she said the words he would know for sure that she had willed it with all her strength.

'I have to go. Before sunrise, for Sehri.'
He moved a thread of hair from her cheek.
'Don't tell me when you're coming back.'
Now his thumb scraped her collarbone.
'Otherwise I'll be holding my breath.'
He nodded, a slight dip of the head.
'Take care of my boy.'

★ ★ ★

Rehana crossed the garden, swinging her arms, past the mango tree and the lemon tree and the rosebush, which was emptied of its secret, and the hydrangeas, which flowered blue and white like a china sky. At the bungalow, Maya was sprawled across the bed like a shipwreck. Rehana made for the kitchen, but then stopped, decided to lie down instead. It was still an hour till sunrise. She closed her eyes and remembered. Just once. Above her, the ceiling fan moved slightly, pushed by the swirl of November air floating through the veranda. Her skin was awash with scents, his watermelon breath, his burned-rubber sweat.

348

She heard the trucks before they turned on to the road; she felt them slowing in front of the bungalow, lining up along the neighbourhood gates. She had time to wake Maya and drag her to the drawing room. *The army is here.* She thought to straighten her hair. She passed a hand across her lips. And then they were perched on the sofa, straight-backed, as though waiting for a guest, except that they were still swimming in the ink-wash of night.

Young men in green uniforms spilled out of their trucks, dozens of them at once, each with identical savage eyes and boots that moved like hammers. They didn't notice the women. Their eyes were for Shona, what Shona would give up. The prayers spilled from Rehana's lips. God, let him be safe.

The boots stomped heavily through the bungalow; they tore books out of shelves, smashed dinner plates, knocked over the brass lamp, ravaged the cupboards. They ripped the posters from Sohail's bedroom, Mao against a red background, Che with a cap and a jaunty smile. A pillow was bayoneted. Yellow cotton scattered like dandelion.

Nobody was arresting them. Through the autumn haze, the sun was making a slow and careful ascent.

A shout went up. 'All clear!' and then the soldiers lined up and stood at attention as a man came through the door, his hand on his hip where a gun was resting.

'Mrs Rehana Haque,' he said in strained, rehearsed English. He had a moustache but no beard. She couldn't determine his age. Youth and age clashed in his face like competing scores. 'My name is Colonel Jabeen. I have an order to search your premises and arrest your son, Sohail Haque.

Now the boots were on the bungalow roof, thudding like elephant feet. Rehana gripped Maya's hand. It was hot and slippery. Next to Jabeen there was another man. He leaned over the window and spat into the hydrangeas. His eyes were on Maya as he swivelled around and cleared his throat. There was spittle still on his lips. He licked them. He looked at Maya — up, down — and licked them again. Maya stared back. Her palms were wet, but she stared back anyway.

Colonel Jabeen did not speak Bangla. He spoke Urdu. He shouted into the spitting man's ear and the spitting man translated for him.

'Tell them they have no choice. Give up the son.'

'Mrs Haque,' the spitting man said, 'Apnar aar kono upai nai.'

'Colonel,' Rehana said in Bangla, addressing Jabeen but looking at the spitting man, 'there must be some sort of misunderstanding. My son is in Karachi, with my sister Marzia. They live in Clifton — you can send someone and see for yourself.'

'Says her bastard's in Karachi.'

Colonel Jabeen didn't reply at first. Then he looked directly at Rehana and said, 'There's no

350

misunderstanding. Your son is a traitor to Pakistan.'

The spitting man said, 'Apnar gaddar cheleke amra charbo na.'

The soldiers returned from the roof, from the garden, from Shona. They brought in the boxes of clothes, saris that would be turned into kathas, the penicillin. No Major. One of them righted an upturned chair, and Jabeen sat down heavily. He looked bored. They laid the boxes at Rehana's feet. A graveyard of evidence.

Rehana said, 'We've been collecting donations for the refugees.' She renewed her grip on Maya's hand, and thankfully, for once, the girl did not have the urge to speak her mind.

'Tell her we know about the cache.'

A rush of cold gripped Rehana's arms. She swallowed. 'We know about the guns you buried under your rosebushes,' the spitting man said.

Rehana opened her mouth to speak.

'No need to explain. We already know everything.'

Rehana waited to see if Jabeen would tell the spitting man what they knew. 'My son is in Karachi,' she repeated, pulling Maya closer to her. Again Jabeen whispered something Rehana could not hear into the spitting man's ear. The spitting man replied. Jabeen smiled. Had she seen him before?

Jabeen and the spitting man looked at each other, serious as new lovers, for a few more minutes before the spitting man said, 'You have more than one child.'

Rehana's legs were slowly, painlessly, turning

351

to jelly. To keep them from buckling under she thought of her bones. She had bones. They stood her up.

'Take the girl into the other room.'

The spitting man turned, a smile settling across his face.

'Ma,' Maya whispered, 'I don't want to go.'

Rehana locked arms with her daughter. The spitting man was at her elbow now, a pair of handcuffs clattering against his palms. Wait, Rehana told herself, just wait one more minute. I'll think of something. She looked at Jabeen. She saw something, a hunger, in his eyes. She saw that he wanted something more, something more savage, than the triumph over two women. She broke free of her daughter and played her only card.

'Colonel Jabeen,' she said in her perfect, native Urdu, 'this cannot be the way you want to wage war.'

Jabeen cocked his head. Had he heard right? He cleared his throat. He mopped his forehead with the back of his arm. There was no electricity and hence no fan, and so everyone was sweating, especially Jabeen, who liked to wear his full army uniform on special occasions such as the routing of traitors.

'You speak Urdu,' he said. It was not a question. The spitting man was still tugging at Maya's elbow, and she was grunting, twisting away from him. The corners of his mouth were wet.

'Stop,' Jabeen said to the spitting man. He obeyed, smiled, taking pleasure in the delay.

352

'Sergeant, go and search the garden again,' Jabeen said, 'and the neighbourhood. Arrest anyone suspicious.'

The spitting man hesitated.

'Go!' Jabeen said. 'Take the boys with you.'

The spitting man saluted and ushered the rest of the soldiers out of the bungalow, leaving Rehana and Maya alone with Jabeen in the strangled afternoon heat.

★ ★ ★

Jabeen turned to Rehana. 'You see the problem,' he said. 'I've already promised my man.'

'Then tell him you've changed your mind.'

He stroked his moustache with the back of his thumb. 'Please, let's be reasonable, Mrs Haque, shall we?' He sat down, gestured hospitably to a chair and tented his fingers. 'I see you are an educated woman. There were three boys on the mission last night. One was your son's friend Joy. The Hindu boy, Partho. And Sohail was the third. We know they would have tried to cross the border. We believe we've picked up their tracks. But something tells me they may also have tried to come home. Especially your son.' He crossed his legs and rocked his foot. 'I have a feeling he may have been prone to . . . prone to sentiment.' He sighed and wove his fingers together behind his head.

Yes, that was true. He was prone to sentiment. For instance, at this moment, his hands scratching with gunpowder, he was not just a man running for his country or for his life. He

353

was also trying to fall out of love. To Jabeen she said, 'I don't know what you're talking about.' And then he smiled again and she remembered where she had seen him before. 'I've seen you. At the thana.'

'Yes, that's right. I spend a lot of time there.'

'You asked for Chinese tea.'

He nodded, impressed. 'I'm not an unreasonable man, Mrs Haque. I would rather not have the sullying of a woman on my hands. Those boys in the field,' he said, shaking his head, 'have allowed the excesses of war to go to their heads. A pity.'

He exhaled deeply, as though blowing smoke. 'However, I have a job. I have to bring those Bengalis back. I have to arrest them. And then I have to shoot them.'

'Then there is no reason why I should tell you where he is.' Rehana swallowed.

'Surely you're more intelligent than that, Mrs Haque.'

The weather was a gale in her stomach.

'Because I could hold him in a nice little cell and not shoot him right away. But perhaps that's not suitable either? You saw what happened to his friend. Poor fellow.'

Jabeen's cheeks were shining. Then he asked, as though the question had just occurred to him, 'Where is your husband, Mrs Haque?'

I once had a husband. His face was round, and his fingers were bread-soft. One day his heart stopped beating. He sank to his knees in front of our house. 'Rehana,' he said, 'Maf kar do.' *Forgive me.*

354

'Dead,' she said, trying to sound as hard as the sewer-pipe woman who had given her the same reply.

'Ah, what a blow for your children.'

My children have not always been my children. My children once belonged to someone else.

There was a sharp rap at the door. A shuffle of feet, a small thud. It was the Sergeant. 'Sir, we've got him.' He kicked a man into the room. His face was streaked with blood. A sickle scar on his cheek. A frame of curly hair. 'Caught him running to Satmasjid Road. Stupid bastard. Right in front of our eyes.'

Jabeen unbuckled his gun and pointed it. Then he changed his mind, turned the gun around and hit him with the muzzle. It collided with the man's chin; Jabeen's arm came down again, and with his other hand he threw a fist into the man's stomach. The man did not try to fight. He collapsed on to the floor, a small triangle of blood on his cheek. He tried to smile. Then he was doubled over, and Jabeen was kicking his back, his arms. 'I should kill you right now, you Bengali sonofabitch. Thought you would take out the lights?'

'Wait! This is not my son.'

Jabeen paused, his boot in the air. 'What?'

'He's not my son.'

The boot landed, heel first, on a hand. A muffled grunt, bitten back.

'Look at him — he's too old to be my son.'

'You want to trick me, woman?' Jabeen was panting, exhilarated with the effort. 'Who is he?'

His breath was hot on her face.

'I don't know. He could be anyone — you just picked him off the street.'

'You think I don't know a mukti when I see one? I know every single one of those bastards — I hunt them for a living. I know them better than you. I am their executioner. You are only their mother.' Jabeen laughed. The back of his mouth was grey. He wanted something more savage. This was it.

'This is not my son. I tell you, this is not my son. I swear on God, on the Holy Koran, on my mother's grave, this is not my son. What good will it do you to catch the wrong man? Where's the glory in that?'

And Jabeen stopped, patting his pockets, shaking off a trickle of sweat at the tip of his nose. 'Dammit!' he said, with a final kick to the man. 'Sergeant!'

'Yes, sir.'

'Get on the radio. See if there's any development.'

'Should I tell them about him?'

'What did I tell you? Go!'

Rehana's head was in her hands. If only she didn't look at him. Maybe it wasn't even him; maybe it was as she said, he was a stranger, caught crossing the road at the wrong time.

The Sergeant came back. 'Colonel, sir, it's on the radio. They've been found.'

Rehana's heart fell to her feet.

'All three?'

'No, sir. Not Sohail Haque. The other two. Tracked them in Comilla.'

Thank you, God. Thank you thank you thank you. But where was Sohail? They were supposed to take the road to Daudkhandi, into the thick autumn rice, threading through villages, swimming across eddies, their trousers rolled up, their guns held over their heads.

* * *

Jabeen crouched, wove his fingers through the man's hair and raised his head. This time he turned to Maya. 'Let's try this again. Is this man your brother?'

She said nothing, pushing urgently against Rehana's arm. 'Is this man your brother?' Jabeen repeated.

'Tell them,' the Major said, the breath whistling out of his mouth.

* * *

She had once told him her secret. Which was not about T. Ali, or about her father's lost wealth, or the stolen jewellery, or her secret love of the cinema, but about the children. How far she would go. Anywhere. Any distance. That was the secret. The shameless, hungry secret.

And with his knowledge, he held her children in his hands, breathing them to life.

It was her choice, not his. She had asked him herself. *Take my affliction.* The rest could only follow as it did. One love that swallowed another. Stacked up like clouds in a hot sky.

She wanted the knowledge back. *I should*

357

never have told you.

I'm so grateful, he said, so grateful you told me.

All my life I've been waiting for this day.

This is the greatest thing I've ever done. All my life I've been waiting for this day. Now say it, and let's be done.

★　★　★

She said it.

'God be with you, my son.'

'And you. My mother.'

Your life for mine.

Take my affliction. She had asked him, and he had answered.

★　★　★

The Sergeant wrenched him away, a hand on his collar, and he was gone, in the dragging, loping walk of a handcuffed man. Maya was pulling Rehana from the window, but she was like a stone. She owed him the looking. She fixed her look. She held him tightly in her gaze, through the black hood they slipped over his head, knowing he could see through it, and through the heart-shaped grille, and into the bungalow, and into her eyes, so that he would know all that she thought, all that she was, at that very moment, belonging to him as he disappeared from sight.

16 December 1971

Dear Husband,
The war will end today.

★ ★ ★

It was winter and the garden was living.

The flowers she had planted at the start of the war now studded the green. Champa, bokul, rojonigondha. The yellow roses. The hibiscus bush straddling the boundary wall.

Dawn was just breaking over the horizon. She knew she had only these few hours before the telephone started to ring and the neighbours began to pour in. People who would come to congratulate her and share their own stories of how they had managed to survive. They would fall on each other, as after a very long crossing.

But it was still early, and still quiet. Only the crows ringing the house.

★ ★ ★

Rehana hugged the shawl around her shoulders, and carefully, slowly, crossed the garden. She had not done it since that day. After the army took the Major away, she had hardly left the bungalow. Shona outside her window she had barely been able to look at.

Her footsteps echoed on the bare cement floor. She opened cupboards, pulled out drawers. Everything empty. Maya had done a thorough job. Cleaned up the broken pots and pillaged bookshelves. Sold the Sunguptas' furniture and sent the money to Salt Lake. The rose-petal carpet was rolled up and pitched against a corner of the drawing room. Rehana crossed the pink-hued dining room, empty except for the portrait of Mrs Sengupta's parents, resting in a corner.

She entered Mithun's room. Coffee-coloured light filtered through the drawn curtain. The projector, the gramophone and the records were all gone. The shelves were wiped clean. There was no trace of him.

Mithun's bed was wedged against the wall. For some reason Maya had left it there, with a colourful bedspread laid out across. Rehana bent to straighten the bedspread, remembering the many times she had reached out just this way, her fingers spread, to smooth his sheets.

On the floor next to the bed was a box of matches. Blue Lion, it said on top. Blue Lion Safety Matches.

Rehana opened the box. Empty. He had used the last one to examine her face. She thought of his finger, sliding the box out of its sleeve, striking the match, watching her face come alive in the sulphur light.

She retraced her steps. Pulled back the curtains. Crossed the drawing room and went through the door. Fastened the padlock.

★   ★   ★

At the bungalow she stepped on to her prayer mat.

Bismillah ir-rahman-ir-raheem.

Dear God, my merciful, my benevolent. *Forgive me.*

Maya was awake, brushing her hair. 'You ready to go so soon? Just give me five minutes, I'll put on a sari.'

'No, you stay. Go with your brother when he comes.'

'OK, but don't be too long. We have to be at Shaheed Minar for the treaty.'

★   ★   ★

The rickshaw turned into Gulistan, crossed the rail line at Purano Polton. People were trickling on to the streets and the rickshaw-wallah had to manoeuvre through the thickening crowd. Every time a plane droned overhead they let up a loud cheer.

Dear husband, she practised, the war will end today.

What else could she say that he didn't already know? That those nine months of the war were like nine generations, brimming with lives and deaths; that Sohail had survived, while his friends had died; and that here was the city, burned and blistered and alive, where she was going to see what remained of the man with the scar across his face who had lived in her house for ninety-six days and passed like a storm through her small life.

★ ★ ★

A boy, no older than fourteen or fifteen, guarded the door. He wore an oversized shirt with the sleeves rolled up; a belt, cinched around his waist, held up his trousers. In his arms he cradled an enormous rifle.

'I'm Mrs Haque,' Rehana said.

'Salaam-Alaikum,' he said, his hand to his forehead. The word had got out about Shona, and how she had sheltered the guerrillas and saved Sabeer. 'They told me you were coming. Follow me.'

The room inside was battered. The police desk was overturned. They stepped through the splintered chairs, the broken glass, the torn-up bits of paper that carpeted the floors.

The gate leading to the cells was guarded by a boy, even younger than the first. The two exchanged a few words, the gate was opened, and Rehana was led through to a corridor with a row of doors. Each door had a small opening, like a letterbox. She thought she could hear the shuffle of bodies inside. The boy took her to the end of the corridor, unlocked a door and swung it open. 'Not to

364

worry, Chachi, I'll stay just behind you.'

The shapes moved in the dark.

This was where they must have brought him. It smelled strongly of sweat and urine. There was a window carved out of a vertical slit in the far wall, but it offered no light. The walls were wet and stained. It was difficult not to turn away.

They squatted in their uniforms.

A man stood up shakily and came towards her. She heard him struggle to breathe. 'Rehana,' he said.

'Faiz.' Dark skin, heavy eyebrows. How much he resembled his brother. His left eye was swollen, the lid squeezed shut.

'Rehana,' he said again. His hands were cuffed. His feet were cuffed. The shackles belled and rattled. 'You've come to get me out — ' He reached out a hand.

'Get back!' the boy shouted.

'No, no, it's all right,' Rehana said. She drew closer.

'Get me out of here,' Faiz said. His beard was matted and soiled. 'Please.'

She couldn't speak; she just looked at him dumbly, this man she had feared and hated.

'Sohail, is he — where is he?' Faiz asked.

'He's fine. He'll be home in a few days.' She had come with a list of questions, but she couldn't remember any of them. It must have been here, somewhere within these walls, that they'd kept him. If I look hard enough, I might find a trace.

Faiz put his palms together. He put his palms together and begged.

365

She had come to ask him about the Major. Where they had taken him. What they had done. But now she knew the questions were useless; she had her answers. The walls, the sound of the chains, told her everything she needed to know.

'Rehana,' he was saying, 'for the sake of my brother. One word from you and they would let me go. Find forgiveness in your heart.'

She searched. It was true, they would let him go if she asked. They were just children, after all, the boys running around with guns, their hearts hungry for revenge. She thought of forgiving Faiz. She imagined telling him to go back to Pakistan, to never come back, never show his face to her again. And saying, It is not for me to punish you but God.

She didn't say anything for a few minutes. Faiz breathed louder and harder as he asked, and asked again. She tried to look into his swollen face. She was about to utter the words *for my husband's sake*, but then the sight of all of them, Joy and Aref and Mrs Sengupta, floated in front of her. Even then she might have forgiven him, but then she remembered the look on Maya's face when they had told her about Sharmeen, and those first few days of the war when it dawned on her that she would not come out of this with her world intact. 'I cannot forgive you, brother. For my daughter I cannot forgive you.'

She turned away, the lock clanging shut behind her. She heard his fist on the door, and the chains, and his fading, strangled cries.

★ ★ ★

The graveyard was cool and dusty. She glanced around for the caretaker, but she was alone. The chill made her half walk, half run, to Iqbal's plot.

She brushed the fallen leaves from his gravestone. She had been nervous about this meeting, wondering what she would say, how she would explain, but now the words came easily.

★　★　★

Dear Husband,
I came to tell you the story of our war and how we have lived.

The war will end today. I have aged a thousand years. I am ugly and tired. But I live.

A man lived in our house for ninety-six days. At first I was angry he was there, because he was training Sohail to be a guerrilla and he seemed to have that savage need to save the country that I saw burning in Sohail's eyes just before he left for the fighting.

But then I was left with him and that poor boy whose brother died and who is lost now, even as it all ends and we have to try to find ways to exist in a country without war. Your son became a soldier and then he lost his friends. They wore each other's shirts. They died in them.

In the midst of all the madness I found the world seemed right for the first time in a very long time. I heard the song of a woman whose voice held a thousand years of sorrow. And yes, I loved him. For the smallest fraction of those ninety-six days, I loved him.

As it was with you, so it was also with him.

367

Only the briefest moment. And I told him everything, about the day I became a thief and the day I became a widow and the day I lost the children. And I told him if I had a chance, just one chance, to choose again I would finally be free of it. So I know he did not blame me for not running to Faiz and Parveen, or to that police station, to beg them to let him go. I let them think they had Sohail. That is what I chose. To let that man pay my debt.

For this, my husband, I pray you will forgive me. And I pray to God to forgive me.

The war will end today. Niazi will sign the treaty and I will walk into the streets. Your daughter will hold my hand. There will be a pressing crowd on the pavement but Maya will elbow us to the front. A boy will sell flags for two taka and everyone will wave and crane their necks to see the road. Coloured paper will sail from buildings; fists will wave in the air; there will be dancing, a man on a flute, a woman beating a dhol slung across her shoulder. Someone will think to plug a megaphone to the radio. The roads are flat and dusty; we are spellbound, love-bound, home-bound, singing 'How I love you, my golden Bengal.' The sky is pale and iridescent and today the war has ended, and today I will clutch my flag, hold my breath and wait for our son.

I know what I have done.

This war that has taken so many sons has spared mine. This age that has burned so many daughters has not burned mine.

I have not let it.

Acknowledgements

I am privileged to be indebted to the following people:

Anya Serota, for her commitment to the book before it was even written and for sheer editorial brilliance. My agent, Peter Straus, who knows more about books than just about anyone, for his wisdom and much-needed counsel. Ellie Birne, Nikki Barrow, James Spackman, Roland Philipps, Sara Marafini and all my friends at John Murray; Lisa Baker, Rowan Routh, Stephen Edwards and the team at RCW. Donna Poppy, magical transformer of the muddy sentence. Myrlin Hermes and Joe Treasure, my genius critics; Andrew Motion for lessons and guidance; David Cross and the Arts Council for their generous support; Liza Glen and Jane Filip for hours around the table. Roland Lamb, for inspiring me to write Rehana better. Michael Veal, Dan Mirsky, Siddhartha Deb and Michele Ashley, for early enthusiasm and confidence;

Shaveena Anam, my co-conspirator. Kaiser Haq, for his timely translation of Shamsur Rahman's 'Shadhinota Tumi'. All my freedom-fighter friends, Habibul Alam, Shahidullah Khan, Naila Zaman, Shireen Huq, Akhtar Ahmed, Shireen Banu, Mofidul Huq, Sultana Zaman, Colonel Nuruzzaman and Aly Zaker; Shahadat Chowdhury, whom we keep alive in our hearts. My mother and father, who told me so many stories about the war that I couldn't help but become a writer.

I will always be especially grateful to Nehal Ahmed, without whose patience and unstinting support this book would have never been written or finished. Thanks also to Najma and Jalaluddin Ahmed, for their unflagging optimism.

Finally, it needs to be said that this book is what it is only because of the place that inspired it. And so, to my beautiful and bruised country, to Bangladesh — my gratitude and love.

We do hope that you have enjoyed reading this large print book.

Did you know that all of our titles are available for purchase?

We publish a wide range of high quality large print books including:
Romances, Mysteries, Classics
General Fiction
Non Fiction and Westerns

Special interest titles available in large print are:
The Little Oxford Dictionary
Music Book
Song Book
Hymn Book
Service Book

Also available from us courtesy of Oxford University Press:
Young Readers' Dictionary
(large print edition)
Young Readers' Thesaurus
(large print edition)

For further information or a free brochure, please contact us at:
Ulverscroft Large Print Books Ltd.,
The Green, Bradgate Road, Anstey,
Leicester, LE7 7FU, England.
Tel: (00 44) 0116 236 4325
Fax: (00 44) 0116 234 0205

Other titles published by
The House of Ulverscroft:

THE INCONSTANT HUSBAND

Susan Barrett

When Patrick McKinley steps into Rose Seaton's life, her heart finds its target. However, this bohemian artist is not the suitor for whom she was groomed: her father demands a Yorkshire son-in-law, with a talent for manufacturing, for his ironworks. What Rose wants is more exciting and dangerous, and Patrick soon ensnares her at a ball to celebrate Queen Victoria's diamond jubilee. But Patrick, for all his charm, is also broke and evasive and his strategies lead Rose into harm and scandal. Then, to indulge his pursuit of artistic utopias, they journey across Europe where Rose meets the other players in Patrick's life. She begins to grasp what it means to be a wife and a mother — and to question her role as a muse.